ORBIT 16

ORBIT 16

Edited by Damon Knight

HARPER & ROW, PUBLISHERS
New York, Evanston, San Francisco, London

Science fiction

FIRST EDITION

ISBN: 0–06–012437–7

LIBRARY OF CONGRESS CATALOG CARD NUMBER: 74–15875

Designed by C. Linda Dingler

Illustrations by Richard Wilhelm

75 76 77 78 79 10 9 8 7 6 5 4 3 2 1

CONTENTS

ORBIT 16

They Say

At that point, my theoretical work complete, I began to look around for those new forms that my theorizing had led me to demand. And I found them everywhere, hiding under a classification which seems designed to guarantee that they are not "serious literature." The classification, as you are all aware, is "science fiction," and it conceals a body of work that is truly astonishing, not just in its "amazing" content but in its range and variety of expression, its present quality and future potential.

—"Stillborn Literature,"
by Robert Scholes, *Bulletin
of the Midwest Modern Language
Association*, Spring 1974

"Science fiction" is a publisher's marketing category like "westerns" or "gothics" or "nurse novels"—a packaging definition. When you walk through a supermarket, you can tell the breakfast cereals from the detergents at a glance, even though they come in boxes of roughly the same size and shape. . . . Science fiction writers have complained that serious literary critics automatically ignore their work, no matter what its merits, and sometimes have spun elaborate theories about the snobbishness of the "literary establishment." But after all, how *can* a serious, conscientious literary critic sort through the year's mountain-high pile of tacky-looking science fiction paperbacks to find a few real jewels buried in this heap of literary mediocrity? He knows

1

what a potentially important book looks like as an artifact, as a physical package, because publishers have consistently packaged most of these books in an identifiable style. He may even realize that one soap box out of twenty contains breakfast cereal, but is he going to chomp through nineteen boxes of soap to find it?

—Norman Spinrad, *Modern Science Fiction* (Anchor, 1974)

MR. BRYAN: . . . During the NERVA experience, I first came into contact with AEC and the methodology they were using. Obviously, since we were developing a nuclear plant that was going to fly over people's heads, we had some of the same problems— in some cases even more severe, since we were moving the plant rather than having a stationary source. We spent a considerable amount of money on research into improved reliability techniques when we entered the NERVA program. This was primarily because you could not build a lot of these and test them like we could in the Apollo program to find out where the problems were. During this experience, we would occasionally be analyzing a potential accident or problem and we'd see the similarity between that and what a power plant would have, so we would go to the AEC or to the industry and try to find out what was going on in analyzing this particular sub-problem.

We were very surprised to find a lack of overall knowledge of aerospace techniques within the AEC, and pretty much a lack of interest in developing them. They were having a lot of problems at that time just with normal QC-type functions—quality control; they were just implementing that as a program, which, of course, had been in aerospace for many years and in industry many years before that. But they were having problems implementing that type of program—which, incidentally, is an inspection-after-the-fact type of program whereas reliability is trying to analyze it before the fact. So we didn't find a lot of help from anything that was going on within the AEC or within the industry. . . .

Since we had spent considerable millions in research to develop some new techniques in the NERVA program for reliability and safety analysis, we were urged by our AEC funding sponsors to contact other AEC people to see what could be salvaged from this program and transferred over to the AEC to use in nuclear power plant analyses. So we made many presentations to AEC personnel on just what we had gone through—what we had learned and the techniques we had developed. We were very disappointed that they elected not to take advantage of this experience—not even to consider, for instance, taking our final documents and reports into a library function to hold until they got to the point in their learning curve where they could use them. What we found was a major concern with their own problems and a very typical resistance to change. . . . I personally concluded, from these many contacts and from discussions with people since those contacts, that in general, the AEC is up to ten years behind the times as far as implementing aerospace reliability and safety techniques is concerned, and as a substitute for good analysis, is pushing phony reliability and safety numbers to assure us of just the opposite. . . .

CHAIRMAN WARREN: Can you explain fault tree analysis?

MR. BRYAN: Yes. A fault tree analysis is where you start with some problem that can occur, some system malfunction, then you start tiering your analysis much like an organizational chart. You start with a box at the top that says you're going to have a loss-of-coolant accident. You then tier it down to the six or so things that can cause a loss-of-coolant accident, and then for each one of those six things, you analyze the things that could cause each of those six, and you just keep tiering down until you're down to the nuts and bolts of the system.

The problem in building a fault tree and getting a number out of the fault tree analysis is obvious. You have this huge tree of possible failure mechanisms that all inter-react and all lead into other events for which you have no quantifiable data. The only possible way to quantify each one of these boxes is to have a

4

failure rate for each one. You'd have to have a failure rate for the bolt. You have to have a failure rate for the inter-reactive effect between two adjoining parts. You have to have a failure rate for the seal leaking between two parts. You just have to have failure rates for every point in the analysis, and there just does not exist that type of information. So you end up doing the same thing we've always done. Where you can get failure rates, you use them. Where there are industrial failure rates, use them. For instance, maybe you can't find anything on the particular burst failure mechanics of a high pressure line that you have, so you go to the oil industry and see what they've got. Obviously, a pipe used in the oil industry is going to fail much differently from one in a nuclear application, but this is the best you have got so this is what you use.

In other cases, where there is no industrial failure rate, you go back to some qualitative method or some guessing game.

If you're consistent in the use of these numbers in the fault tree, when you get done you certainly can compare one design against another and say this design is better than the other, if you used a common data base.

CHAIRMAN WARREN: But only for comparison?

MR. BRYAN: Only for comparison. The absolute value of the number is totally meaningless. There is just no way that number can mean anything in terms of the real-world probability of failure.

—William Bryan of the National
Institute for Applied Research,
testifying before the Subcommittee
on State Energy Policy of the California
State Assembly, Charles Warren,
Chairman, February 1, 1974 (excerpted
in *Not Man Apart*, Mid-May 1974,
under the title *"Nothing* Can
Possibly Go Wrong, Go Wrong, Go Wrong")

By 1919 the German bourgeoisie must have felt any means to be justified in the defense of its power. As of this time, myths and magic moved out of the drawing-rooms and coffee-houses to fight against reason and revolution. The flood of pseudo-scientific pamphlets and treatises became overwhelming. SF, read by the social classes that were not reached by pseudo-scientific and philosophic pamphlets, also succumbed to such irrationality. The idea that the time was ripe for a "spiritual re-orientation" in literature too was ceaselessly suggested by such authors. They called for sensations and imaginative fantasies that would help to conquer gross "materialism" and its literary counterpart, realism. One seemingly non-political articulation of these tendencies went as follows:

There are many indications that mechanistic materialism—derived from the exact sciences—which has impressed its stamp on the last decade, is at last dying out, due to the recent spiritual revolution. Obviously, the transcendental longings of the majority of humanity cannot be suppressed in the long run. . . . To begin with, we have again arrived at the point of view of "wonder"—i.e., we no longer dismiss as nonsense all things that are not explicable in terms of the known laws of physics. Mysterious connections between human beings, independent of spatial and temporal separation, spooks, the appearance of ghosts, all are again in the realm of the possible.

This quotation comes from the magazine *Der Orchideengarten,* which was devoted to publishing only fantastic fiction and drawings—analogous to American "weird" and "fantasy" SF magazines. Max Valier, the later rocket pioneer and chairman of the "Society for Space-Flight," who toured the country lecturing about the end of the world, about Atlantis and Lemuria, about Glacial Cosmogony and the breakthrough into Space, and in 1929 made an unsuccessful attempt to interest Hitler in the military potential of rockets, was even more explicit—

Our present time, more than any other, requires a truly cosmic source and center for spiritual orientation. We need a tremendous, even super-Terran shock, in order to regain a sense of our identity which we have lost in the whirlpool of everyday selfishness. . . . On the basis of a new theory of cognition we will seek a more profound knowledge; and for our emotions, we will seek sensations of truly primeval shock, so that even the end of the world and of this Earth shall be a constructive experience.

—"SF, Occult Sciences, and Nazi Myths," by Manfred Nagel, *Science-Fiction Studies*, Spring 1974 (excerpted and translated from Nagel's *Science Fiction in Deutschland* (Tübinger Vereinigung für Volkskunde, Tübingen, 1972)

MOTHER AND CHILD

The king, the smith and the alien all loved her:
and she? She loved all three.

Joan D. Vinge

PART I: THE SMITH

All day I have lain below the cliff. I can't move, except to turn my
head or twitch two fingers; I think my back is broken. I feel as if
my body is already dead, but my head aches, and grief and shame
are all the pain I can bear. Remembering Etaa . . .

Perhaps the elders are almost right when they say death is the
return to the Mother's womb, and in dying we go back along our
lives to be reborn. Between wakings I dream, not of my whole
life, but sweet dreams of the time when I had Etaa, my beloved.
As though it still happened I see our first summer together herd-
ing shenn, warm days in fragrant upland meadows. We didn't
love each other then; she was still a child, I was hardly more, and
for our different reasons we kept ourselves separated from the
world.

My reason was bitterness, for I was *neaa*, motherless. The winter before, I had lost my parents to a pack of kharks as they hunted. My mother's sister's family took me in, as was the custom, but I still ached with my own wounds of loss, and was always an outsider, as much from my own sullenness as from any fault of my kin. I questioned every belief, and could find no comfort. Sometimes, alone with just the grazing shenn, I sat and wept.

Until one day I looked up from my weeping to see a girl, with eyes the color of new-turned earth and short curly hair as dark as my own. She stood watching me somberly as I wiped at my eyes, ashamed and angry.

—What do you want?   I signed, looking fierce and hoping she would run away.

—I felt you crying. Are you lonely?

—No. Go away.   She didn't. I frowned. —Where did you come from, anyway? Why are you spying on me?

—I wasn't spying. I was across the stream, with my shenn. I am Etaa.   She looked as if that explained everything.

And it did; I recognized her then. She belonged to another clan, but everyone talked about her: Etaa, her name-sign, meant "blessed by the Mother," and she had the keenest eyesight in the village. She could see a bird on a branch across a field, and thread the finest needle; but more than that, she had been born with the second sight, she felt the Mother's presence in all natural things. She could know the feelings and touch the souls of every living creature, sometimes even predict when rain would fall. Others in the village had the second sight, but not as clearly as she did, and most people thought she would be the next priestess when she came of age. But now she was still a child, minding the flocks, and I wished she would leave me alone. —Your shenn will stray, O blessed one.

Old hurt pinched her sun-browned face, and then she was running back toward the stream.

—Wait!   I stood up, startled, but she didn't see my sign. I threw a stone, it skimmed past her through the grass; she stopped and turned. I waved her back, guilty that my grief had made me hurt somebody else.

She came back, her face too full of mixed feeling to read.

—I'm sorry. I didn't mean to make you unhappy too. I'm Hywel. I sat down, gesturing.

Her smile was as sudden and bright as her disappointment, and passed as quickly. She dropped down beside me like a hound, smoothing her striped kilt. —I wasn't showing off . . . I don't *mean* to . . . Her shoulders drooped; I had never thought before that blessedness could be a burden like anything else. —I just wanted to— Her fingers hesitated in mid-sign.—To know if you were all right. She looked up at me through her long lashes, with a kind of yearning.

I glanced away uncomfortably across the pasture. —Can you watch your shenn from here? They were only a gray-white shifting blot to me, even when my eyes were clear, and now my eyes were blurred again.

She nodded.

—You have perfect vision, don't you? My hands jerked with pent-up frustration. —I wish I did!

She blinked. —Why? Do you want to be a warrior, like in the old tales? Some of our people want to take the heads of the Neaane beyond the hills for what they do to us. I think in the south some of them *have.* Her eyes widened.

The thought of the Neaane, the Motherless ones, made me flinch; we called them Neaane because they didn't believe in the Mother Earth as we did, but in gods they claimed had come down from the sky. We are the Kotaane, the Mother's children, and to be *neaa* was to be both pitiful and accursed, whether you were one boy or a whole people. —I don't want to kill people. I want to be farsighted so I can be a hunter and kill kharks, like they killed my parents!

—Oh. She brushed my cheek with her fingers, to show her sorrow. —When did it happen?

—At the end of winter, while they were hunting.

She leaned back on her elbows and glanced up into the dull blue sky, where the Sun, the Mother's consort, was struggling to free his shining robes once more from the Cyclops. The Cyclops' rolling bloodshot Eye looked down on us malevolently, out of the wide greenness of her face. —It was the doing of the Cyclops, probably, Etaa signed. —Her strength is always greatest at the Dark Noons, big Ugly-face; she always brings pain with the cold! But the Mother sees all—

—The Mother didn't see the kharks. She didn't save my parents; She could have. She gives us pain too, the Great Bitch!

Etaa's hands covered her eyes; then slowly they slid down again. —Hywel, that's blasphemy! Don't say that or She will punish you. If She let your parents die, they must have offended Her. She lifted her head with childish self-righteousness.

—My parents never did anything wrong! Never! My mind saw them, as they always were, bickering constantly. . . . They stayed together because they had managed to have one child, and though they'd lost two others, they were fertile together and might someday have had a fourth. But they didn't like each other anyway, and maybe their resentment was an offense. I hit Etaa hard on the arm and leaped up. —The Mother is a bitch and you are a brat! May you be sterile!

She gasped and made the warding sign. Then she stood up and kicked me in the shins with her rough sandals, her face flushed with anger, before she ran off again across the pasture.

After she was gone I stood throwing rocks furiously at the shenn, watching them run in stupid terror around and around the field.

And because of it, when I had worn out my rage, I discovered one of my shenn had disappeared. Searching and cursing, I finally found the stubborn old ewe up on the scarp at the field's end. She was scrabbling clumsily over the ragged black boulders, cutting her tender feet and leaving tufts of her silky wool on every rock and thorn bush. I caught her with my crook at last and dragged her back down by her flopping ears, while she butted at me and stepped on my bare feet with her claws out. I cursed her mentally now, not having a hand to spare, and cursed my own idiocy, but mostly I cursed the Mother Herself, because all my troubles seemed to come from Her.

Scratched and aching all over, I got the ewe down the crumbling hill to the field at last, whacked her with my crook, and watched her trot indignantly away to rejoin the flock. I started toward the stream to wash my smarting body, but Etaa was ahead of me, going down to drink. Afraid that she would see me for the fool I was, I threw myself down in the shade of the hillside instead and pretended to be resting. I couldn't tell if she was even looking at me, though I squinted and stretched my eyes with my fingers.

But then suddenly she was on her feet running toward me, waving her arms. I got up on my knees, wondering what crazy thing—

And then a piece of the hill gave way above me and buried me in blackness.

I woke spitting, with black dirt in my eyes, my nose, my mouth, to see Etaa at my side still clawing frantically at the earth and rubble that had buried my legs. All through her life, though she wasn't large even among women, she had strength to match that of many men. And all through my life I remembered the wild, burning look on her face, as she turned to see me alive. But she didn't make a sign, only kept at her digging until I was free.

She helped me stand, and as I looked up at the slumped hillside the full realization of what had been done came to me. I dropped to my knees again and rubbed fistfuls of the tumbled earth into my hair, praising Her Body and begging Her forgiveness. Never again did I question the Mother's wisdom or doubt Her strength. I saw Etaa kneel beside me and do the same.

As we shared supper by my tent, I asked Etaa how she'd known when she tried to warn me. —Did you see it happening?

She shook her head. —I *felt* it, first . . . but the Mother didn't give me enough time to warn you.

—Because She was punishing me. She should have killed me for the things I thought today!

—But it was me who made you angry. It was my fault. I shouldn't have said that about your parents. It was awful, it was —cruel.

I looked at her mournful face, shadowed by the greening twilight. —But it was true.   I sighed. —And it wasn't just today that *I* have cursed the Mother. But I'll never do it again. She must have been right, to let my parents die. They hated staying together, they didn't appreciate the blessing of their fertility, when others pray for children but can't make any.

—Hywel . . . maybe they're happier now, did you ever think? She looked down self-consciously. —To return to the Mother's Womb is to find peace, my mother says. Maybe She knew they were unhappy in life, so She let them come back, to be born again.

—Do you really think so?   I leaned forward, not knowing why this strange girl's words should touch me so.

She wrinkled her face with thought. —I really think so.

And I felt the passing of the second shadow that had darkened my mind for so long, as though for me it was finally Midsummer's Day and I stood in the light again.

Etaa insisted on staying with me that night; her mother was a healer, and she informed me that I might have "hidden injuries," so gravely that I laughed. I lay awake a long time, aching but at peace, looking up past the leather roof into the green-lit night. I could see pallid Laa Merth, the Earth's Grieving Sister, fleeing wraithlike into the outer darkness in her endless effort to escape her mother, the Cyclops, who always drew her back. The Cyclops had turned her lurid Eye away from us, and the shining bands of her robe made me think for once of good things, like the banded melons ripening in the village fields below.

I looked back at Etaa, her short dark curls falling across her cheek and her bare chest showing only the softest hint of curves under her fortune-seed necklace. I found myself wishing that she would somehow magically become a woman, because I was just old enough to be interested; and then suddenly I wished that then she would have me for her man, something I'd never thought about anyone else before. But if she were a woman, she would become our priestess and have her pick of men and not want one without the second sight. . . . I remembered the look she'd given me as she dug me out of the landslide, and felt my face redden, thinking that maybe I might have a chance, after all.

Through the summer and the seasons that followed I spent much time with Etaa and slowly got used to her strange skills. I had never known what it was like to feel the Mother's touch, or even another human's, on my own soul; and since I had few close friends, I didn't know the ways of those who had the second sight. To be with Etaa was to be with someone who saw into other worlds. Often she started at nothing, or told me what we'd find around the next turn of the path; she even knew my feelings sometimes, when she couldn't see my face. She felt what the Earth feels, the touch of every creature on Her skin.

Etaa's second sight made her like a creature of the forest (for all animals know the will of the Mother), and, solitary like me, she spent much time with only the wild things for company. Often she tried to take me to see them, but they always bolted at my coming. Etaa would wince and tell me to move more slowly, step more softly, breaking branches offends the Earth . . . but I could never really tell what I was doing wrong.

The next year on Midsummer's Eve I was initiated into manhood. During the feast that followed, while I sat dripping and content after my ducking in the sacred spring, Etaa sat proudly at my side. But when midnight came I left the celebration to walk in the fields with Hegga, because for that one could only ask a woman, and Etaa was still a child. Which she proved, by sticking her tongue out at Hegga as we passed. But it made me smile, since it meant she was closer to being a woman, too.

Now that I was a man, Teleth, who was the village smith, asked

me to be his apprentice. Smithing is a gift of the Sun to the Fire
clan, and a man of that clan is always the smith, whatever clan he
marries into. Teleth, my mother's cousin, had a son who would
have followed him, but his son was farsighted, and not much
good at the close work smithing required. I was Teleth's closest
nearsighted kin; but he signed that I was good with my hands and
quick with my mind too, which pleased him more. And pleased
me too, more than I could tell him; because besides the honor,
it meant that I'd have a better chance of impressing Etaa.

Though she was still a child, whenever I saw her passing in the
village, or watched her sign to the people who came to see her,
the grace of her manner and her words left me amazed; especially
since for me words never came easy, and my hands showed my
feelings better by what they made from metal and wood. But
often I saw her, from the smithy, going off alone on the path to
the Mother's Glen, and I remembered the burden she always
carried with her, and how she had lightened mine. And then I'd
go back to work, and work twice as hard, hoping Teleth would
take pity on me and let me go early.

But usually Teleth kept me working every spare minute; he was
young, but he had a lung sickness that made him cough up blood,
and he was afraid he wouldn't live long. When I could be with
Etaa at last, my hands tangled with excitement while I tried to set
free the things I could never share with anyone else. With me
Etaa was free to be the child she couldn't be with anyone else; and
though sometimes it annoyed me, and I thought she would never
grow up, I endured it, because I saw it was something she needed:
and because she would pull my head down and kiss me sometimes as lightly as the touch of a rainbow fly, before she ran away.

We were always together at the Four Feasts and for other
rituals, because until she became a woman she wouldn't be our
priestess. We saw each other in the fields at planting and harvest
too, when everyone worked together, and sometimes in the summer she'd come foraging and berry picking with me. Having eyes
that saw both near and far, she could choose whatever task she

liked; and, she said, she liked to be with me.

Usually our berry picking went crazy with freedom, and more berries got eaten and stepped on than ever went into our baskets. But one windless, muggy day in the second summer after my initiation, we went in search of red burrberries and Mother's moss for healing. All through the morning Etaa was strangely reserved and solemn, as though she were practicing her formal face in front of me now too. I tried to draw her out, and when I couldn't, I began to feel desperate at the thought that I'd offended her by something I didn't know I'd done—or worse, that she was finally losing interest in me.

—Mother's Tits! I jerked back from a thorn, cursing and fumbling all at once, and lost another handful of berries.

Etaa looked back from the stream bank, where she was peeling up moss, sensing sharp emotions as she always did. —Hywel, are you all right?

I nodded, barely able to make out her signs from where I stood. —Just save some of that moss for me. I'm being stabbed to death.

She came scrambling up the bank. —Let me pick, then, and you get the moss. It will soothe your hands while you work.

—I'm all right. I felt my old sullenness rise up in me.

—I don't mind. My scratches are better already . . . Look! There's a rubit. It's the Mother's bird; She wants you to change places with me.

—How do you know what it means? You're not the priestess yet. I squinted along her pointing finger. —And that's not a rubit, it's a follower bird.

—Yes it is a rubit, I can feel its—

—It is not! I crossed my arms.

—Hywel— She stared at me. —What's wrong with you today?

—What's wrong with *you*? All day you've acted like you barely know me! I turned away, to hide the things my face couldn't.

At last she touched my shoulder; I turned back, to see her blushing as red as the burrberries and her hands twitching at her waist. —I didn't mean to . . . but I couldn't tell you . . . I thought

. . . Oh, Hywel, will you walk in the fields with me on Midsummer's Eve?   Her face burned even redder, her eyes as bright as the Sun.

Laughter burst out of me, full of relief and joy. I caught her up in my arms and swung her, my body saying *yes* and *yes* and *yes*, while she hung on and I felt her laugh her own relief away. I set her down, and straightened the links of my belt to cover my speechlessness. Then I looked her over, grinning, and signed, —So, brat, you've finally grown up?

She stretched her face indignantly. —I certainly have. So please don't call me "brat" anymore. As a matter of fact, my mother hasn't cut my hair for nearly six months, and you never even noticed!

I touched the dark curls that reached almost down to her shoulders now. —Oh. I guess I didn't. I'll have to make you a headband, to go with your necklace.

Her hand rose to the string of jet and silver beads I had made for her. —My necklace doesn't hang straight anymore, either.

—I noticed *that*.   I grinned again, moving closer.

She caught my head and pulled it down to kiss me, as she always did; but this time she didn't pull away, and her kiss was more like fire than a rainbow fly's wing.

I jerked away instead. —Hai, I never taught you that! Who have you been with?

—Nobody. Hegga told me you liked that!   She danced away, and hands waving wildly, slipped and fell down the bank into the bed of moss.

I leaped down the bank after her, landing beside her in the soft, gray-green moss. —Gossip about me, will you?   I signed. And then I taught her a few things Hegga hadn't told her about.

It seemed to me that Midsummer's Eve would never come. But it came at last, and I found myself laying my cape out on the soft earth between the rows of wheat. I drew Etaa down beside me, her woman's tunic still clinging wetly against her. And then we made love together for the first time, asking fertility for the fields and for ourselves, while I wondered if I was dreaming, because I'd dreamed it often enough.

After, we lay together in the gentle warm night, seeing each other's smiles bathed in green glow, watching the Cyclops like a great striped melon overhead. I gave her the earrings I'd made for her, silver bells shaped like winket blossoms, the symbol of a priestess of the Mother. She took them almost with awe, stroking them with her fingers, and signed that they had a beautiful soul. And I thought of how she would become our priestess tomorrow on Midsummer's Day, and pulled her close again, wondering what would happen between us then. Etaa wiggled her hands free, and asked if she was really a woman now, in my eyes. I kissed her forehead and signed, —In every way, feeling her heart beating hard against me. And then, proudly, as if she had read my mind, she asked me to be her husband. . . .

We didn't return to the village until dawn; and the harvest that year was bountiful.

But cold drizzling rain falls now, the sky is gray with grief, I lie below the cliff and even yesterday is beyond the reach of my crippled hands. Only yesterday . . . yesterday Midsummer's Day came again, the Day of Fruitfulness, the greatest of the Mother's sacred feasts—and the day that should have been our joy, Etaa's and mine. Yesterday our Mother Earth escaped the shadow of the envious Cyclops, and was united again with her shining lover the Sun, once more defying darkness and barren night. And yesterday the priestess of our village took the Mother's part in ritual, and a man of the appointed clan was her consort, to ensure a safe passage through the seasons of Dark Noons and a better future for our people. Because the priestess of a village is the woman most blessed by the Mother, each Midsummer's Day by tradition she joins with a man of a different clan, in celebration, and in the hope of creating a child blessed as she is, who will strengthen the blood of its father's clan.

This year, as in the past seven years, Etaa was our priestess; but

this year my own clan had chosen her consort, and they had
chosen me. Etaa's face mirrored my own joy when I told her;
because though I was smith now, and though I was her husband,
that highest honor usually went to the clansman most gifted with
the second sight.

And then on Midsummer's Day Etaa shook me awake at dawn,
her eyes filled with love. She wore only her shift, and already her
Midsummer garlands twined in the wild dark curls of her hair.
She smelled of summer flowers. —Hywel, it's Midsummer!

I felt myself laugh, half a yawn. —I know, I know, priestess! I
could hardly forget—

—Hywel, I have a surprise.   She glanced down suddenly, and
her hands trembled as she signed. I saw her silver earrings flash
in the light. —I missed my monthly time, and I think—I think—

—Etaa!   I touched her stomach, still flat and firm beneath the
thin linen of her shift.

—Yes!   Her smile broke into laughter as I pulled her down
beside me into the hammock. Eight years of marriage and seven
Midsummer's Days had passed, and we had begun to think Etaa
was barren, like so many others; until now—

I held her tightly in the soft clasp of our hammock, swaying
gently side by side. —We're truly blessed, Etaa. Maybe the
Mother was waiting for this day.   I began to kiss her, pulling at
her shift, but all at once she pushed me away.

—No, Hywel, today we have to wait!

I grinned. —You take me for an old man, me, the father of your
child? I won't slight the Mother today—but neither will I slight
my wife!

Yesterday was all it could have been, the Sun's glory dazzling
the sky, the bright fields of grain . . . Etaa's radiant face in the
Mother's Glen, on the day when she became Wife and Mother to
us all, and I was her chosen.

But then, this morning, she asked me to let her ride with us
when I went to trade with the Neaane. We have traded with the
Neaane since we first settled on their border, longer ago than

anybody can remember. They are a strange, inward people who
have lost all understanding of the Mother. Their lives are grim
and joyless because of it; they even persecute their people who
are blessed with the second sight, calling them witches. They
believe in gods who live in the sky, who abandoned them, and,
they say, caused the plague that took the Blessed Time from all
people.

We never liked their beliefs, but we liked their possessions:
soft-footed palfers to carry burdens or pull a plow, new kinds of
seed for our fields—even a way to keep the fields fertile over
many years, which gave us a more settled life. They wanted our
metalwork and jewelry, and the hides of wild animals, because
they like to show wealth even more than we do, especially the
ones who have most of it. Settled farming has given them time
to develop many strange customs, including setting some people
above all others, often for no good reason as far as we could see,
not wisdom or courage or even good vision.

Still, our trade was good for both of us, and so we lived together in peace until, in the time the elders still remember, the
Neaane's gods returned to them—or so they believed. With the
gods' return the Neaane turned against us, saying it proved their
beliefs were the only truth, and we, the Kotaane, were an abomination to their gods. Ugly rumors had come to the village of
incidents farther south, and even here ill-feeling hurt our deal-
ings with the local lord and his people at Barys-town. I didn't
want to see it grow into war, because I had never wanted to kill
anyone, and because a war with the powerful Neaane could only
bring us death and pain. I also didn't want to expose my priest-
ess-wife with her unborn child to the hostility and insults I'd
gotten used to in Barys-town. But she insisted, saying she wanted
adventure; she was as irresistible as the summer day, and as
beautiful, and I gave in, because I wanted to share it with her.

When we reached Barys-town, we found it choked with the
soldiers of the king, the most powerful lord in their land. He was
making a rare visit to his borderlands, probably to make certain

they were secure against us. I saw the king himself, not thirty feet away but hardly more than a blur to my eyes; he sat on his sharp-footed horse, watching with his nobles as we began to barter. But then his soldiers crowded around us, waving at Etaa and mocking her, calling her "witch" and "whore." One tried to pull her from her palfer, but she hit him with an iron pot. The king made no sign to stop them, and angrily I ordered my goods taken up, not caring who my nervous palfer stepped on in the crowd. I had taken too many insults from the people of Barys-town in the past, and while they gathered sullenly around I told them this insult to my wife was the last one, and they would get no more metal from me. We turned and rode away, passing the fat local priest of the sky-gods, who had come for the jeweled god-sign he had commissioned from me. Seeing him, I threw it onto a dunghill. I didn't look back to see whether he ran to fetch it out. Etaa was very pale, riding beside me; she signed that it was an evil place behind us, and begged me to keep my promise and never go back, because she'd seen hatred in too many eyes.

Then horror froze her face, though I didn't see anything; she turned in her saddle, looking wildly back at the town. —Hywel!

My palfer lunged sideways as an arrow struck its flank. I jerked its head back, saw the mounted men coming fast behind us, the sunlight sparking on chain mail. Etaa pulled at my arm and we kicked our palfers into a gallop, getting drenched with spray as we plunged through the stream that crossed the trail.

We rode for the hills that separated our village from the Ne-aane, hoping to lose the soldiers in the rough brush where our palfers were surer-footed. But the Neaane seemed to know our every move; again and again we lost sight of them, but they never lost us, and always they cut us off from escape. We knew nothing about the broken uplands, soon we were lost and scattered until only Etaa and I still rode together; but the soldiers followed like hounds on a trail.

Until at last the rigid black-striped hands of a stream-cut gorge brought us to the end of our run—the edge of a cliff where the

snow water dashed itself down, down to oblivion, and there was
nowhere left to go. My palfer sank to its knees as I slid from its
back and went to look down. The drop was sheer, a hundred feet
or more onto the wet-silvered rocks below. I turned back,
stunned with despair. —They still follow?

—Yes! Etaa threw herself off her palfer, her dappled gown
mud-smeared, the summer blossoms torn from her hair. She
clung to me, breathing hard, and then turned back to face the
brush-filled gorge. —Mother, they're coming, they still come!
How can they follow us, when they can't *see*? She trembled like
a trapped beast. —Why, Hywel? Why are they doing this?

I touched her cheek, bloody with scratches, with my own
scratched hand. —I don't know! But . . . My hands tried to close
over the words. —But you know what they'll do, if they take us.

Her eyes closed. —I know . . . Her arms closed in fear around
her body.

—And burn us alive then, so that our souls can never rest. I
glanced toward the cliff, trembling now too. —Etaa—   Her eyes
were open again and following my gaze.

—Must we—   Her hands pressed her stomach, caressed our
child.

I saw the riders now, a shifting blur down the shadowed canyon. —We have to; we can't let them take us.

We went together to the cliff's edge and stood looking down,
clinging together, dizzy with the drop and fear. Etaa threw out a
quick handful of dirt and prayed to the Mother, as it drifted down,
that She would know and receive us. And then she looked up at
me, shaking so that I could barely understand her. —Oh, Hywel,
I'm so afraid of heights . . . Her mouth quivered; she might have
laughed. She drew my head down then and we kissed, long and
sweetly. —I love you only, now and always.

—Now and always—   I signed. I saw in her eyes that there was
no more time. —Now!   I fumbled for her hand, seeing soldiers
at the mouth of the gorge, her stricken face, and then—nothing.
I leaped.

And felt her hand jerk free from mine at the last instant. I saw her face fall upward, framed in dark hair, through cold rushing eternity; and then my body smashed on the rocks below, and tore the bitter anguish from my mind.

Why I ever woke again at all I don't know; or why I still live now, when I would gladly die and be done with my pain. But I woke into nightmare, trapped in this broken body with my shame: knowing I had jumped and Etaa had not. I had let her be taken by the Neaane. I tortured my eyes for some sign, some movement above the face of the black-striped cliff; but there was nothing, only the glaring edge of day, the red Eye of the Cyclops. Etaa was gone. The falling river leaped and foamed beside me, mocking my grief and my aching mouth with cold silver drops. I strained my head until my metal collar cut into my throat, but nothing moved. And so I lay still finally, and prayed, half in dreams and half in madness, and couldn't even form her name: Etaa, Etaa . . . forgive me.

Overhead the clouds gathered purple-gray, darkening the noon; the Mother in Her grief drew Her garments close and rejected Her Lover. The crops will fail. She has cursed Her children for this abomination; for the unbearable sacrilege of the Neaane, for the pitiful weakness of Hywel, Her Lover and son. She tears the clouds with knives of light, crying vengeance, and Her tears fall cold and blinding on my face. I drown in Her tears, I drown in sorrow . . . Mother! If I could move one more finger, to make Your sign . . . Giver of Life, let me live! Give me back my body, and I will give You the heads of the Neaane. I will avenge this desecration, avenge Your priestess . . . my Etaa . . . Mother, hear me—

Who touches my face? Work, eyes, damn you . . . Smiling, because I'm still alive . . . they wear black and red. They are the king's men! And they will take my soul. Mother, let me die first. No. Let me join my Etaa, on the wind. And have pity on us. . . .

PART II: THE KING

It's hardly an army fit for a king. . . . But Archbishop Shappistre
tells my people openly these days that King Meron is bewitched
—and they believe him. They believe anything the Church tells
them. My poor people! Though with my only child lost, and the
Kedonny eating away Tramaine while the Gods do nothing, who
can blame them? But if I angered the Gods by wanting the Kedonny Witch, if I brought myself ruin, it wasn't because my mind
was not my own. It was because it was too much my own, and I
knew exactly what I was doing.

And yet, when I look back and remember how I came to this,
perhaps there was a kind of bewitchment about it. For it was on
the day I first saw her that the plan came into my mind, as I
watched her ride into the border village with the Kedonny traders: my Black Witch, my Etaa . . . The Earl of Barys' priest pointed
her out to me, signing she was a pagan priestess, his fat hands
trembling at how these godless Kedonny worshipped wanton-
ness and *hearing;* at which point he spat religiously. I fumbled for
my lenses to get a better look, and was surprised to see, not some
debauched crone, but a fresh-faced girl with masses of dark hair
falling loose across her shoulders.

The Kedonny believe that hearing is a godly blessing, and not
a curse, as our Church considers it to be; and for my own part,
all my life I've questioned the practices that teach us to suppress
it. Why should any gods who had our best interests in mind ask
us to weaken ourselves? Why, when my own father had passing
good vision, had he felt guilty about it, and chosen for my mother
a woman who could barely see his face—so that without the
lenses so kindly presented me by the Gods, I must stumble into
doorframes in a most unkingly manner? Now, watching the Ke-

donny priestess, revered as the most gifted of her people, my old
discontent was transformed. Suddenly I realized that my own
heirs didn't need to suffer the same weakness and dependency.
I would get them a mother who could give them the strengths I
could not. . . .

I snapped out of my thoughts to see the Kedonny traders
riding abruptly away, their faces set in anger, while my men-at-
arms gestured curses and the villagers shuffled sullenly between
them. Almost without thinking, I summoned my carriage and
gave orders to my men for pursuit.

As my carriage rose into the air over the heads of the gaping
locals, I looked down on the earl's priest digging inexplicably in
a dunghill. If I were a religious man, I might have taken it for a
sign.

My carriage was made by the Gods, a smooth sphere with a
texture like ivory that not only moved over land without using
palfers but could take to the sky like a bird. From the air I could
track the fleeing Kedonny easily, and guide my men in separating
the woman from the rest—all except one man, who stayed stubbornly at her side even when we drove them into a trap. But in
the end he was no problem, because he flung himself from the
cliff, apparently afraid of being burned alive. I saw his body
smashed on the rocks below, and turned away with a shudder,
thinking how close I had come to losing what I sought—for my
men said that the woman had pulled back from the edge at the
last second, and they had barely gotten to her in time. Some of
them had thrown her down on the ground, with obvious intent,
and I disciplined those with the flat of my sword, in a fury edged
with shame. Then I took her up myself, her face the color of
hearth ash, and carried her to my carriage.

Being king, I had no need to explain my behavior to anyone
at Barys Castle, though there was a flutter of knowing amusement
among the nobles as I said an early good-night. I went directly
to my chambers, where the Kedonny priestess waited, and left
orders with my watch that they were not to disturb me.

The woman sat huddled at the window slit, staring out into the sodden twilight; but as I entered she jerked around, fixing her wide, burning eyes on me. I smiled, because it proved she could hear, and because I saw again that she was a beauty. But seeing me, she pressed back against the cold stone slit as though she wanted to throw herself out.

"Your lover is dead—"

She hesitated, her face blank, and I realized she couldn't read lips. I repeated with my hands, —Your lover is dead. You tried to follow him, and failed. I wouldn't try it again.

She understood the common sign-speech at least, for she sank back down on the seat with her face in her hands. I brought my own hands together sharply, and she glanced up again, startled. I noticed a meal, untouched, on the carven chest beside her. —Will you eat?

She shook her head, her face still frozen.

—Stand up.

She rose stiffly, her hands clutching at her torn gown, her slender arms bare except for bracelets and burned as dark as any peasant's. Her unbound hair gleamed black in the flickering fire-light, tangled with wilting flowers and twigs. On her face the dust of flight was smeared and tracked by tears, but I was relieved to see she wasn't the dirt-encrusted barbarian I had half expected; she looked cleaner than some members of my own court. Her ragged dress was coarsely woven and dull-colored, but somehow it brought to my mind the pattern of green leaves and the muted light of deep woods . . . This was my wanton priestess, the fertile Earth incarnate, who would strengthen the royal line. And even now her witchy beauty went to my head like wine.

It must have shown, for she shrank back again. I pulled off my cloak, amused. —What, priestess, am I so hard to look at? They say a Kedonny priestess will lie with any man who wants her. I touched my crown. —Well, I'm king in this land; surely that makes me as good as any Kedonny shennherd. I caught her arms, and suddenly she came to life, fighting with a strength that stunned me. She struck at my face, knocking off my lenses, and I felt more than saw them shatter on the floor. Angry, I dragged her to the bed and threw her down, pulling off the rags of her dress.

And then I forced her, ruthlessly, in the way I thought befitted a whore of the uncivilized Kedonny. On the bed she did not struggle, but lay limp as a corpse under me, biting her lips while fresh tears of humiliation ran down her face, staining the satin pillows. Her eyes were as brown as peat, the only part of her that showed life, and they tore at me in grief and outrage and supplication. But I looked away, too angry and too eager to admit I had no right to make her mine.

And whatever else may come to pass, that is the one thing I will never forgive myself. Because I did not use a pagan slut that night: I raped a gentle woman, on the day she saw her husband die. Because later I came to love her; but I could never undo the wrong, or hope to change the bitterness I had caused in her heart.

She slept far into the next day, the sleep of exhaustion; but she sat waiting, clad in her rags, when I came back to my chamber after making ready for our departure. She looked as if she hadn't slept at all, or as if she had wakened to find herself still caught up in a nightmare. But she lifted her hands and made the first words I had seen from her, strangely accented: —Will you let me go now?

It took me a moment to realize that she thought I had done all this merely for a night's pleasure. —No. I'm taking you with me to Newham.

—What do you want of me?   Her hands trembled slightly.

I pushed my new lenses higher on my nose. —I want your child.

Her hands pressed her stomach in an odd gesture of fear, then leaped into a series of words that meant nothing to me; I guessed she was pleading with me in her own language.

I shook my head and signed patiently, —I want you to bear me sons. I want your—your "blessings" for them. They will be princes, heirs to the throne of Tramaine. They'll have luxuries you can't imagine—and so will you, if you obey me.

She twisted away hopelessly to gaze out the window slit. I could see the line of hills that separated us from the Kedonny, gray land merging into gray sky in the silver rain. Her hands pressed her stomach again.

I clapped and she looked back at me. —What is your sign, priestess?

—Etaa.

—The serving women will bring you new clothes, Etaa. My fingers tangled on the unfamiliar word. —We leave within the hour.

We returned to the palace at Newham, since continuing in the marches would only have made an incident likely; our return took several days, because my carriage had to go more slowly than usual for the sake of my retinue. But we outdistanced the rain at last, and though the roads were mired, the fresh rolling green of the land, the fertile fields and dappled groves of horwoods filled me with pride. Looming Cyclops, which the peasants called the Godseye, merged its banded greens with the green of the earth, and to one side I could see the gibbous outer moon paled by its magnificence. The outer moon was swirled with white that the court astronomer said was clouds, like the ones on Earth. When I was young I had thought of taking the Gods' carriage and flying out to see it, having been told that men once lived there too. But the Gods said the air grew thin as you went higher, and told me I would suffocate if I tried. I tried anyway, and found they were right.

The Kedonny woman accepted the matter of flight without the terror I had expected, only asking, —How does it do this?

—The Gods give it power. It was a gift to my grandfather on their return to Earth.

—There are no gods; there is only the Goddess. A small defiance flickered on her face.

I glanced briefly at the forward compartment, where my coach-man tended our flight. —I agree: there are no Gods. But never say it again, priestess, since you know well enough what happens to heretics. You're under my protection, but my archbishop will not welcome a pagan at court.

She settled back into the velvet cushions, and into her quiet resignation, confined and incongruous in the stiff, brocaded gown and the modesty of her headdress. Small silver bells shaped like winket blossoms dangled from wires piercing her ears; she toyed with them constantly. Sometimes as she did she would almost smile, her eyes fixed on nothing.

As I watched her, the image came to me of a pitiful wild child I had seen as a boy, kept in a cage at a fair. The kharks had stolen human children and raised them as their own, until the Gods came and destroyed the kharks. The wild humans could never adjust to normal life again, and I had wondered if there was something about being wild that was better than being a prince, and it saddened me to think that all the kharks were gone. I looked away from Etaa, falling into another memory of my child-hood and the Gods: of the time I had inadvertently spied on them during hide-and-hunt with the pages—and seen the grotesque, inhuman thing they treated as a brother. And somehow I knew that this *thing* was the Gods' true form, and that the too-perfect faces they showed to us were only enchantments. I slipped away and ran to tell my father, but he was furious at my blasphemy, and beat me for it, forbidding me ever to speak against our Gods again. I never did, for I realized quickly enough that whatever they weren't, they had powers even a king dared not question. I often wondered if my father had realized that too. But privately I never gave up my heresies, and because of that I found less and less that was deserving of reverence in the teachings of the Church. Which is why my cousin, Archbishop Shappistre, and I have never been much in accord. Why, indeed, he would gladly see me dead and damned.

The archbishop was quick to inform me of his displeasure in

the latest instance, after my arrival at the palace at Newham. My good wife, the queen, did not come out to meet us, sending word that she was indisposed. I wondered if she had heard that I was bringing back a mistress; but since through fifteen years of marriage she had rarely been disposed to come and greet me, it hardly mattered. I espied her brother the archbishop among the nobles, however, marking my progress across the banner-bright courtyard from the carriage, with Etaa at my side. He alone was not amused; but then, like his sister, he rarely was. I anticipated a visit from him before the day was out.

I was not disappointed, for early in the evening my watchman entered the room, standing patiently with his face to the door until I should happen to notice and acknowledge him. Etaa started at his entrance, and I caught her motion in the mirror I had fixed at the side of my lenses; it occurred to me that her very presence could be a useful thing. I went to touch the watchman's shoulder, giving him audience, and was informed that the archbishop desired to speak with me. I sent for him, and returned to the table where I was laboriously reviewing the reports sent to me by my advisers. Etaa watched from the long bench where she befriended the fire, avoiding me. Even though she did, after so many years alone I found that the constant presence of a woman was oddly comforting.

The archbishop did not appear to share my feelings, however. His gaunt, ascetic face had always seemed at odds with the flaming richness of his robes; but the look of pious indignation that he affected on seeing Etaa touched on the absurd. "Your majesty." The modish sleeves of his outer robe swept the flags as he bowed low. "I had hoped I might speak with you—alone."

I smiled. "Etaa does not read lips, my lord. You may speak freely in her presence." I gained a certain pleasure at his discomfort, having been made uncomfortable by him often enough in my youth . . . and more recently.

"It is about—this woman—that I've come to your majesty. I strongly protest her presence at court; it's hardly fitting for our king to take a pagan priestess for a leman. Indeed, it smacks of blasphemy." I fancied seeing hungry flames leap behind his eyes; or perhaps it was only firelight reflecting on his lenses. "The Gods have expressed their displeasure to me. And the queen, your lawful wife, is extremely upset."

"I daresay the queen, your sister, has little reason to be upset with me. I have allowed her all the lovers she wants, and the Gods know she has enough of them."

The archbishop stiffened. "Are you saying she is not within her right?"

"Not at all." Divorce was forbidden by the Church, which places duty far above pleasure. As a result, it was common that childless couples would seek an heir from formalized liaisons; though most of the queen's were far from being that. "But we were married, as you know, when I was sixteen, and in all the years since she has not produced a child. If I couldn't give her one, I would gladly acknowledge someone else's. But she is ten years my senior—frankly, my lord, I've begun to give up hope." I didn't add that I'd even given up trying—our marriage had been arranged to bind factions, and it had never been a love match. "This woman pleases me, and I must have an heir. Her beliefs will not affect her childbearing."

"But she is not of noble breeding—"

"She is not a Shappistre by blood, you mean? You would do well to contemplate the scriptures and the law, my lord. The relationship between church and state is a two-edged blade; take care that you don't cut yourself on it."

He bowed low again, his bald head reddening to match his jeweled cap. "Your majesty . . ." Abruptly he glanced at Etaa and clapped his hands. Etaa, who had returned to her fire-watching, started visibly and turned. A smile of triumph crossed his face. —She hears. I must request that your majesty have her ears put out as soon as possible . . . in accordance with the scriptures, and the law. His hands moved carefully in the common signing.

My fists clenched over an angry retort. Then, evenly and also by hand, I replied, —She is a foreigner. While under my protection she is subject to neither the religion nor the laws of Tramaine. And now, good night, Archbishop; I am very weary after my long journey. I crossed my arms.

My archbishop turned without another word and left the room.

I joined Etaa by the fire, noting how she drew away as I sat down, and asked if she had understood us.

Her eyes met mine briefly, and wounded me with their misery, before she signed, —He would hurt me. He fears the blessings of the Mother.

I nodded, reminding her that here her "blessings" were sins, but assuring her that she would not be hurt while she was under my protection. —Tell me, Etaa, what did you think of the archbishop? He's the high priest of my people.

—He does not like you.

It surprised a laugh out of me.

—And he is a poor man to be priest, who cannot feel another creature's soul. To deny the second sight is to deny one's—gods.

—But the Gods say they wish it that way.

—Then they are false gods, who do not love you.

Then they are false Gods. . . . I watched the flames eat darkness for a long moment. —But they're here, Etaa, and powerful; and so is their Church. The archbishop would gladly see you burn as a witch, and so would almost anyone. But I believe as you do, that hearing is a blessing—and I want to share it. You will give my children the "second sight." And you can give it to me.

—From now on, if you hear anyone come into my presence you will tell me immediately, wherever we are. It's not an easy thing to be king in these times, or any times. I need your help . . . and you need mine. If anything should happen to me, there's no one who would protect you. You'd be burned alive, and suffer terrible agony, and your soul would be lost to your Goddess forever. Do you understand me? I knew that she had understood everything, from the changes that crossed her face. Slowly she nodded, her hands pressing the stiff, gold-embroidered russet that covered her stomach.

Unthinking, and somehow ashamed, I reached out in a gesture

of comfort, only to have her wither under my touch like a blossom in the frost. Gently I went on touching her, but to no avail, and when at last I took her to the bedchamber, she lay as limp and deathly unresponsive as ever. As she turned her face from a final kiss I caught her shoulders and shook her, saying, "Damn you, you heathen bitch!" I let her fall back against the pillows, remembering that she didn't understand me, and raised my hands into the lamplight. She lifted her own defensively, as though she thought I was going to strike her, and I brushed them aside. —Watch me! Do you think a man enjoys taking a corpse to bed? I know what you are with your own people, why should you turn away from me? I'll have an heir from you whatever you do; you're mine now, so why not enjoy it—

Her fist flew out and struck me across the jaw. I jerked back in painful disbelief, while her hands leaped in hysterical fury.

—I serve my Goddess in holiness, I am not a Neaane whore! You have stolen a priestess, you have defiled Her, murderer, and She will never give you heirs. Neaa, you murdered my husband, whom I loved. Soul-stealer, I would burn a thousand times and weep forever in the wind before I would give you pleasure! Never will I . . . never . . . Hywel . . .   She crumpled into sobbing and meaningless gestures, and buried her face in the cover.

Slowly I rose from the bed, and groping for my lenses, forgave the only woman who had ever struck a king of Tramaine.

I still took her to my bed as often as I could, although her wretchedness had driven all the pleasure from it; for, priestess of fertility though she might be, and king though I might be, children are a rare gift of fortune since the plague. And the Gods have done nothing to change that. I was away from her much of the time after our arrival in Newham, though, being engrossed as usual in affairs of state. And so I could scarcely believe my eyes when fat old Mabis, whom I had sent to serve Etaa, informed me gleefully of seeing signs that I was going to be a father. She was my nurse as a child (and so accepted most of my quirks, including

a godless mistress), and assured me that if anyone could tell, it
was Mabis. Giddy with pride, I forgot the quarreling of my nobles
and the complaints of the burghers; I left even my watchman
behind and ran like a boy to find Etaa.

She sat as she so often did, gazing out the high windows, her
hair hanging at her back in a heavy plait, for Mabis couldn't get
her to wear a covering. She looked up in amazement as I entered;
composing myself with an effort, I managed to keep from de-
stroying the moment by lifting her up in my arms. She seemed
to know why I had come, and I thought, relieved, that maybe
traces of pride hid behind her dark eyes as I bent my knee before
her. I gave her my heartfelt thanks and asked what gift I could
give her, in return for the one she had given me.

She glanced out the open window for a moment, her face lit
with rainbows from the colored glass; when she looked back, her
hands were stiff with emotion. —Let me go outside.

—That's all you want?

She nodded.

—Then you shall have it. Carefully I took her hand, and
ordering my watch to keep well behind, led her outside into the
palace gardens. Etaa somehow belonged in the beauty of roses
and pale marisettes, her own wild grace set free from the gray
stone confines of the palace walls. I took her to the limit of the
green slopes overlooking the placid Aton and the edge of New-
ham-town on the river's farther shore. I tried to describe for her
the city that was the heart of Tramaine, the bright, swarming
mass of humanity, the marketplaces, the pageantry of New Year's
and the celebrations of Armageddon Day. She gazed and questioned with a hesitant wonder that pleased me, but I thought she
seemed glad when the peaceful bowers closed her in again.

We made our way along drowsy, dappled paths heavy with the
heat of a late summer's afternoon, and I found it hard to believe
the sun was already half hidden as it sank behind Cyclops. And
as we walked I saw the drawn, anguished look fade from Etaa's
face for the first time since midsummer. At one point, we unex-

pectedly came upon young Lord Tolper and his sweetheart, in a compromising position on the grass. I took Etaa's arm and led her quickly away, before the blushing lord felt required to rise and make a bow; as we turned to go I saw a quick, sweet smile of remembrance touch her lips, and felt a pang of envy.

Because I had so little time to myself, I instructed Mabis to accompany Etaa in the future into the gardens—and to do anything else that might be required for her health and comfort. Mabis confided that she had already been gathering healthful herbs for the babe at Etaa's request; for, bless her pagan soul, the girl had the skill of ten Newham physicians, and had even told her of a poultice to ease the ache in an old woman's back. Mabis was deeply religious in her own way, but she had never liked the queen, and Etaa's thoughtless kindnesses and lack of vanity had won her heart.

Etaa had little contact with the court in the beginning, partly at my wish and partly at her own. Yet she found another friend in the palace before long, a fellow outcast of sorts: young Willem, who was one of my pages. He was a strange, nervous boy, his hair as flaxen as her own was black, who seemed to be constantly starting at unseen sights and sometimes even to see around corners. He stuttered in both noble and common speech, as though not only his lips but even his own fingers wouldn't obey him. One afternoon I came to call on Etaa in her chambers and found him sitting at her feet before the fire, their faces half in the green light of waning eclipse, half ruddy with fireglow. They looked up at me almost as one, and Willem scrambled to his feet to bow, barely concealing his dismay at the arrival of his king. I gathered that Etaa had been telling him a story, and asked her to continue, feeling that I would be glad of a little diversion too.

She took up her story again almost self-consciously, a Kedonny tale of how a wandering people had come to settle and find a home at last. I grew fascinated myself by the realism of it, even though it was riddled with allusions to the supernatural powers of the Mother. It struck me that this must be the story of how they had come to our borders, in the time of the second Barthelwydde king, nearly two hundred years before.

I was fascinated too by the motions of her hands, so quick and bold compared to the refined gestures of the court poets, whose graceful imported romances usually left me yawning. Occasionally she would stumble, breaking the trancelike rhythm of her tale, and I remembered that she had to translate as she told, a feat that would leave my poets ill with envy.

When her tale was finished I sent Willem away to his neglected duties, and, impulsively, asked Etaa if she would come with me to see our own collected lore. She nodded, politely curious. The child growing within her seemed to have given her a thing to love in place of the man she had lost; perhaps because of it—and because I no longer touched her—she tolerated me now, and sometimes almost seemed glad of my company.

I led the way into the part of the palace given over to the Gods; it was hung with gilt-framed paintings and ornate tapestries of religious scenes. I went there often, not for homage, but to visit the repository for the holy books. It had taken all the power and influence of the kingship to defy the clergy successfully, but I had been determined to study on my own those remnants of the Golden Age that the Gods deemed too complex—and possibly too heretical—for the layman. The priests who were entrusted with the books spent the greater part of their lives studying them, since they were presumably protected by their faith (or, I sometimes suspected, by their ignorance). I had had the best possible education, but even I found to my frustration that most of the learning from before the plague time was far above me. The Gods would give me no clues, of course, though they claimed omniscience, since they opposed my right to study the sacred lore. But then, they also refused to give guidance to the priests.

As we entered the corridors of the Gods a viridian-robed priest came to meet us, and I recognized him as Bishop Perrine, the archbishop's chief lackey. His bow was scarcely adequate, his lips moving in rigid formality. "Your majesty. You cannot possibly bring that—that woman here! It would be sacrilege to reveal the holy works to a—a pagan."

I smiled tolerantly, suspecting that after the morning's usual strife with the archbishop, this very scene had been secretly taking shape in my mind. "Bishop Perrine, this woman is acting as my watchman. I am quite sure she can't read—"

Etaa started, and I glanced past the bishop's shaven head to see one of the very Gods coming toward us down the hall. Bishop Perrine turned, following my gaze, and together we dropped down on one knee. Too late I noticed that Etaa still stood, defiantly facing the towering, inhumanly beautiful figure in robes lit with an unearthly inner glow. I signaled her to kneel but she ignored me, caught up in fearful amazement.

I waited while God regarded priestess in return, my knee grating on the unaccustomed hardness of the floor and my head thrown back until a crick began to form in my neck. At last an expression passed over his face that I almost took for appreciation; and remembering us, he gave us permission to rise, signing, —My pardon, your majesty, for causing you discomfort; but I forgot myself, at the sight of the opposition.

Bishop Perrine began apologies, his fingers knotting in nervous obsequiousness, but the God stopped him. —No need, Bishop Perrine—I understand. And she is charming, your majesty. I see why they say the Black Witch has enchanted you.

I inclined my head while I mastered a frown, and signed with proper deference, —She is no witch, Lord, but merely a handsome woman. Her beliefs are of no consequence; only primitive superstition.

—I am relieved to learn that. His hands expressed a faint mockery, each move slightly too perfect. —Etaa, can you deny the presence of the true Gods, now that you see one before you?

Slowly she nodded. —You are beautiful to see. But you are a man, and so you cannot be a god. There are no gods other than our Mother. Her face was serene, her eyes shone with belief. I had often envied unshakable faith, but never more than now.

Bishop Perrine shuddered visibly beside me and clutched his god-sign, but I saw the God laugh. —Well signed, priestess. Your belief may be misguided, but not even I can deny its purity. Bishop Perrine, I take it you sought to keep this woman from entering here. I commend you—but I think you should let her pass. Perhaps some further exposure to our beliefs would do her soul good.

Bishop Perrine dropped to the floor, and I sank grudgingly down beside him as the God passed. And as I led Etaa on to the repository, I wondered that a God should have treated us so affably. I knew that the various Gods who called on us had different manners, just as they had different faces when you were used to their splendor. But they were seldom so kindly disposed toward heretics, or anything that threatened the stability of their Church.

Etaa brushed the blue velvet of my sleeve. —Meron— She seldom called me by name, although it pleased me. —How is it that you do not believe in your own gods, when you've seen them all your life? Her hands moved discreetly, half hidden by her wide fur-trimmed sleeves.

I remembered my comment to her in the carriage, so long ago. —You don't believe in them because you say they look like men. Our scriptures tell us that they *are* like men; but I've seen them when they were not. I told her what I'd seen as a child. —So whatever they are, they're *not* the Gods of the scriptures who abandoned us long ago. But they control the lives of my people, and the peoples of all the adjoining lands, through the church: these—false Gods.

She frowned. —It was only after the gods came that your people began to hate us. Are they cruel, then, to make your people cruel? Her eyes stole glances at the dark scenes displayed along the walls.

I shook my head. —No . . . they're not cruel to us. But they don't condemn cruelty toward nonbelievers. They want no competition, I think. I looked away from a woven witch-burning.

—They've done good, useful things for us—driven the wild kharks from the countryside, helped us grow better crops, shown us how to control the shaking fever . . . they've made us—comfortable. Too comfortable, I sometimes think. As though . . . as though they wanted us to stay here forever, and be content never to regain the Golden Age again. And there *was* a Golden Age, I've seen proof of it, in the volumes we go to see now.

—Volumes? Books? Excitement lit her face.—We have a book in our village, that I've studied with the elders; it's said to be from the Blessed Time, when all people knew the touch of the Mother.

—You have that legend too? I stopped moving. —Then it must have been widespread—perhaps the whole world! Think of it, Etaa! But what knowledge we have left, the Gods keep hidden from anyone who could use it. My bitterness made my hands tighten. —The Church teaches us "humility"—not to strive, not to tempt fate, or the Gods, but follow the old worn path to sure salvation. It teaches the people to hate the "second sight" that could give them such freedom, and to hate your people most of all, because you make a religion of it. The Gods make us comfortable, but not because they love us. Damn th—

Etaa caught my hands suddenly, in a graceful grip that was like a vise; she forced them to her lips in a seemingly effortless kiss. I stared at her, astounded, and caught movement in the mirror at the side of my lenses. Down the hall, the archbishop stood watching us intently; she had kept me from cursing the Gods in his presence. I let her know by my tightened hands that I understood. She freed me, and I signed, —Come, love, first go with me to see the holy relics. We continued to the repository; the archbishop did not follow us. I wondered if he had seen enough.

I thanked Etaa, and for a moment she touched my hands again; but then she only looked away, signing stiffly, —Your life is my life, and my child's, as you have said. You need not thank me for that.

But I felt she had been repaid when her hands rose in wonder as we entered the repository and she saw the books—thirty-five

volumes resting on yellow satin, above the elaborately embell-
ished study table. Two priests were at their contemplation; not
having attendants with me, I went myself and tapped them on the
shoulder, asking them to leave. Their faces flashed surprise, acceptance—and a hint of scandal as they passed Etaa and left us
alone. Etaa went to stand by the sloping desk, looking down
reverently on the smooth, timeless pages of the open books. And
then I learned one more thing about the barbaric Kedonny—that
their priestess read the printed words of the old language as well
as any man of our own priesthood.

And so, though I had taken her with me originally out of a
certain obstreperous pride, and because I valued her as a watchman, I began taking her with me for her opinions as well. Word
of the pagan woman studying the holy books got rapidly back to
the archbishop, and when he came to make his complaint I was
forced to remind him sharply that he spoke to his king. I think
despite his hunger for personal power he believed in the
Church's tenets and its Gods, and was torn by the dilemma they
created for him: he believed I committed sacrilege, but because
a God had approved it there was nothing he could do to stop me.
Or so I thought, even though I knew well enough he would do
anything to get at the kingship, for the aspirations of his family
and the furtherance of Church power.

As the dark noons of autumn passed into the bright, snow-
blind days of true winter, I continued to take Etaa with me to
study the books, and to have her beside me as my watchman and
companion whenever the occasion allowed. Her coming mother-
hood grew obvious to all, and was the target for much discreet
levity, and also more serious speculation. Also for some unpleasant and ugly rumors revolving on witchcraft, whose sources I
thought I knew. I didn't bother to deal with them, however, being
more concerned with other matters; particularly with the rebel-
lious Kedonny, who stubbornly harried our borderlands even
though the snows lay heavy on the earth. There were rumors that
a new leader had emerged, using the defiling of a priestess to

rally them, and so I sent messengers to my most trusted border lords, telling them to be on guard. But the Kedonny would strike whenever a back was turned, and then fade away into the hills, and their Mother shielded them in Her snowy cloak, as Etaa would have signed—if she'd known. My best leaders seemed helpless against the determined fanaticism of the Kedonny chief, a man called only "the Smith," who was becoming a bogeyman in Tramaine fit to compete with the Godseye that looked down on my people's sinful lives.

At last came Midwinter's Day—a day I would not have marked except that I found Etaa kneeling awkwardly at her hearth, wearing dappled green velvet. She was tossing stalks of ripened wheat into the fierce blaze and reciting a ceremony of the Mother. Pale Willem crouched watching as if hypnotized, while his spotted pup chewed unnoticed at the tail of his jerkin. Mabis sat spinning in the far corner of the chamber, her round chill-reddened face set in righteous disapproval. I was mildly disturbed to see Willem so caught up in Kedonny ways; but his friendship with Etaa cheered them both, and lately I found it hard not to prefer Etaa to our own dour ways myself. But I chided Willem, and he disappeared, ghostlike as always, when I took Etaa away to visit the holy books.

That day she sat beside me as usual, though lately she found it hard to bend forward at the ornate table's edge. (Mabis had said my son—for I was sure it would be a son, just as I was sure he would hear like his mother—must be a strapping babe, perhaps even twins.) Her ungainly roundness charmed me even more than her former grace.

I had taken my lenses off, in order to read close up, for with Etaa there, I had no fear of being caught unawares. She glanced down as I set the lenses on the table, and then suddenly she caught at my arm. —Meron, look— She picked up the end of the thin, dark strip that lay pinned under them, curling it between her fingers. —What is this? It's like glass, but soft as paper. And look—look! Tiny words, under your lens—

I squinted, unable to make them out, and reached for a magni-

fying glass. —It's plastic, that the Gods use . . . and that we used,
once, in the Golden Age.   A strange excitement filled me as Etaa
pulled the rest of the tape out from under the shelf into the
lamplight. —How did it get here? Could the Gods have forgotten—

Etaa took up the glass and held it over the plastic strip.

—Can you read it?

She didn't see me, but sat frowning, breathless with concentration, her hand toying with the silver bell at her ear. At last she
looked up, her fingers barely moving as she signed, —I can read
it. It is part of a book in the old language. . . . But it's from *before*
the plague time.

—Are you sure?   All our holy books had been written after the
plague; though they mentioned the wonders of the Golden Age,
they were clouded with the despair of a failing people, and many
references were unclear. My hands shook. —Read it to me.

I held the glass and Etaa translated, until her eyes were red and
her hands trembled with fatigue. And though many things were
still unclear, because they were so far above us, one undeniable
truth stood out: —All men *could* hear, in the Golden Age. I was
right! Men weren't meant to be less than the Gods—men *were*
Gods. The Church has lost the truth in fear since the plague time,
and these false "Gods" use our superstition to control us.   I
took Etaa's weary hands and kissed them. —But our son will be
the beginning of a new Golden Age, he'll hear and see clearly,
and show my people the truth. He will be our greatest king.
Etaa smiled, caught up in my dreams, and if she smiled for her
son and not for me, it didn't lessen the fullness of my joy.

And then the moment was torn by a lash of pain that raked my
back, a blow that knocked me from my seat. My useless eyes met
billows of indigo as I rolled, and a streak of light arcing down at
my face; desperately I threw up my hands. But before the blade
could find me again, a sweep of green velvet blocked my sight as
Etaa flung herself on the attacking priest. Fair hands dimmed the
shining blade, and somehow she drove him back from me while

I got to my feet. I caught up my lenses and drew my dagger, only to see him fling her against the wall and bolt toward the door. I brought the priest down as he tried to get past me; his skull cracked against the flags, and the knife flew from his grasp.

And beyond him I saw Etaa curled on her side on the floor, racked with a spasm of pain. She pressed her stomach, staining the velvet with blood from her slashed hands. I looked down again into the face of my attacker, full of terror now as my dagger rested on his throat. And saw that he was no priest: dirty hair slipped from under his cap, his face was young, but grimy and pinched with hardship. He was a paid assassin out of the Newham stews, and I was sure he was a hearer as well. And I couldn't touch him—or his master—for the Church claimed jurisdiction here. My hand tightened on the dagger hilt, and I would have slit his throat. But as blood traced my blade across his neck I felt Etaa's eyes on me, and I sickened. "Let the archbishop try you, then, for your failure, 'priest,' " I said. "And I pity you—" I struck him on the head with the dagger's butt, and felt him go limp.

Then I went to Etaa and fell on my knees beside her, raising her head. Her eyes sought me almost with hunger, and for a moment they filled with wild joy as her wounded hands brushed my face. But they tightened into fists with another spasm as she tried to form signs. —Meron . . . my child. My child . . . comes—

My throat tightened with despair. It was scarcely half the year since her conception, and that was too soon, too soon . . . I felt the back of my tunic soaking with blood, but the assassin's knife had caught in the folds of my cape and the wound was not deep. I picked Etaa up in my arms, gasping with pain, and started back through the endless halls.

Halls that were endlessly empty, until suddenly I came on the archbishop and Bishop Perrine. The archbishop saw us first, and laughter fell from his face, leaving blank horror. He hurried toward me, arms outstretched, until he met my eyes; then, and only then, did I ever see my cousin afraid. He stopped. "Your majesty—" His lips quivered; Bishop Perrine's eyes went to the trail of red on the stones behind us, and he dropped to his knees, babbling incoherently.

"My lord . . . bishop." I staggered against the wall to save my precious burden. "If my son dies, my lord, not even the Gods will find sanctuary from me." I pushed grimly past him, and saw in my mirror that he was hurrying on toward the repository.

I found a guardsman and friendly halls at last, and summoned aid. My physicians swarmed around me like flies, binding my wound and begging me to rest; but I stood at the door of the chamber where they had taken Etaa, until finally my knees buckled and I could not stand. And then I remember little except my helpless fury, at events and my own weakness, until I woke in my canopied bed, hemmed in by kneeling attendants, to face a God. I struggled toward the only thing of real importance: —Etaa . . . my child—?

I thought the God smiled, though I couldn't focus. —I have been with them—

"No!" I lunged at him, and was pulled back by my horrified attendants.

They gibbered apologies, but he waved them aside. —The lady is well, and asks for you. And your son—yes, your majesty, your son—will live. He is well grown for one born so early, and we will watch over him.

I sank back into the pillows. —Forgive me, lord, I—I was not myself. I thank you. And now, doctor, with your aid I would go to see my Etaa . . . and my son.

The Church proclaimed that my assailant was a mad priest, who had wrongly believed me guilty of sacrilege concerning the Church's holy books; he had been summarily excommunicated and put to death for his treason, upon order of the archbishop. There were mutterings in the Church faction at court that the priest was hardly mad, but in the celebration at the birth of a royal heir they were scarcely heard. I named my son Alfilere, after my father, and to me he was the most beautiful sight on Earth. And second only to him was his mother, her own face shining with pleasure as she gazed down upon him in his golden cradle or caressed him with bandaged hands.

I began to take her with me everywhere now, seeking her impressions of the things she saw at court; and though she protested, I seated her openly beside me at table. The queen still sat at my other hand, unwilling to give up any of her position, though her eyes drove daggers into my back. Her brother absented himself from the great hall these days, and I wondered if he was sharpening a new blade of his own. But he would never dare such a blatant attack on me again, and though my advisers knew of his treason and urged me to act against him, I refused. If I attacked my cousin I would risk civil war, and I would not bring that on my people for the sake of personal revenge. But I no longer went anywhere without attendants, and I saw that my guard kept watch at all times over Etaa and her child.

But though tension whispered in the halls like the chill drafts of winter, it could not discourage the spring that brightened my heart at the thought of my newborn son, or the nearness of Etaa. For the Armageddon Day festivities, I taught her, amid much laughter, to dance. I had always hated memorizing intricate patterns and steps, the watching of ceiling mirrors, the need to be constantly keeping count. But she was enchanted at this new challenge to her imagination, and her enthusiasm caught me up and made me feel the beauty of the dance.

The Armageddon celebrations, mirrored in Etaa's delighted eyes, had not seemed so bright since I was a boy, and as I carried my son in my arms I imagined how the same wonders would delight him too: the poets and jugglers and acrobats, the trained hounds and morts, the magicians flashing colored fire, even the Gods who presided, resplendent in their shining auras. All the gaudily clad folk feasting and dancing, driving away the cold bleakness of dark noons that marked the equinox and the grating end of a cruel winter beyond the walls.

I think, looking back, that I had never been happier than on that evening, when Etaa danced beside me. Gowned in the fragile colors of spring, her shining hair bound with pearls, she was the very goddess of the Earth. Her cheeks were flushed with excitement and her dark eyes radiant; after the last dance I took her in my arms and kissed her, and she did not pull away. Anything seemed possible to me then, even that someday she might come to love me . . . as I had come to love her, this captive goddess, in a way that I had never loved any woman.

But, as I have always known in my saner moments, not all things are possible, even for kings. And not long afterward Etaa turned cold eyes on me as I entered her chamber, looking up over Alfilere's dark curly head as he fed at her breast.

I hesitated. —Etaa, is something wrong?

Mabis got up heavily from her stool. She moved to sit facing away from us, still knitting, her ruddy face showing trouble and concern.

Etaa did not answer me for a moment, but rose and took Alfilere to his cradle near the fire, where she stood smiling and rocking him gently. She had refused a new nurse, preferring to feed and care for her own babe, another virtue which had pleased old Mabis. And indeed, my son's mother was better than any nurse, for she could "feel" his needs; she grew uneasy if he was ever beyond her hearing. At last she came back to me, the smile fading again, and I repeated my question.

Her pink-scarred hands snapped up with accusation. —Meron, I know the truth now, about my people. That they're making war on Tramaine, and being killed, because you've stolen me. I know that they demand my return—and beyond that, only to be left in peace by your witch-burners. But instead you send them soldiers, to kill and burn all the more. And you have kept it from me! And made me . . . made me forget . . .   A strange emotion tormented her face, her hands twitched into stillness.

—Where did you learn this, Etaa?

She shook her head.

—Willem—

—You will not hurt him!   Anger and fear knotted her fingers.

—I would not hurt a child for repeating gossip.

—But it's true?

—Yes.

Her fingers searched the rough edge of the tapestry that swayed in the draft along the wall. —Then let me go home to my people.

I looked away, feeling disappointment stab me like an assassin's blade. —I . . . I cannot do that. You wouldn't leave your child. And I will not give up my son. Are you so unhappy here? Can't you tell your people you're content to stay? I'll make peace with them, pay whatever restitution . . . I—need you, Etaa. I need you here with me. I depend on you now, I—

She shut her eyes. —Meron. The man who leads my people, who demands me back, the man you call "the Smith": he is my husband.

—Your husband is dead!

—No!   Her foot stamped the floor.

—You saw him yourself, broken on the rocks! No man could survive that. He was a coward; he killed himself, he abandoned you to me, and I won't let you go.   I drew a breath, struggling for control. —Your people raid and slaughter mine, and take their heads. You damn *our* souls—by our beliefs dismembered spirits cannot be freed by cremation. If there's war, then the Kedonny bring it on themselves!

Etaa drew herself up stiffly. —If you won't release me, he will come and take me!

I frowned. —If he can rise from the dead, then perhaps he will. But I doubt if even you can expect that of the Mother.

She crossed her arms, her eyes burning.

I left the chamber.

She stayed in her rooms from then on, refusing to accompany me anywhere, the drawn look of grief she had first worn returning to her face. When I came to see my son she would sit by the fire and turn her back on me, wordless. Once I came and sat beside her on the cushioned bench, with Alfilere squirming bright-eyed on my knees, wrapped in a fur bunting. I clapped my hands and saw him laugh, and as I offered him ringed fingers to chew on, looked up to see Etaa smile. I took back my fingers and signed, —Who could ask for a handsomer son? But he doesn't favor his father, I fear, little dark-eyes— I smiled hopefully, but she only looked away, brushing the silver bell at her ear, and tears showed suddenly on her cheeks.

Angry with Willem, at first I had forbidden him to visit her again; but I'd relented, knowing her solitude and sorrow. Not long after, I found him with her, his pale head in her lap, his thin shoulders shaken with sobs. She looked up as I came toward them, her eyes filled with shared pain; but Willem did not, and so she lifted his head from her lavender skirts. He rose unsteadily to make a bow, then sank exhausted onto the wine-red cushions beside her, wiping his face on his sleeve.

But I stood frozen in my place, because I had seen the thin tracks of drying blood that ran down his neck and jaw. Suddenly all his strange, frightened prescience fitted into place, and I realized the truth: my own page was a hearer, and somehow until now his family had managed to keep it a secret. Until now. My stomach twisted: his ears had been put out by the Church.

As though she had followed my thoughts, Etaa signed bitterly, —It was your Archbishop Shappistre. He hounded Willem for being with me, until he learned that Willem felt the Mother's touch—and see what he's done! He persecutes all who have Her blessings, he almost killed my child—he almost killed you! Your own kinsman! How can you let him go free, if you are king; why don't you challenge him?

I reached to the crooked scar along my back, caught in my own bitter outrage. The archbishop's open attempt to destroy me had failed, and now he waged a subtler war, spreading rumors, subverting those I trusted, tormenting those I loved. I had the power

to strike him down, even in the face of the Gods; but I could not.
. . . —Etaa, it's not that simple. This isn't some villager's dispute,
I can't take him out on the mead and thrash him! The royal line
is split in two, and with it the loyalties of the nation; I rule a land
at peace because I have tried to keep them reconciled. The archbishop is my counterbalance, but he'd upset the scales if he
could, with his dreams of a Church-ruled state. He would throw
this country into civil war to achieve it; he cares nothing for
consequences. If I charged him with treason I'd do the same. He
will stop at nothing; but I stop a long way before that.

Etaa stroked Willem's drooping head. —I don't understand the
needs of nations, Meron . . . and you don't understand the needs
of women and men.   Suddenly she looked up at me, her face
anguished. —He'll destroy you, Meron! Don't let him, don't
. . . Her hands dropped hopelessly into her lap; she rose and
turned away, going to the baby's cradle to comfort her gentle
son.

Two days later, Willem was gone. The other pages said he had
run away home. But one of Etaa's earrings, the tiny silver bells
that she always wore, was missing too. I asked her where it was,
and too carelessly she signed that she had lost it. And so I knew
that Willem had gone east to find the Smith.

Slowly, with all the pain of birth, winter gave way at last to
spring, while the Kedonny raided on our borders. Etaa mourned
in her chambers, and the New Year's revels on the green were a
bright, shallow mockery of the past.

And while I slept that night and dreamed of happier times, Etaa
and my son disappeared.

Frantic with loss, I had the countryside searched and searched
again, but there was no sign of them. There was no rumor, no
clue; it was almost as if they had never been. I could get no rest,
and my own lords said openly that I looked like a man possessed.
The archbishop, smiling, said that perhaps the Earth had swallowed them up—and I almost came to believe him. But I learned
my coachman had disappeared on the same night as Etaa, and

some said they thought my carriage had gone in the night, and come back carrying no one. And so I wondered if the truth lay not in the Earth but in the sky . . . and the Gods had taken their revenge on me.

But the Kedonny ate deeper into my lands, and finally I was forced to abandon my search. I planned to raise a full army and put them to rout; but as I sent out calls to gather men, I discovered how well my archbishop had done his ungodly work. His rumors of my bewitchment had taken hold: my own people believed the Black Witch had snared me in a spell and addled my mind, then disappeared like the accursed thing she was, stealing even my son to be put to some terrible blasphemous use. They believed I would betray them to the Kedonny in battle, and that the Gods themselves had abandoned me.

Even lords who were always loyal to my father's line have deserted me for the archbishop, and those who still support me get little support themselves for the raising of an army. The word is abroad in the land that it is suicide to ride with me to war— that if I am denied, and destroyed, then the forces of Right will be served, and the Gods will save them from the pagan hordes. Damn the Church! The Gods have never intervened in a war of men; I doubt they'll do it now.

And so I leave today, with what forces I can gather, to go and save my kingdom myself, if I can. Perhaps then this new storm of ignorance will pass, and not inundate us all. Perhaps. Or perhaps it is already too late . . .

If so, then maybe it is best that Etaa has gone, and taken my son. I only pray, to whatever true Gods may be, that they are safe, and that some day her son will return to claim his throne, and be the greatest of our kings. If she chose to leave me, I cannot blame her, for I never had the right to take her as I did. But I loved her, and I pray she will remember that too, and forgive me a little.

I often wonder if she ever loved me. If so, it was more than I deserved. But sometimes there was a look, or a sign —The hands of the summer wind are as warm and light as your touch, Etaa;

it may be that your Mother has stolen you home after all. Watch over my son, and forgive his father. Give him your blessings, as you gave them to me. Etaa . . . I think I will not see you again.

But come, my lords; the Godseye keeps watch on us, and the sun is already high. They say a smith may look at a king: then let it be the last thing he ever sees!

PART III: THE GOD

I understand that I'm speaking today because you wondered how a "naïve kid" in the Colonial Service was inspired to solve the Human Problem. The answer is simple—I loved Etaa, and Etaa was the mother of Alfilere.

You probably all remember the situation at the time. The Colonial Service had come upon the Humans not long before: an intelligent life form based on carbon rather than silicon, but oxygen-breathers and compatible with roughly the same temperature range that we are. That made them another competitor, but only marginally; and if they were anything else but Humans, we could have expected to coexist with them. But our studies of their ongoing culture, and the scanty records of their past, indicated they were the most unrelentingly and irrationally aggressive species we'd ever encountered. Combined with a high technology, it would have made them the most dangerous, too. We'd live in peace with them willingly enough, under the circumstances, but the question I'd always heard was whether *they* would live in peace with *us*. The majority Conservative opinion was that it wasn't likely, and so our sector council ordered us to intervene, and stall their cultural progress. The Liberal faction in the Service objected, doing their best to prod the Human status quo, and that was how the trouble started.

I'm a xenobiologist, and at the time I was just beginning my

career; I was also too inexperienced to question policy then, and
so I blindly supported the majority's stand on Humans. Especially since I'd had to live among Humans, to study (and watch)
them, as the "coachman" for the God-hating king of Tramaine.
When the Libs gave restricted records to the king, and then
openly incited the neighboring Kotaane to war, we Conservatives
retaliated by kidnapping Etaa, the king's Kotaane mistress, and
her son, his heir. I was chosen to do the actual deed, because of
my strategic position—and, frankly, my naïveté. All I had to do
was keep the pair safely out of the way, they told me, and at the
same time I could experience my first change-study of an unknown world. . . . All I had to do was spend an eternity alone, I
discovered, on a desolate abandoned world with no one for company but a superstitious alien woman and a squalling alien brat.
I didn't know whether to be honored by the responsibility, or
ashamed of being used. But I did my duty, and stole her away to
the outer moon.

I sent Etaa drugged wine, and shuttered all the ports; she never
knew what had happened, even when I brought the shuttle down
near the ruins of the dead colony and opened the lock. I watched
her on the screens as she stepped outside, waiting while the first
rush of stunned dismay took her. She stumbled back, clutching
her child protectively against her as the cold wind gusted, swirling the drab rust-brown grit into stinging clouds. Beyond us the
naked, stony slope swept upward toward the ruins of the Human
town, fangs of bitterness snapping at the clouds. I'd seen it once
before, but never like this, knowing I couldn't leave it. My own
eyes burned with the bleakness and the memory of the stinging
wind. It would be hard to learn the unity of this world . . . it was
easy to see why the Humans had failed to.

I don't know what thoughts were in Etaa's mind then; only that
they probably weren't the ones I expected. But confusion and
despair were on her face as she started down the ramp, the wind
tugging at her long cape and stiff, ungainly skirts. Her baby had
begun to cry, wailing with the wind. For the first time she was real

for me, touching my emotions and stirring—pity. This was the stolen woman, used by a ruthless king, whose misery I seemed to be tied to from the start, when I'd piloted the king's carriage in her capture. She was only another victim of the cruel and senseless schisms that divided these wretched Humans, and she'd suffer more now and never understand why, because of them, and because of us. . . . I felt unease pull down pity: Did I have the right—? But she'd been a pawn, she would be a pawn; maybe that was her destiny, and this was mine.

I left the controls at last, bracing myself to deliver the final horror to her. I'd gotten rid of my Human makeup, and knew my form would be starting to slip after the stress of the flight. And no Human had ever seen a "God" unmasked, even a God who passed for a coachman. Avoiding the velvet cushions on the floor, I went to stand at the lock.

—Meron—?   She turned with a gasp to stare up at me, her hands asking the question. I remembered she was a Kotaane priestess, and could hear; the speculation was that the king had taken her precisely because she *could*, out of his hatred for tradition. Her eyes had brightened with hope and something more as she turned. It froze into terror as she saw me, and she backed away, her fingers stiffening out in a sign to ward off evil. It was too much like an obscenity popular with the king's retainers; I almost laughed. That would have been the final cruelty. I caught it in time and only spread my hands in a peace gesture. I signed, —I will not harm you, Lady Etaa. Have no fear. She shook her head, keeping her distance. I wondered what I must look like to her—a mockery of a Human made of bread dough, or clay. I ducked back into the king's "carriage" to get my hooded jacket, thinking the more I covered the better. But as I disappeared I heard her startled cry and footsteps behind me on the ramp. She appeared at the lock in a swirl of dust, and dropped to her knees at my feet. —Oh, please, don't leave me here!   The baby whimpered as her signing jostled him, inside her cape. I stared down at her, stunned; but seeing my face again she faltered, as if she

saw her own doom instead. Looking away, she placed her wrig-
gling child tenderly on a red velvet cushion, then forced her eyes
back to mine, signing, —Then have mercy on my child. Take him
with you, he's no harm to anyone! He is a prince, return him to
—to his father, King Meron. You'll be rewarded! Give him to
anyone . . . but let him live—

I bent down and picked up the child; he gazed at me in fascination, and suddenly he began to laugh. Inexplicably delighted, I
held him close; then, slowly, I passed him back to his mother's
arms. Hope shattered on her face, and she flinched when I
touched her.

I stepped back. —Etaa, you aren't being abandoned in this
godforsaken place. I am your guardian; I'll stay with you here, to
look after you and your child. You've been . . . exiled, and it will
be a hard life for us both. But it won't last forever, only until—
certain matters are settled in Tramaine. But it has to be this way
until then; you have no choice. This is your new home.

She watched rigidly, the need to ask a hundred questions struggling against the certainty that she didn't need to ask, but only
accept, and endure, this new trial. She looked down at last, and
I saw the trembling lines of her face grow quiet with resolve; she
would adapt. I felt relieved, and somehow surprised.

—Who has ordered this? Not . . . not the king? Her dark eyes
flickered up again with a kind of urgency.

—No. I reassured her, thinking how she must hate the man,
and not wanting the truth to seem any harsher than it was. —It
—is the will of the Gods, Etaa.

Her flush of relief turned to a sudden frown, and she looked
hard at me for a moment. But she pulled back into her silence,
and signed nothing more, waiting for me.

I gave her a clingsuit and boots like my own to replace her
awkward gown, then waited outside the craft in the wind, knowing the preoccupation with bodily shame that these heterosexuals
had. She appeared at last, with her hair bound up and her child
slung at her back in the folds of her cape. The heavy jacket

flapped around her like a tent, but I could see that the suit had adapted to her well enough to keep her warm. I sealed the clasps on her jacket while she watched me, intent and suspicious. Then I unloaded supplies, and sealed the hatch behind us. The lifeboat rose silently; the king's carriage would be home before he missed it. I wished we could have been, too.

We struggled up the hill toward the ruined town, battered by blowing grit and dead, unidentifiable vegetation. The ragged maze of the tree-eaten ruins broke the back of the wind as we reached the summit; we stood panting and rubbing our burning eyes while the wind moaned and clattered in frustration overhead. I led Etaa through the rubble to a shelter that stood intact, a prefabricated box that still had its roof. As we stumbled along the street she watched with awe, but without the sickly dread Tramanians had for the cities of their dead past. I wondered if she had ever seen a pre-plague Human city even on her own world, not knowing she didn't understand that this wasn't her own world.

The Humans had colonized the inner, major moon of a gas giant they had named Cyclops, which circled the yellow star Mehel. This outer, barely smaller moon was just marginally habitable, and they had only tried to establish a colony here to escape from the disease that decimated them at home. They had failed, and all that remained was this town, under skies that were endlessly gray with clouds. Etaa never saw the change in the heavens, and never knew there had been one because she never asked a question: we communicated as little as possible, and often I caught her staring at me, her eyes somewhere between fear and speculation.

But once she insisted that she needed to gather healthful herbs for the baby, and when I tried to tell her that our supplies had everything she would need, she gathered him up protectively inside her jacket and slipped out the door. I went after her, armed, because I still wasn't sure exactly what else was making its home in this dead city. For over an hour I watched her search for a trace of the life she knew, but nothing had survived the departure of the Humans. At last, shivering and defeated, she brushed past me without meeting my eyes, and returned to the shelter. After that she communicated less than ever, only glaring at me as if this terrible strangeness were somehow my doing too. She never ventured outside again by choice, and never left her son alone with me.

I spent most of my time outside, struggling with equipment in the bitter wind as I tried to gather background data for my eco-logical change-study. The deserted Human town crouched like a tethered beast on the rim of the plateau, waiting with un-Human patience for the return of its masters while time and the gnarled hands of the tree-shrubs worried it toward oblivion. Beyond the plateau's rim eons of sediment from some murky forgotten sea lapped away to grim distant peaks. But closer in, the stone had been shattered by countless faultings, eroded by the winter rains and the sand-sweeping wind until a network of twisting sheer-walled canyons had been eaten into its undulating plain. The eternal wind sang through the maze, whipping the iron-reddened dust of the washes, where flashing water roared and passed with every drowning downpour. The wind was a bully, tumbling the slow, heavy clouds, breaking them open for a sudden glimpse of burnished heaven and shutting them again before you found it. Land and sky merged at the dusky horizon, and everywhere the colors repeated, shadow-violet and rust, burnt orange and fragile lavender, all merging toward gray in the somber light.

What flora there was was carbon-based, mainly lichen and an omnipresent hummocky dark moss. The sparse scatter of higher forms climaxed in the tree-shrub that dotted the ruins, a gro-tesque thing that looked like it was growing upside down. I knew almost nothing about the animal life, the preliminary survey hav-ing been so cursory; from time to time dark things scuttled at the edge of my vision, and in the updrafts above the canyons I could sometimes glimpse a shadowy, undulating form. As I began to watch these "gliders" in flight, I first felt the change stir within me, a blind groping toward understanding, a restlessness, a formless need to seek the new equilibrium . . . for the first time I wasn't being forced into a preset mold, this time my body would find its own place freely in the unity of a new unknown. I was fulfilled in the knowledge that now I knew nothing of the life on this world . . . but soon, in a way, I would know everything.

And I wondered whether that was the true reason why we feared the Humans: for all the studies we'd done, we had never been to their origin place or really "gone native" among them. Because we were forced to non-natural imitation among this transplanted stock, we had never really *felt* what it was to be Human. We wore false faces, false bodies; we saw them act and react around us, but never knew what moved them to it.

Exploring the dead Human town, I found myself thinking of how it would feel to colonize an unknown world, to think you were secure and settled—and then to be struck by an alien epidemic: to see half the population die, the survivors left genetically mutilated, sterile and deaf and blind . . . to lose contact with the rest of the Human kind, to see your proud civilization torn apart by fear and your technology crumble to barbarism . . . to lose everything.

And then to come back, to begin again from nothing in a treacherous, silent universe, and come so far—only to be stopped again, by us. They had adapted; and there was nothing we admired more. Yet the Colonial Service held them back; we counted ourselves lucky that they had suffered so much. And I'd never had any doubt about the morality of our position.

But then I shared a deserted world with Etaa, and passed through the change, and was changed in ways I had never meant to be.

The changes were resisted, in the beginning, as change always is. My physical deterioration of form had slowed, while my body chemistry fumbled toward an understanding of its new environment; but I stayed longer and longer out in the bitter days of the alien spring. My physical change was also slowed by the presence of Etaa; I went on instinctively mimicking the form of my closest companion—my only companion, for dreary weeks on end, until the return of Iyohangziglepi with supplies, and with them, the chance to hear a spoken word again and see a friendly face. And hear the gradually more agonizing reports that things in Tramaine continued unresolved. The Liberals had aroused the Kotaane, and now there seemed to be no stopping them. And as long as the uncertainty lasted, the king's son had to be securely out of it.

I began to worry sometimes that Etaa would break down in her endless solitude, since she rarely even had my escape into the greater world around the dead town. But she came from a people used to long, buried winters; and if she sometimes tended the fire below the window needlessly, or slept too long, and cried in her sleep, I tried to leave her alone. We all cope however we can, and she wouldn't have listened anyway. But I watched her with her child, as I watched the gliders by day wheeling over the maze, and again I felt an indefinable shifting in my soul.

Her thoughts were wrapped in her eternal cloak of silence, and only the baby, Alfilere, could draw her out. She would sit rocking him for hours while rain dinned on the roof, the silver bell she wore on one ear singing softly. She made him toys from scraps, smiled when he pulled her hair, tickled him while he played naked on her cloak by the fire, until their laughter filled the bleak room with light. She made the best of their new captivity, and so her son thought the world was a delightful place.

But sometimes as he fed at her breast her gaze would drift out of the present; a wistfulness would fill her eyes like tears and pass into a deeper knowledge that was wholly alien, and wholly Human. Sometimes too she would look into her child's face as though she saw someone else there, and then cover his face with longing kisses. She called him by a Kotaane name, "Hywel," and never "Alfilere," and I suspected that she knew he was her husband's child, and not the king's—this child of hope and sorrow. This child who was the center of her world—to whom Etaa, who was named "the blessed one," could never give the most unique and wonderful "blessing" she possessed, the gift of speech. Because she would never know she possessed it.

Her Alfilere was a bright, gentle baby who smiled more than he cried, and only cried when he had a reason. His awareness of the world grew every day, and soon I shared Etaa's fascination at each change. But when he first found his voice, babbling and squeaking to himself for hours on end, she only watched him with perplexity. Her people believed that hearing was the manifestation of another's thoughts and soul, and I knew this was her first child. Though she clapped her hands to get his attention, she never made another sound for him except her laughter, only moving her hands over and over while he watched, repeating the signs for simple words. Usually he would only catch her fingers and try to stuff them into his mouth.

And watching this woman, who was strong and fertile and gifted with full hearing and sight, who represented everything a Human could be . . . or should be . . . I suddenly realized what it would be never to find fulfillment, because you had even lost the sound of the word . . . the *feel*— In desperation I began to recite, "I am the eye that meets my gaze, I am the limb . . ."

Etaa started and stared at me; I'd never spoken before in front of her. Surprise and consternation pulled at her face; she looked back at her son, whose cheerful babbling must have made as much sense as mine, and then across the room at me again. On an impulse I repeated the lines, and she frowned. She picked up the baby and moved to the far corner, huddling inside her tent-like jacket on her ruined mattress . . . touching her throat. She coughed.

It wasn't long before I caught her mimicking the sounds her baby made. In a week or so more she had learned to hum for him. At first I was half guilty about what I had done; but gradually I convinced myself that it wouldn't come to anything. Though I wasn't even sure anymore that I'd done anything wrong.

And then the day came when the clouds parted. As I prowled the rim of the canyons, grateful for the slowly warming weather, brilliance suddenly opened up around me and all across the canyonlands a shower of golden sunlight was falling. For a moment I stood gaping at the incomprehensible glory until, glancing up, I saw the red "eye" and the banded green face of Cyclops peering back at me, filling a ragged piece of sky so bright it was almost black. I had taken off my braces to free my legs for change —running had gotten to be awkward and nearly ridiculous—but I ran back to the shelter and ducked in the open doorway. "Etaa, come and look!"

She stopped Alfilere in mid-whirl as she danced him around the room, and blinked at me, her smile fading. I realized I'd been shouting. I repeated it in sign language. —You can see the sky.

She followed me outside, and set Alfilere down to roll in the springy moss while she stood beside me, entranced by the sun-brindled, golden land and sky. I had almost forgotten the majesty of Cyclops wearing the sun for a crown, only a little diminished even from this outer moon. I remembered again that the sky the Humans took so much for granted was the most beautiful one I had ever seen. —Look, Etaa, can you see that dark spot against the face of Cyclops? That's your Earth.

She reddened as if I had insulted her. Only then did I realize that she had no idea we were on another world, and in my blind inexperience I had no idea of what that could really mean. —We traveled to Laa Merth, the moon you see from Earth, in the king's carriage; the Gods can make it travel between the worlds. You can see your Earth, up in the sky now instead; both these worlds are moons of—

She shut her eyes angrily, refusing me. —The Mother is the center of all things. *This* is the Earth!   She folded her arms, then turned away toward the edge of the cliff, a small, stubborn figure plucked by the wind. She was still the Mother's priestess, and I suddenly realized that she was as true a believer as any Tramanian, and that her chthonic Goddess was just as tangible and real. As if by her will, the clouds closed over the last shining piece of the sky and rain splattered down, pocking the russet dust with spots the size of kiksuye buds.

Etaa turned back from the cliff's edge as the rain began, her eyes scanning for her child—and screamed. I jerked around, following her gaze, to see the shadow-form of a glider plummeting like dark death out of the clouds toward little Alfilere. She came running, her arms waving desperately. I pulled my stunner and fired, not knowing where a glider was vulnerable, but hoping the shock would divert its strike. I ran too, and saw the incredible, leathery balloon of the glider billow with the shock, heard myself shouting, "Here, here—damn you!" And heard the piercing shrill of outrage, saw the sky darken as the glider swerved to strike at me. Warty mottled skin flayed me, I staggered with the impact of its shapeless bulk. I heard my own scream then and the glider's moaning wail as a pincer beak closed over my arm, sank in, and snapped my body like a whip into the air. The glider shuddered at my weight, and hysterically I saw myself being crushed where it fell. . . . But then suddenly my arm was free, the air brightened—and I slammed back down onto the earth. The glider soared out over the canyon's rim, still keening.

I lay in the patch of blessed moss staring up into the rain, feeling as if a stake had been driven through me, pinning me to the ground. My torn arm throbbed with the beating of my heart, and I drew it up, strangely light, to see that the end was gone, bitten through. I studied the oozing stump where my hand had been, somehow unimpressed, and then let it drop back to my side.

But it didn't drop, for Etaa caught it in her own hands, making small moans of horror while Alfilere wailed his fright against my leg.

" 'S all right, 's all right . . ." I said stupidly, wondering what had happened to my voice, and why she didn't seem to understand me. I managed to sit up, shaking her off, and then stand. And then finally to realize that I didn't know what I was doing, before I fell to my knees again, weeping those damn sticky silicon-dioxide tears and cursing. But strong arms pulled me up again, and with Alfilere on one arm and me on the other, Etaa led her two weeping children home out of the rain.

I collapsed on my bedding, just wanting to lie in peace and sleep it through, but Etaa badgered me with frantic solicitude. —I'm a healer, let me help you, or you will die! The blood—

And I discovered that with a hand missing, there was no way I could explain. I frowned and pushed her away, and finally I held up my wounded arm and shook it at her; it had closed off immediately, and there was no more blood, nothing that needed to be done. She pulled back with a gasp of disbelief and looked at me again, her eyes asking the questions I couldn't answer. Then she brushed my cheek gently with her fingertips, and there was no revulsion in her touch. At last I let her bury me in warm covers and build up the fire, and then I slid down and down into darkness, through layers of troubled dreams.

I slept for two days, and when I woke my mind was clear and fully my own again, and I was starving. As if she knew, Etaa plied me with hot soup that I almost gulped down, though it probably would have poisoned me. I rejected it unhappily, unable to explain again. She looked down, hurt and guilty, as though I were rejecting her. I touched her face, in the gesture of comfort I'd seen Humans use, and signed, one-handed, —Can't . . . can't. Mine . . . cans— I waved at my own food supply, stacked by the Human supplies on the dusty shelves by the door. Her head came up, as if she should have known, and she left me. I looked at my wound and saw signs that the tissue was regenerating already. But it only made me realize the bigger problem: I'd been slowly reabsorbing all my limbs. Now that there was a need, and a reason, how could I communicate anything?

Etaa returned with an armful of cans and dropped them beside me on the floor. Then, kneeling, she held out the pad and stylus

I'd been using for my sketches outside. I took them; she signed, beaming with inspiration, —Write for me.

I'd heard the king had taught her to read the archaic "holy books," but I hadn't believed it. I printed, clumsily, "Can you read this: 'My name is Etaa.' " I handed back the pad.

She smiled and signed, —My name is . . . She glanced up at me, puzzled. We used an arbitrary sign/symbol system based on the Human alphabet to record the Human hand-speech, and she had never seen her name written down at all. I pointed at her. She smiled again. —My name is . . . The middle fingers curled and straightened on her left hand, she held her right hand turned palm down, toward the earth. —Etaa. I am a priestess, I can read it.

I smiled too, in relief, and showed her how to pull open cans.

After I had eaten she brought Alfilere to me, half asleep, and gently sat him in my lap. I cradled him in the crook of my wounded arm; he settled happily, trying to nurse my jacket. Etaa laughed, and a feeling both strange and infinitely familiar came to me like spring, and left me breathless . . . and content.

—Thank you for saving my child. Etaa's dark eyes met mine directly, without loathing. —I was afraid of you, before, because of your strangeness. I think there was no need to be afraid. You have been . . . have been very kind. Again her eyes dropped, heavy with guilt. I thought of the king.

I printed laboriously, shamed by my own hidden prejudices, "So have you; though you had every right to be afraid, and hate me. Etaa, my strangeness will keep growing with time. But believe me that it will never harm you."

She nodded. —I believe that . . . Can't you eat the food I make? It's better than those— Her wrist flicked with faint disdain at the emptied cans; I wondered if they looked as disgusting to her as the coarse Human meals did to me.

I hesitated before I wrote an answer. "I can't eat meat." I didn't add that I couldn't eat anything at all that wasn't on a silicon base like my own body.

—The Gods do many things strangely, besides changing their shape. Meron was wiser than he knew; you are false gods indeed to his people. She watched me coolly, almost smug in her conviction. I remembered hearing of her confrontation with another God, back in the dreary halls of the royal palace.

She was probably gratified by my stupefaction. I wrote, "How did you know?"

—The king knows. He saw a God once in an inhuman form; he knows you are not the ones promised to his people.

I frowned. So that was why the king scorned the Gods: he had discovered the truth. Suddenly his repressed anger and his ill-concealed hatred of the Church fell into perspective, and I realized there could have been more to the man than royal arrogance and consuming ambition. But that hardly mattered now. "Who does the king think we are?"

—He doesn't know . . . and neither do I. We only know your power over us, over our people. She studied me, and her dark-haired child blissfully asleep again in my lap. —Who *are* you . . . what are you? Why do you interfere in our lives?

"Because we're afraid of you, Etaa."

Her eyebrows rose as she read the answer, and her hands rose for more questions, but I shook my head.

She hesitated, and then her face settled into a resigned smile. She signed, —Why is it that you don't wear golden robes like the other Gods?

I laughed and wrote, "I'm a young God. We don't have all the privileges." Besides which, it was impossible for a biologist to make valid observations of any xenogroup while wearing golden robes.

She smiled again, the conspiratorial smile of one who was herself a Goddess incarnate. —What shall I name you?

"Name me Tam." I gave her my name-sign among Humans, since Wic'owoyake would have been unmanageable. I felt myself yawn, a trait I'd picked up from the Humans too, and reluctantly gave up Alfilere's sleeping form to my own need for sleep. He clung to me with his strong, tiny hands as his mother lifted him away, and I felt a rush of pleasure that he had taken to me so. I slept again, and had more dreams; dreams of change.

I don't know exactly when I decided to teach Etaa to speak. The desire arrived on a wave of exasperation, as it got to be more and more trouble to write out every word of every answer I made. My hand regenerated, but the change overtook it, and my other hand was getting too stiff and stubby to make signs or hold a stylus. Teaching Etaa speech meant going against the rules in a way I had never even considered before, interfering with Human society by adding a major cultural stimulus. But then, I thought, what was I doing here with her in the first place, and what were the Libs doing waging war back in Tramaine? I'd be guilty of Liberalism too, but I had to be able to communicate—and so I convinced myself that even if she could learn to speak, it would never come to anything among a people who were still mostly deaf.

And so while the final drenching storm of the rainy season battered the helpless land and rattled on the roof, I explained to Etaa how she knew there *was* rain on the roof, when other Humans didn't. I called her attention to the sounds her child made, and the ones I'd made—and the ones she had begun to make herself. I showed her the patterns they could weave, as her hands wove patterns in the air. I sang her a song from one of the pre-plague Human tapes, and twice again she asked me to sing it, her whole body tight with excitement—and, almost, fear. The third time I sang it she began to hum along, tonelessly at first, while Alfilere sat in her lap chewing a strip of plastic and adding his own delighted babysong. But abruptly she broke off, glancing from side to side nervously. Wrapping her cloak of silence around her again, she signed, —This is not right! The Mother tells us that we feel—hear—the inner soul of all things. This "voice" is not from the soul, not real . . . perhaps we weren't meant to use it, or we would *know.*   Her earring jingled with her desire and uncertainty.

"Etaa," I scrawled patiently, "your people did know, once; all Humans did. But after the plague they forgot how to use their voices, because no one could hear them. You've seen the Tramanian nobles move their lips, and understand each other—they've forgotten their voices too, but they remember how a mouth was used to make signs. A voice was given to every Human, so they could let people know how they felt. Think how much more you know about other creatures because you can hear their voices—feel their souls. Think how much more you'd know about people, too, if they knew how to use their voices fully!"

She stared at the message for a long time, and then she made a series of signs in Kotaane; I realized she was praying. She gathered up a handful of dust from the floor and let it drift between her fingers. At last she took a long breath, and her eyes told me before her hands did, —I will learn it.

Once she had decided, she was never silent, practicing her sounds to me or to Alfilere, or to the gliders on the warming winds of summer if no one else would listen. She immediately learned to tell one sound from another as she heard it, to my relief, and I put away my pad and stylus once I had taught her the phonemes of the pre-plague speech. Making them herself was harder, and in the beginning she answered in an earnest singsong of slurred and startling imitations, making her own translations by hand as she went along. But slowly her instinct for forming sounds sharpened; she laughed and marveled at the endless surprises hidden in her own throat. And so did I, as though together we had triumphed over ignorance and fear, and had begun to find our own private unity.

We began to spend more and more of our time together in conversation, too. She told me of her people and her life as their priestess, and about the man she loved, who had been her other half and made her whole. And that she had lost him . . . but no more than that. She kept Alfilere close in her arms as she spoke, the living symbol of her lost joy. It moved me in ways I couldn't explain, that would have made no sense to her; and somehow for the first time I began to feel the real nature of heterosexuality, and sense the kinds of love and desire that made it possible, the ties that could bind such a terrible wound of dichotomy.

I almost told her then that I had seen her husband, and that I knew he was still alive. She had asked me often for news of the king, and of the Smith, who led her people against Tramaine. When she asked about the Smith, sorrow and longing for the past made her tremble. But I thought she couldn't know that the Smith and her man were the same: that the Libs had found him broken at the bottom of the cliff and saved his life, and had used his own love and outrage to make him their tool for change. He fought for her now like a hero out of Kotaane legend . . . and he might still die for her in the end. And so, though I told her what I'd heard about the Smith and the king, to spare her further anguish I never told her what I knew.

Etaa pressed her curiosity about my nature too, as we began to feel more free with one another. Who was I? What was I? Why were we here among Humans? I was forbidden by my training to give her the answers; but I gave them to her anyway. Cut off from everything, with even my own form getting unfamiliar, this separate world I shared with Etaa and her son was suddenly more important than my own—and in a way, more real. If I had been less impulsive, or more experienced, maybe I wouldn't have become involved; but if I hadn't, this galaxy would be a different place today.

But Etaa had been open with me, and so I opened myself in return. I told her about my "home" far off among the stars, farther away than she could ever imagine—so far away that I had never even seen it; how I had been born in space, and followed my parents into the Colonial Service. I tried to tell her how many worlds there are, and of the limitless varieties of form to be found upon them, all lit by the unifying fire of life. How much of it she believed, I'll never know, but her eyes shone with the light of other suns, and she always pressed for more.

I never intended to be fully open about our purpose on her world, but I felt she had a right to know something about why she had been stolen into exile. So I told her we had come to make things comfortable for people on Earth—so that they would never want to leave it and intrude on our stars. We had helped the Tramanians to lead better lives, and if the Kotaane ever "needed" us we'd help them too. I explained to her about the starfolk faction that wanted to stir up trouble among her people (and stir up progress too, but that I didn't say): how they had encouraged the Kotaane to fight a painful, vicious war they could only lose, and caused endless suffering and misery, when the rest of us wanted only to bring peace to her Earth. But Tramaine's king had begun the war by stealing her, and so we had rescued her from him, to help stop the ill-feeling (but primarily to keep the king from raising an heir to the throne who would be hostile to us, but I didn't say that, either). Let the angry king win the battle with the Kotaane but lose the war for progress, and the Libs would suffer a policy setback it would be hard to get over.

Etaa listened, but when I finished I noticed her dark eyes fixed on me, as bright and hard as black diamonds in the firelight. She said, "If you have taken me to save me from the king, then why won't you let me go to my people? You say it would stop the war—"

I hesitated. "Because the war wouldn't stop now, Etaa. Too much else is involved. When the war is over you can go home; it's not safe for you now, while the king could still search for you." And so could the Liberals, and they would have found her.

She set her silver bell ringing softly, with fingers that were still nervous to form a reply. "I *know* why the war will not stop. You say your starfolk want peace for us, and comfort, and only a few wish us trouble. Then tell me why the 'Gods' urge the Neaane to burn my people and persecute them! My people are not fools to be misled, they fight because they have good cause, and the cause is you! The Neaane were our friends until you came to them, and now they spit on us. You offer us your help, 'God.' Spare us, we've had enough of it." She caught up Alfilere, who had been placidly stuffing a rag doll into my empty boot, and stood glaring at me before she turned away to her pallet in the corner.

"You've learned to speak very well, Etaa," I said weakly.

She glanced up at me from the shadows, disappointment softening her words. "Better than you do, Tam."

I settled down in my own darkened corner, listening to the sounds of Alfilere nursing himself to sleep, and his mother's sighs. And thought about the strains on a culture when new ideas come too fast, and the need for an escape valve to ease the pressure, a catharsis . . . the Humans had needed a lot of them, in their past, and the Tramanians had needed one now, so we let them have it. We let them kill the Kotaane. It was a vicious escape, but they were vicious creatures. . . . But did that make it right? Not by our philosophy of unity; not by our standards. And we upheld those standards, or I thought we did. All life is our life, and so we do not wantonly destroy any species, no matter how repulsive or threatening it is to us. We meddle, yes, to protect ourselves. But how far should it go? What about the kharks, the wholesale destruction of so many, for the "comfort" of the Humans? The kharks were the most highly developed species indigenous to the planet. Was it right to put them so far below the Human intruders? Had the Human lust for destruction infected us too—or did this politic blindness to the philosophical ideal go on everywhere?

I hadn't been everywhere—I'd hardly been anywhere, and I'd never questioned my teachings; I'd never had cause. The Liberal faction argued for more xeno self-determination, and I couldn't see the point, because with Humans it was suicide. The Libs tampered with Human society to overthrow our settled status quo, to force the sector council to accept a "better" one, and to do it caused Human bloodshed and chaos. The Libs revolted me —but had we been more honest, or only bigger hypocrites? Suddenly there were no answers, there were only Humans who suffered and died for their "Gods," and the words "More atrocities are committed in the name of religion than for any other reason." A Human quotation. I fell asleep at last, aching with fatigue and indecision, and dreamed that I met the Human empire, come to reclaim its lost colony: a colony of the deaf and blind, living in ignorant stagnation. And with the guns of their warships trained on me the Humans said, "What have you done to our children . . . our children . . . our children . . . ?"

While Etaa went through the greatest change in her life, the evolutionary changes my body was undergoing speeded up, as though my instincts had finally become attuned to the rhythm of this new world, and my body had chosen its most suitable form. Etaa never referred to the change at first, too unsure even to ask me questions. But at last, one evening, she came to stand beside me while I played with Alfilere, now more awkward than he was, and making him bounce with sudden baby laughter. Cool, dry breezes fingered her dark hair, and she asked with lips and hands, "Must you change?"

I nodded as much as I could. "I'm committed, now."

"Why?"

"Why must I change? Because it was planned that I would, for the protection of us both on an unknown world. It helps me know what to expect." The specter of a glider struck behind my eyelids: I'd recorded that this world was too unknown, that the adaptation had left me vulnerably in-between for too long. "Or why do I change?" I opened my eyes. "Because . . . every living creature changes as its environment changes, that's called evolution; but my people have the ability to change very fast. What takes most creatures many lifetimes to do, we can do in months, instinctively —in a way, like your rainbow flies change the colors of their wings in an instant, to match a flower. We've learned to control the changes when we want to, and freeze them—but when we need to understand the system behind the form, nature has to take its own course."

"*Her* course," Etaa said mildly. "Will—will you still speak with me when you are changed?"

I smiled, and Alfilere giggled, blinking up at me with wide

brown eyes. "I think so. I need my voice now."

Her smile broke apart, her speech broke down into gestures.
—I wish I could change, as you do! Mother, let me change my
being and start again; let me lose my memories, and . . . and my
sins— She rubbed her hand across her mouth like a child,
pressing back the bitter misery.

"Etaa . . ." I raised myself up, holding Alfilere. "However you
changed, your mind and soul would still be the same—with all the
bonds to hold you. But however you changed, you couldn't
choose better than to be who you are." I remembered how I'd
looked forward to my change, my hope and anticipation, and
said, "If you knew the truth, I wish I didn't have to change. I—
I'd rather stay Human with you." I laughed. "I never thought I'd
hear that—but it's true. It's true."

She took Alfilere from me and slipped open her clingsuit as he
nuzzled her in hunger. She stroked his curly head and smiled
again at me, her eyes so strong with feeling that I could barely
meet them. "Thank you," she said, very clearly; and I knew I had
been given my reward.

The change reabsorbed and reformed my Human limbs, and
I settled squatly to the ground. My skin mottled rust and gray,
expansible air sacs made my leathery hide sag into whispering
folds: I was becoming a glider—a creature of the air, bound to
the earth by my own unsureness. To be an earthbound glider was
clumsy and exasperating; it was difficult even to use a recorder
for my observations, and, worst of all, I itched all over with the
changes, and couldn't scratch. Etaa reconciled herself with her
usual determined grace; she spent her evenings singing off-key
to her child while she sat beside me scratching my back with a
stick, and my alien body sang with relief.

During the days I haunted the cliffs, watching the gliders swing
and soar, hunting far out over the maze—or sometimes closer in.
Seeing me, they would set up a moaning that started tonal vibra-
tions in my own air sacs; they lured and cajoled . . . until at last

my alien desires slipped free of my inhibitions and I threw myself from the cliff and joined them. My flaccid body ballooned as the sacs expanded and filled with air: I could fly. Battered and caressed by the wind, my elemental god, mindless with exhilaration and terror, I probed the limits of the constant sky. I was one with the wind and the cloud-shadow; without thought, with only the flow of light into darkness, time into eternal timelessness, motion to rest to motion.

At last I came back to myself and remembered my duty, and my reality. I returned to the shelter, to find the hot, rising winds had turned cold in the long shadows of evening. Etaa looked at me strangely, as if somehow she knew where I had been. For a moment I saw envy in her eyes, the envy of one who could feel the unity of all things for one who could share in it.

But as I grew apart from Etaa in one way, suddenly and unexpectedly I found that I had become much closer to her in another, more profound way: I discovered that I had become pregnant. I was very young for that, barely twice her age, and separated from my own people, everyone I cared for; there was no stimulus—and yet I was pregnant. And then I realized my stimulus had been Etaa and her laughing Alfilere. But they were aliens. There was no one here of my own people to share a birth with, no one I loved, not even a pregnant stranger. How could I bring a child into the world without conjugation, to be a part of no one but me: a solitary-child, not a child of shared love, and without namesakes or a family? I struggled alone with my despair, hiding it from Etaa behind the growing strangeness of my face, until the supply shuttle came again. But Iyohangziglepi could only report "no change" in Tramaine, and sharing my misery only seemed to deepen it in the end, as I watched the shuttle climb toward the sullen clouds and turned back alone to the ruined town.

But like all natural things, I was prepared by nature to be glad, and when finally I was ready for the first partition, my fears disappeared and astonished pride filled the void they left behind. A secret pride, which I kept hidden from Etaa as I had hidden my pain, because I didn't know what her reaction would be. She had accepted everything until now—because Human culture had not progressed to the point where "miracles" were impossible—but my protective instincts kept me silent. I only made her promise to avoid a darkened back room of our shelter, and hoped she would obey.

Not trusting her with that one secret of the differences between us, thinking that one mother of a child could not learn to understand another, was the worst thing I could ever have done. And somehow I knew it, when I heard her shriek of horror; knew it, as I struggled frantically back to the shelter from the fields: she had entered the forbidden room and found my child.

"Etaa, no!" I floundered to the doorway, wild with frustration and grief.

"Tam, hurry, help me, a beast—!"

"Etaa!" My voice broke with fury—she froze with the stick in her hand, over the formless bleeding lump of gray still quivering on the floor. Its piteous cries shrilled in the range that only I could hear, fading now as its life faded. "Etaa"—the words burned my mouth—"what have you done?"

Etaa dropped the stick and backed away from me, frightened and confused. She lifted Alfilere, crying now with his own confusion and fright, and stood staring from me to the bundle of living parts that cowered on their nest, all that remained of my half-finished child. Her lips trembled. "Hywel . . . Hywel crawled into this room. And when I came after, I found—I found—*that* creeping around him."

"Etaa, that . . . is my child."

"No!" Revulsion flared in her eyes, against the truth, or against her deed, or both.

"Yes . . ." I moved to the quivering cluster, avoiding the part that lay still and silent now, and the rest gathered close, mewing for comfort and warmth.

An anguished cry tore itself from Etaa; I looked up to see her bury her face against her own child. She sank down on the dusty floor, sobbing her desolation.

I held my little ones close, and groped for the strength, the words, to help us both. "I should have told you . . . I should have warned you. They're helpless, Etaa, they wouldn't harm your son. Among—among my people, we don't have children the way you do, all in a finished piece. We form them a part at a time, by duplicating each part of ourselves; the way I was able to grow another hand, when I needed one. Some parts serve an extra purpose, protecting the rest, that are more specialized; they might have stung him . . . but it's harmless."

She looked up at me, shaking her head, her mouth drawn too tight for words.

"I should have told you, Etaa."

"They . . ." She took a long breath. ". . . they are—yours?"

"Yes."

"But, I th-thought . . .?"

"You thought I was a man? I am. But I'm also a woman. We don't come together with another to form a child; we form our own and choose someone we love for sharing: a part of our child for a part of theirs, after the birth."

She groaned again, softly, fighting for acceptance. "Oh, Mother, help me . . . Oh, *Tam,* what have I done to you?" She clutched Alfilere against her so hard that he squalled in protest.

I looked away. She had done what all Humans did, acted from fear, reacted with violence, inflicted pain and death blindly out of ignorance. I had been a Human once, and had despised them; but only now, after I'd lost Human form, had I really learned anything about the Human mind and spirit—and now, in the face of this most terrible act, I found I could only blame it on myself. "It—wasn't your fault. And this hurt can be mended . . . we're more fortunate than you that way. It would never have happened, if you'd known all along."

But she only sat rocking her child, the bell on her ear singing softly with her helpless grief.

Etaa spent long hours alone in the days that followed, gazing out across the sighing, broken world from the doorway of the shelter or walking the rim of the cliffs with her baby at her back.

The clouds that filled the sky now were only wind clouds, dark and licked with lightning, never dripping enough moisture to settle the endless dust. The wind had grown hot and parched, shredding the clouds and sweeping the dust high into the upper air, to fade the brazen blue that sometimes broke through into this land of somber hues. She watched the sky with yearning as Midsummer's Day approached, and when it came she performed makeshift Kotaane rituals; but clouds hid the triumph of the Sun, and she left them unfinished, her eyes haunted and empty.

At dusk she came to me where I crouched in the doorway watching the luminous fantasy-face of billowing Cyclops wink behind the clouds. I heard Alfilere murmur as he slept, somewhere in the firelight behind us. She pushed a dark curl back from her eye, brushed at it irritably as it slipped down again. At last she said, "It's true, isn't it, Tam?"

"What?" I waited, knowing there was more troubling her than the secret of my child.

"What you told me: that we're not on the Earth anymore. That we're on Laa Merth? And—" she struggled to keep her voice steady— "and that little speck that you see, passing over the face of the Cyclops like a fly . . . that's the Earth? I've watched the sky, and it is different; the Cyclops is shrunken, the bands on her robe are twisted . . . everything is different here. I think it must be true."

"Yes. It's all true."

"Our legends tell how Laa Merth once had children of her own, but the Cyclops destroyed them. This must be their town, and so that must be true too."

"Yes." I wondered if there was any truth in the Kotaane myths about the source of the Human plague.

"But our legends say that the Mother is the center of all things, She is greater than all things. How can She be a speck on the face of the Cyclops!"

My throat tightened with the pain that shook her voice, and I couldn't answer.

"Tam." Her fingers reached down, scraping my rough hide. "I

know nothing, it is all lost on the wind. Tell me what is true, Tam." She sank down beside me, her voice wheedling and her eyes wild. "What shall I believe in now?"

"Etaa, I—can't . . ." Her fingers convulsed on my back, telling me that I *had* to, now: that my pitiless, self-centered world had torn her world away and thrown her into the darkness of the void. Her faith was her strength against adversity, and without faith she would shatter, we would all shatter. "Etaa, the Mother is—"

"There is no Mother! Tell me the truth!"

I closed my eyes, wondering what truth was. " 'Mother' and 'Earth' . . . are the same to you, in your language, in your mind. But the Earth is also the world where you live, and a mother is what you are, and I am, a bearer of life. And those things are both still real, and wonderful. Your Earth looks very small now, but only because it's far away; like Laa Merth, in your sky at home. When you return you'll see again how large it is, and beautiful —full of everything you need for life. It's like a mother, and that will still be true. The Kotaane are very wise to call themselves the Children of the Earth, and be grateful for its gifts."

"But the Cyclops is greater, and stronger."

"Greater in size. But only another world." And only a brightness behind the clouds now. "Your myths are right, it doesn't love your people—it would poison you to live on Cyclops; but the Earth is strong enough to stay out of its reach, and will always care for you. And the sun will always defy its shadow, making the Earth fertile, able to give you life. You see, you've known the truth all along, Etaa."

"But . . . the worlds are not alive . . . they do not see all, or *choose* to interfere in our lives, as you do—"

"No. But really in the end they are more powerful than any of us. All our lives depend on them; even starfolk need air, and water, and food to survive. We're very mortal, just as you are. Everything we know of is mortal, even worlds . . . even suns."

"Isn't there anything else, then? Is there no God, or Goddess, to give us form?"

"We don't know."

Etaa gazed out into the growing darkness, silent, and her hands formed signs I didn't know. And then, slowly, she reached up to her ear and removed the silver bell. She dropped it into a pocket of her jacket as if it burned her fingers.

"Oh, Meron," she whispered, "how did you bear it for so long, never knowing what was true, or whether anything is, at all?"

I glanced over at her, surprised; but she only got up and went to her pallet, seeking her answer in the closeness of Alfilere. I slipped into my darkened nursery to see my own child, thinking of the sorrow we two had given to each other, and the joys. And as I lay beside my forming child, I wished there could have been a way for us to give each other the greatest gift of all.

We stayed on Laa Merth for more than a third of a Cyclopean year, nearly half a natural Human year. Bright-eyed Alfilere took wobbling steps hanging onto his mother's fingers, and my own baby, full-born now, soft and silvery and new, opened enormous eyes of shifting color to the light of the world. I marveled to think that I could have been so beautiful once, for S'elec'eca was both my child and my perfect twin.

Etaa loved "her" on sight (Humans have only gender terms reflecting their basic dichotomy, and she refused to call my baby "it"); and if it was partly out of guilt and need at the start, I saw it grow into reality, while she watched both children and I studied the world outside. She called my child "Silver," her term for S'elec'eca, the name I had chosen. She said nothing more about religion or belief, and her love for the children filled her empty days; but when she absently invoked the Mother a painful silence would fall, and her eyes would flicker and avoid me. Sometimes I noticed her touching her throat, as if in finding her voice she had eaten the bitter forbidden fruit of a Human myth far older than her own and found the cost of knowledge was far too high.

When the supply shuttle came again I slithered and slid down the hill to meet it, oblivious to everything but the chance of good news for us; Iyohangziglepi nearly stunned me, thinking I was an attacking alien beast, before I remembered to call out to the ship.

But after the initial shamefaced apologies, I finally heard the news I had been waiting for so long: the war between Tramaine and the Kotaane was over. But the Kotaane had won—and not just won concessions as the Libs had planned, but won Tramaine. The king had been killed in battle, fighting to save his people; because, thanks to our Archbishop Shappistre, the people wouldn't fight, cursing the king and expecting us to take their side when we couldn't. And so the Liberals had won too, and the Service would have to support the Kotaane; but the Kotaane didn't know what to do with their victory now that they had it. They wanted only their priestess, and their peace, and the shattered Tramanians filled them with disgust: so signed the warrior Smith. Once I would have said that he was lying or insane, or else he wasn't Human. But he was Etaa's husband, and I believed him.

But if it was true, then nothing was settled, and Etaa's world teetered on the brink of more chaos. Iyohangziglepi said bitterly that even the Libs were appalled at their success in changing the world: because of it, we were faced with leaving the Humans to worse grief than we had caused already, or interfering in their culture to a degree that would destroy all that was left of our faltering integrity. Etaa could go home at last, and so could I. But to what kind of a future?

Etaa was still waiting eagerly at the top of the hill, watching my return from the ship. She held a child in each arm, masked against the blowing sand, and I could almost see hope lighting her eyes as I scrabbled back up the gravelly hill and the shuttle stayed on the ground behind me.

"Tam, are we going home? Are we?"

"Yes!" I reached her side, puffing.

She danced with delight, so that one baby laughed and one squeaked in surprise. "It's true, it's true, little ones—"

"Etaa—"

She stopped, looking at me curiously.

"The ship will wait for us. Let's get our things, and—and I'll tell you the news. But let's get out of the wind."

We threw together our few belongings in minutes, and then she settled with the children on the piled moss beside the ashy fire-ring. I crouched beside her, and our eyes met in the sudden realization that it was for the last time. Taking a long breath, I said, "The war is over, Etaa. Your people have beaten the Tramanians."

She shook her head, wondering. "How can it be—?"

"Your people are brave warriors. King Meron is dead, because the Tramanians wouldn't fight them anymore; they expected the Gods to—"

"The king is dead?"

I nodded, forgetting it wouldn't show. "Long live the king." I finished the Human salute as I smiled down at Alfilere, who had come over to me and was trying to climb up my face. Etaa cradled my own little rainbow-eyes in her lap, as I longed to do, and would do, soon, at last. "Your suffering has been avenged, and the suffering of your people."

"How—how did he die?"

"Struck by an arrow, in battle against your people."

A spasm crossed her face, as if she felt the arrow strike her own heart; her head drooped, her eyes closed over tears. "Oh, Meron . . ."

"Etaa," I said. "You weep for that man? When your people hate him for taking you, and defiling their Goddess? When his own people hate him for keeping you, and bringing the wrath of their Gods? Even the Gods have hated him . . . But you, who deserve to hate him more than any of us, for shattering your life —you weep for him?"

She only shook her head, hands pressing her eyes. "I am not what I was. And neither is the world." Her hands dropped, her eyes found my face again. "One's truth is another's lie, Tam; how can we say which is right, when it's always changing? We only know what we feel . . . that's all we ever really know."

I felt the air move softly in the cavities of my alien body and
the currents of alien sensation move softly in my mind. "Yes. Yes
. . . I suppose it is. Etaa, do you still want to return to your
husband, and your people?"

Her breath caught. "Hywel . . . he is alive? Oh, my love, my love
. . ." She picked up her curly-haired son, covering him with kisses.
"Your father will be so proud! . . . I knew it must be true, I knew
it!" She laughed and cried together, her face shining. "Oh, thank
you, Tam, thank you. Take us to him now, please! Oh, Tam, it's
been so long! Oh, Tam . . ." Her face crumpled suddenly. "Will
he want me? How can he want me, how can he bear to look at
me, when I betrayed him? When he jumped from the cliff to save
his soul from the Neaane, and I pulled back? How can he forgive
me, how can I go home again?"

"Why did you pull back?" I said softly.

"I don't know! I thought—I thought it was because of my
child." She held him close, resting her head on his while he
squirmed to get free. "For half a second, I drew back—and then
it was too late, the soldiers . . . But how can I know? I was so
afraid, how can I know it wasn't for *me*? To let him die, thinking
. . ." She bit her lip. "He will never look at me!"

"But who was the coward, Etaa? Who threw himself from the
cliff and left you to the Neaane? Was it you who betrayed, or
Hywel?"

"No! Who says that—"

"Hywel says it. He is the Smith, Etaa, the victor in this war; and
whatever the reasons that others fought, he fought for you. All
he wanted was to find you, and to repay you for his wrong. He
wants you brought to him, that's all he wants—but only if it's what
you want, too. He cannot send you his feelings, but he sends you
this, and asks you to—remember." Carefully I produced, from a
pouch in my hide, the box Iyohangziglepi had given me.

She took the box from me and opened it, lifting out a silver bell
formed like a flower, the mate to the one she had worn on her
ear. She searched in her pockets for the one she had taken off,

and laid them together in the palm of her hand. Her fist closed
over them, choking off their sound; her hand trembled, and more
tears squeezed out from under her lashes. But then, slowly, a
smile as sweet as music grew on her face, and she pressed them
to her heart.

Alfilere had drawn Silver off her lap, and they rolled together
in the moss beside her, sending up a cloud of dust. Etaa's exile
and sorrow were ended at last; she would return to her people,
and I would return to mine. Probably we would never see each
other again, and the children . . . I looked away. What sort of a
life would Alfilere have, in the world we had left him? The son
of the Smith, the heir to Tramaine, the strong, gifted child of
Etaa, the Blessed One . . . who would have been my child too if
there had been a way; who was as dear to me as my own child.
The child of unity in a broken world. The child of unity—

And suddenly it was so obvious: the answer to everything had
been here in my keeping, all along. We could raise Alfilere to
inherit his birthrights, and be a leader such as his people had
never known—one who could give them back their rights and
give us back our pride.

"Etaa?" She looked at me vaguely, still half lost in reverie. I
tried to keep my voice even, not knowing if she felt the same way
I did, or what her reaction would be. "You know the situation
back on your Earth is very unstable right now. The Kotaane have
won a war they didn't expect to win, and they don't know what
to do about it. Your husband wants only to go home with you,
not to rule a kingdom. Your people despise the Tramanians, and
now the Tramanians despise themselves. They don't even know
what to think about their Gods, they have no leadership; all the
nations that surround Tramaine will be shaken, and there'll be
more war and hardship that could involve your people, unless
something is done—"

She frowned, and reached to catch up the escaping children.

I released air from my sacs in a sigh. "Yes, I know. *We've* done
too much already. Even the Service can see that, finally. But if

some new answer isn't found, some compromise, things will keep
on getting worse. We could destroy you, Etaa, with our meddling,
unless somehow you stop being a threat to us. And if we did that
to you, we would have destroyed ourselves as well."

She shifted the babies uneasily on her knees. "You have a plan
to stop it?"

"I do . . . I *think* I do. . . . When I met you, I thought all Humans
were violent and cruel without reason. That's why we were afraid
of you, why we wanted you to stay where you were. But now I
don't believe it. Your people are more aggressive than we are,
and you have to learn there are responsibilities to progress that
can't be ignored, you have to grow in understanding as you grow
in strength.

"But your cultures are still young, and maybe if you begin to
learn now how to live with one another, when you come to us as
equals between the stars you'll be able to live with us as well. The
time is perfect now, in the balance of change, for a religion to
show Humans the unity of all life, and how to respect it—as your
people do, when they follow the teachings of the Mother. And
there is the perfect sign of that unity, the perfect *Human* to begin
it: your son." I shifted nervously, trembling with hope and love.
"Etaa, will you give me your son? Let me raise him, among my
people, and give him the chance to change your world forever."

Her eyes stabbed me with incredulity and betrayal. "My son?
Why should you take my son?"

Blindly I said, "Because he's the child of the Kotaane and the
child of the Neaane. Let him inherit his father's throne, and close
the wound between your peoples forever."

"He is not the king's son! He is mine, and my husband's."

"Only you know that, Etaa. The Tramanians believe he's the
heir to their throne."

"My husband knows! He would never agree, he would never
give up his son and clan-child."

"Hywel would be proud to give his child such an honor! I know
he would, I . . ." I faltered, in my terrible need to be right.

"No!" Her hand rose in a fist. "I will not! Do you think we're less than animals, that you can take our children and we'll never mind?" Her voice broke. "Tam, eight years we waited for this child—eight *years*. How can you think we could give him up?" She looked down at me, her eyes changing. "But I forget; you aren't even Human." It was the first time she had made that an insult.

And I suddenly remembered that I wasn't, that we were still two totally alien beings who would never really know each other's needs or share each other's dreams; and there would never be an answer that was right for both our peoples. "I didn't know what I was asking, Etaa. I'm sorry, I—"

"Would you give up your child, Tam?"

I saw Silver from the corner of my eye, and tiny mock hands contentedly exploring Etaa's real one. I forced my eyes to meet Etaa's. "For this, I would give up my child, Etaa. Even if it was the only child I would ever bear. If it meant the future of my people, I would. And it *can* mean the future of both our peoples."

Coldly she said, "Would you give me Silver, Tam, if I gave you my son? To raise in his place?"

"Yes . . . *yes!*" I wondered wildly what emotions showed on my glider's face. "Etaa, if you could only know how you honor me, how much it means, to share a child with you. If you knew how much I've wanted you to love my child the way I love yours—it's all I could ask; to share with you, and bind our lives together."

She searched my eyes desperately, holding the children, and the future, in her hands. At last she looked down, into the two small flower faces peering up from her lap, and asked, "Would you teach him to use his voice?"

"And write, and read; and hand-sign, too. And to respect all life, and make others want to do the same. He's a good, beautiful baby, Etaa; let him be a great man. Let him be all he can be. He could save your world."

She shook her head aimlessly and no silver song answered now to give her comfort. "Is this true? Is it the only way to help? Will it help everyone in the world?"

"It's the only way, if you want the Humans to have any say in

their own future, Etaa. If you want to save yourselves from our
meddling." The knowledge tore at me that I was the biggest
meddler of all, not shifting the fates of anonymous aliens, but
tearing apart the life of someone I knew about and cared about,
who had suffered so much—for a dream that might never come
true. And what if I was wrong? "Etaa—"

"All right," she said softly, not even listening. "Then it must
be, if we are to have our future. If you will love my son, if my son
will be all he can be; if the *world* can too, then . . . I will share my
child with you." The final words fell away to nothing. But she
looked up, and for a moment her voice was strong and sure.
"There is no one else I would do this for, Tam. Only for you.
Don't let me be wrong."

I kept my un-Human form hidden in the shuttle when we
returned to Tramaine, to the town by Barys Castle where it all
began. Etaa rose from her seat as the lock opened; beyond, in the
darkened afternoon of early autumn, I could see the congrega-
tion of resplendent artificial gods—and goddesses, our "manifestation" of the Mother's willingness to accept this new union of
beliefs. Beyond them were the milling Human representatives,
and somewhere among them, a dark-haired warrior who only
wanted his wife. Etaa took Alfilere up in her arms for the last time
wrapped in a royal robe, and I saw her shiver as he nuzzled her
neck, cooing. Her face was the color of chalk, frozen into a mask
too brittle to melt with tears. She left Silver squirming forlornly
alone on the foam-cushioned seat.

"Etaa—?" I said. "Won't you share my S'elec'eca?"

In a voice like glass, she said, "I couldn't take Silver, Tam. I
love her, I *do*—but how could I teach her what she was meant to
be? And my people wouldn't understand her. It wouldn't be fair.
I will try . . . try to help them be ready for my son. And maybe
someday for Silver, too. Will you bring her to see me then?"

"I will," I said, wanting to say something else. Tears crept
down my face like glue.

"Will you always be with him, and Silver too?"

"Yes, always . . . and never let him forget you." I hesitated, looking down. "Etaa, you'll have more children. And it doesn't have to be eight years again. There are ways, we can help you, if you want us to."

Her mouth stiffened in angry refusal; but then, softening, she bent her head to kiss Alfilere and said very faintly, "I would like that . . . Tam, I should hate you too, for everything you've done. But I don't. I can't. Good-bye, Tam. Take care of our children." She knelt and stroked my mottled hide, while I caressed her with the sighing hands of the wind, the only hands I had.

Etaa left the cabin, and Iyohangziglepi came to pick up Silver, who began to cry at being held in a stranger's arms. Together we watched the viewscreen as Etaa presented Alfilere to the waiting deities, with the small speech I had trained her to recite for effect. She delivered it flawlessly, standing as straight and slender as a rod of steel, and if there was any sign on her face of the agony inside her, I couldn't see it. But Archbishop Shappistre stood nearby, still tolerated by the grace of the Gods, watching with an expression that surprised and disturbed me. And then after one of the Goddesses had accepted Alfilere, Etaa turned on him with pointing finger and charged him in sign language with treason, in the name of Alfilere III and his father Meron IV before him. The archbishop turned pale, and the Gods glanced back and forth among themselves. Then one of them made a sign, and guards appeared to lead King Meron's betrayer away. Fleetingly, as if for someone beyond sight, I saw Etaa smile.

But already she was searching the Human crowd, and I saw it part for the tall dark man in Kotaane dress, the warrior known as the Smith—Etaa's husband. A fresh puckered scar marked his cheek above the line of his beard, and he still walked with the small limp that bespoke his terrible fall. He stopped beyond the crowd's edge, across the clear space from Etaa, and his grim, bespectacled young face twisted suddenly with uncertainty and longing.

Etaa stood gazing back at him across the field, a bizarre figure in a flapping dusty jacket, her face a mirror of his own. Two strangers, the Mother's priestess who had found her voice and lost her faith, the peaceful smith who had taken heads; strangers to each other, strangers to themselves. And between them they had lost the most precious possession this crippled people knew, a new life to replace the old. The frozen moment stretched between them until I ached.

And then suddenly Etaa was running, her dark hair flashing behind her. He found her and they clung together, so lost in each other that two merged into one, as though nothing could ever come between them again.

THE SKINNY PEOPLE OF LEPTOPHLEBO STREET

"Leptophlebo" is from two roots that mean
"slender" and "vein": but as you will see in a
moment, Mr. Lafferty is in his richest vein here.

R. A. Lafferty

—and turned into Leptophlebo Street (it's always a scruffy sort
of delight to come into it). It was a minor discovery and a sudden
entrance, like going through a small and florid door into a whole
new world, a world of only one street.

The chattering of the monkeys was what struck him first, and
then the chattering of the people in a kindred tone, and then the
absolute cleanliness of the place, and the pleasant bouquets of
selected and superior smells. Close on that was a whole dazzle of
details that would take days to assimilate.

The poverty of the street struck him last of all, and then it
seemed a more pleasant poverty with some other name. It was
picked-clean poverty, as if every speck of dust had been hand-
gathered from between the cobblestones, as if it were as valuable
as lepto pepper or gold.

Canute Freeboard, adventurous investor and freebooter-at-large, had come to Leptophlebo Street for what money could be found there; but the street seemed bare of value. He had come looking for a man named Hiram Poorlode. Canute needed money, and that was the year that money was very tight. There were those who said that money might be got in Leptophlebo Street, but they all laughed when they said it.

"Could you tell me where I might find a man named Hiram Poorlode?" Canute asked a friendly-looking young fellow there.

"Kmee–fee–eee–eee–eee," the young fellow said, and Canute saw that a mistake had been made. "I'm sorry," he said. "I hadn't noticed that you were a monkey."

The monkey nodded as if to say that it was quite all right, and he motioned for Canute to come along with him. They stopped in front of a man who was sitting cross-legged on the stones of the street. The man had a sign, "Nuts, Wholesale and Retail": he had a pandanus leaf in front of him, and on the leaf there were seven filbert nuts and two almonds. The monkey pointed the man out to Canute and Canute to the man and he said, "Kmee–fee–eee–eee–eee." Then he skittered away.

"Yes, I am Hiram Poorlode," the nut man said. "Thank you, Hoxie." He spoke the latter to the skittering monkey.

"Get your clothes rewoven, sir. Get your clothes rewoven," a young boy chanted at Canute. "My father reweaves clothes free. Turn those baggy clothes into trim fit real fast."

"My clothes aren't baggy," Canute said.

"Boy, they sure will be baggy in a little while," the boy said. "Better get it done now."

"Get your teeth cleaned, sir!" another young boy chanted at Canute. "My father cleans teeth excellent free."

"Is he your son?" Canute asked the street-sitting nut merchant Hiram Poorlode.

"Oh, no. This one is Marquis Shortribs," Hiram introduced. "His father is Royal Shortribs who is a tycoon in teeth. And I am Hiram Poorlode, nut merchant, investor, moneylender. Sit down on the cobbles, sir, and talk to me. You are the only customer in my shop at the moment, so I can give you my full time."

"I am Canute Freeboard, a stranger in this country and in this town. I expressed strong interest in obtaining investment money. The man to whom I had introduction must have been a humorist and he played a lopsided joke on me. Ah, how *is* the nut business?"

"It hasn't been a bad morning," Hiram said. "I received twelve filbert nuts on consignment this morning and I have already sold five of them. With my markup, this gives me enough equity in filberts that I can eat one myself and still have enough cash on hand to cover those sold. This is known as eating free, and it is the first rule of economic independence. As to the almond nuts, I own them outright. I started the day with five of them and I have sold three for cash. This is the best sales record that I can remember, up to this time of day, for almonds. I also own the pandanus leaf. That being so, I am almost insulated against misfortune. If I sell nothing for the rest of the day it will still not be a complete catastrophe."

"Haircut, sir? Haircut, sir?" a small boy cried in set chant. "My father does supreme haircutting and head grooming free."

"No, I don't believe so, boy," Canute mumbled. "Is he your son, Mr. Poorlode?"

"Oh, no. This is Crispin Halfgram, the son of Claude Halfgram, the biggest man in hair and heads in Leptophlebo Street. Some of the finest garments here are woven by his wife Rita from the hair that Claude collects in his studio. You are looking for investment money? I am the most promiscuous moneylender in Leptophlebo Street. How much do you need?"

Hiram Poorlode, as did all the skinny people of Leptophlebo Street, wore a very large, flat, wide-brimmed hat that was crawling all over with rambling greenery. Canute now saw that what Hiram really wore on top of his head was a growing vegetable and fruit and grain garden. And all those garden-hats were tilted to catch all the sun possible.

"I'm afraid that we're not thinking on the same scale," Canute said dourly. "I need eighty-five thousand dollars for an opportune deal, such a deal as will come only once in my life. I need the sum at no more than seven percent interest and I need it today. Yes, my acquaintance in this city must be a humorist."

"Here are the shoes back again, Mr. Poorlode," a small boy said, and he set a good-looking pair of smooth shoes down beside Hiram. "He will not need them again for two hours, but he believes that Mr. Shortribs may want them before that."

"Thank you, Piet," Hiram said, and the boy skipped off. "That is Piet," Hiram told Canute, "the son of Jan Thingruel who gathers more astatic grain out of cracks than does anyone else on the street. We have but one pair of shoes here, and whatever person goes to make a prestigious visit will wear the shoes. They fit all persons in the street, since Claude Halfgram had the finial joints of four of his toes removed last year. They are good shoes and we take excellent care of them. I am shoe custodian this week." Hiram Poorlode lifted up one of the flagstones of the street and put the shoes down into a shoehole that was underneath it.

"I have the money by me now," Hiram said then. "Nothing is easier than eighty-five thousand dollars in gold. And, with me, a man's face is his security. Give me half an hour to consider you, for I am a cautious man. Spend the time pleasantly: visit and observe our rather odd Leptophlebo Street here. Enjoy yourself, sir, and be assured that your case is under active consideration. I can tell a lot about a man by watching how he reacts to Leptophlebo Street."

"All right," Canute said. "I'd given up hope of raising the money anyhow. Money is tight this season. Ah, but it was a sweet, once-in-a-lifetime opportunity! Yes, it's an odd little street here. How much do you sell the filberts for?"

"Three for a mill. Oh, it's the standard coin of the street. One tenth of a cent."

One might as well enjoy the drollery. Really, Canute had never seen anything quite like Leptophlebo Street; never such skinny monkeys or such skinny people. There were mysteries about the relationship of the monkeys and the people. The monkeys couldn't talk properly. There's an old saying that whenever monkeys *do* talk there's some monkey business going on. Well, there was plenty of it going on here, but all that the monkeys could say was "Kmee–fee–eee–eee–eee." The monkeys wrote notes on little pieces of paper and gave them to the merchants of the street. They brought in fruit and they traded it or sold it. From the merchants they bought a few nuts that were out of season in the woods, bought them for clay coins or in trade for their in-season fruits or nuts. The people asked the monkeys about their families and about the situation in the woods, and the monkeys wrote the answers on little pieces of paper.

"The monkeys are so smart," Canute said, "that it seems as if they could talk. As long as you are doing business with them anyhow, you could teach them speech."

"People of the monkey caste are not allowed to talk," Effie Poorlode said. (She was the wife of Hiram the nut merchant.) "Everyone has his niche in the world, and the monkeys don't have talking niches. And it would be no profit to us to teach them speech. We have plenty of time to wait for them to write out their notes, and we do make a good profit on the paper that they write them on."

The people of Leptophlebo Street were the skinniest folks that Canute had ever seen. How the ribs stood out on them! Two ribby young ladies were in a booth down the street.

"What? Do you sell the paper to the monkeys?" Canute asked Effie Poorlode.

"Get your teeth cleaned free, sir!" the boy Marquis Shortribs was soliciting a passer-by. "My father does excellent tooth cleaning free." But the passer-by continued on.

"If the tooth cleaning is free, and if there are no customers anyhow, then where is the profit?" Canute asked.

"Oh, there will always be customers," Effie told him. "Suppose that ten thousand persons go by and do not avail themselves of this service. But then the very next person might stop at the Shortribs' booth, and you can see how that would make all the waiting and solicitation worthwhile. As to your question, no, we don't sell the pieces of paper to the monkeys. The monkeys make the paper in the woods, and they make the ink too. They write their notes on the paper and they give them to us. You can see that the profit will be enormous. If we get only eight or ten of these little pieces of paper a day, look how they will count up. We dissolve the ink off the paper, and when we have a thousand pounds of the ink we can sell it to the ink bottlers or pen makers of the city."

"How long will it take to accumulate a thousand pounds?" Canute asked.

"Oh, it would probably take us a thousand years, but what's time so long as we keep busy? And we find all sorts of uses for the little pieces of paper. I tell you that there is money in paper; there is money in everything."

"How much money *is* there in everything, Mrs. Poorlode?" Canute questioned.

"Yesterday my husband and I cleared one cent and three mills from all our businesses," Effie answered. "And we also achieved equities in three other mills. This is better than most of our days, but all our days are good. Oh, the wealth does accumulate!"

Mrs. Poorlode was like the valiant woman in scripture as she stood proud and skinny, with her garden on top of her head and with her hands busy leaching nutshells in a bowl.

"This processes the nutshells for industrial use," she said, "and we have the Nutshell Bitter Tea left over to drink. It makes the bones glossy. My husband gives a rebate to every purchaser of one of our nuts if he returns the shell after he has eaten the meat out of it. We are blessed to live on a street that has so many business opportunities."

There was something very interesting about the gaunt ribcage of Effie Poorlode.

"Yes," she said, reading the thoughts of Canute Freeboard, "the townsmen lust after our ribs and after our ossuary generally. There is nothing wrapped up about us. There are some persons in the town with so much flesh grown onto their bones that their fundamental persons and passions are buried away and their real impact is never felt. Luckily that is not so with the people of Leptophlebo Street."

"How is the street kept so clean and swept?" Canute asked.

"Brooms with both astatic and static bristles are the secret," Effie told him. "Organic dust clings to the static bristles, and the nonorganic dust is swept clean into gathering vessels by the astatic bristles. Then we pass the brushes over degaussing jets that release the organic particles, and we make soup from them. And the nonorganic dust is separated into flammable and inflammable piles."

"They mean the same thing," Canute said.

"Not on Leptophlebo Street they don't," Effie insisted. "So we make briquettes to burn as fuel out of the one sort. And we make bricks and flagstones and face stones for buildings out of the other sort. So we have our soup and our fuel and our bricks, and we keep the street clean all the time."

A medium-sized bird, probably a grackle, came down onto the rim of the garden-containing hat that Effie carried balanced on her head. And the bird was stuck fast. Canute saw that the edge of the hat was bird-limed to catch anything that landed there.

"I will wait," Effie said. "The pot wants a bird, but the pot must wait also. These grackle birds attract one another for a while. This is not one of our own grackles that I know; it's one of the newly arrived grackles from the countryside. They will not be wary of one bird stuck there, nor of two birds stuck. They will not be wary of less than three stuck birds. I will be patient and I will have three grackles for food and for byproducts. Will you not stay with us this evening and have a look at our night life on Leptophlebo Street?"

"I don't know what I will do," Canute said. "I haven't comprehended it all yet."

"Lose weight free in seven-minute surgery, sir," a small boy chanted. "My father does good free work. He is one good loser."

"No, not right now, boy," Canute said.

"Have your appendix out, sir? Have your appendix out?" Another small boy was putting the shill on. "My father performs faithful appendectomies free."

"No, not right now," Canute said.

"This boy is Pat Thingruel, the brother of Piet and the son of Jan Thingruel," Effie told Canute. "The father is as stylish a free appendectomist as you will find anywhere."

"I do not understand how all the people of Leptophlebo Street can work for free," Canute said. "How do they profit by it?"

A second curious grackle bird came down and got itself squawkishly stuck in the bird lime of the edging of Effie's garden-hat.

"Oh, there's lots of profit!" Effie exclaimed. "A vermiform appendix, especially when inflamed, is a veritable storehouse of richness. Master microchemists like ourselves can manufacture all sorts of useful things from such rich material. And the teeth that Royal Shortribs cleans, do you realize just how superorganic are the deposits taken from teeth? Do you know how many things can be woven and fabricated from the hair that Claude Halfgram cuts? Garments, rugs, tents, seines, modish gowns for the modish ladies in the town. Almost solid profit. And the head grooming that he does, do you know that there are some very lively products to be had from that? Our greatest industry, though, is the night soil that we gather from the cooperative people of the town. And I will tell you something else if you will promise not to tell the monkeys."

"No, I won't breathe a word of your secret to the monkeys," Canute promised.

"We pay the monkeys only half as much per equal weight for their night soil as we pay the people in the town. And the monkeys bring theirs to us; we don't have to go and get it. Ah, there is profit everywhere you look, in the stones, in the air, in the very rain. What a money harvest we do have! Mills and mills and cents

and cents, and at the end of a week we may even have another
nickel for our hard work."

"It's a wonder you don't gather belly-button fuzz and process
it for profit," Canute laughed.

"Of course we do," Effie cried. "We gather more than a pound
a year of it from the people of the town, and this in spite of the
fact that many of the burghers will not cooperate with us and say
that the whole thing is silly. But there are a few friendly people
in town who wear wool. The woollies are the best for the fuzz.
And it can be made into the softest of all sheens. Oh, do stay over
and have a look at our night life tonight, Mr. Freeboard! Really,
it's wonderful the times that we do have."

A third grackle came and stuck itself in the bird lime on Effie's
head-garden. And then was heard "Sorrow in Three Voices by
Grackles": but only those three would be stuck there. Others
would veer away from the three birds in trouble.

But a fourth grackle did come, a bird carrying a long piece of
broken looking-glass in its beak. It was too wise to get caught in
the bird lime, but it was watched with avid eyes. Sometime it
would drop that broken piece of silvered glass, and some person
would rush in and catch it before it hit the ground. There's profit
to be had from old mirror glass.

A man with affluent gestures arrived at Hiram Poorlode's
booth in a sudden hurry. He had the sharp, lean, craggy face of
a bird of prey. He was taut and of a restless thinness in every part.
Why, he was none other than the Lean Eagle from Lean Eagle
Street!

"Hiram, I'm caught short," said that opulent man who wore
diamonds on every finger. "I have to cover. I'm overextended. It
will be only for a few days. I need two and a quarter million
dollars and I need it now. I have my dray here."

But the Lean Eagle was the highest-flying and the most rapa-
cious moneyman ever. Why should he come to Leptophlebo
Street to borrow?

"With me, a man's face is his security," Hiram Poorlode said, "and I know your face, Mr. Schlemel kurz Karof. A man of such a name and reputation is security itself."

Hiram removed three of the largest flagstones from the street on which he had been sitting. He passed the heavy bars of gold up to the nine lackeys who served Mr. Schlemel kurz Karof. It took a fair number of gold bars to amount to two and one-quarter million dollars.

"There has to be an explanation to this!" Canute Freeboard howled out loud. "Oh, but by all the equivocating things that be, there *can't* be any explanation to it!"

When the lackeys had loaded all the gold bars onto the dray, Mr. Schlemel kurz Karof signed a note and gave it to Hiram Poorlode. Then that opulent man went away with his dray and his lackeys, and Hiram Poorlode replaced the three flagstones in the street.

Canute Freeboard hummed a little tune to himself. There were some notes missing from that tune. "How long did it take you and your husband, at a nickel a week, to get to a position where you could make instant loans of two and a quarter million dollars and still have lots more gold glinting in your gold-hole under the street?" Canute asked Effie.

"It sure did take a long time," she said. "There just aren't any shortcuts." Effie took from her husband the note that Schlemel kurz Karof, the Lean Eagle, had given him. She dissolved the ink off it and put it with the ink accumulation. And she put the de-inked paper with the paper accumulation.

"How will you collect, when the writing is dissolved off the note for the ink?" Canute asked Hiram.

"Ah, a man's face is his security to me," Hiram said. "He will pay me back. And if he does not, what is the difference? In time I will accumulate that amount again, and I have lots of time."

"Hey, is the handsome man going to stay around for the night life this evening?" two pretty young skinny ladies asked. "We sure do have a lot of fun at night-life fiesta."

"These nice young ladies are Regina and Maharana Short-ribs," Effie Poorlode introduced them. "I believe that a good-looking young man like you could have a lot of fun just skylarking with them at night life, Canute."

"You know what we do for the climax of a night-life go-it-all?" Maharana asked. Oh, the skin and bones of that young girl! They'd send shivers of delight through anyone.

But sometimes one must put second things first.

"Ah, about that loan," Canute said to Hiram. "Oh, by the swept cobbles of Leptophlebo Street, there has *got* to be an explanation to this! About that loan, Mr. Poorlode?"

"Oh, certainly," Hiram said. "I've been observing you, and I now have complete confidence in you. I'll lend you the money. Eighty-five thousand dollars, was it not? Do you want it in gold or in certified cash warrants?"

"In gold, in gold. Oh, what a beautiful, hardscrabble, skinny street this is!" Canute rejoiced. "How have you done it? How have you accumulated millions of dollars in gold on a nickel a week?"

"In bad weeks we don't make near that much," Effie Poorlode said.

"Ah, but where does the gold *come from?*" Canute pursued the matter.

"Oh, there's several legends about the origin of the gold," Hiram told him. "One story is that it's rabbit gold and that it reproduces itself, that it all comes from two nuggets that got together under the flagstones."

"But there is raw nugget gold there. There is bar gold and ingot gold. And there is coined gold of various coinages," Canute protested. Hiram had already removed the stones that covered the gold in the street.

"Yes," Hiram agreed, "several pairs of different forms of rabbit gold would be required, wouldn't they? Then there's the story that it's all monkey gold. The monkeys find it and refine it in the woods. Then they give it to us noble burghers of the street. They are afraid to keep it. It is said that they did keep it when they were men, and that that's what made monkeys out of them. You don't believe that entirely? Oh, I see that Hoxie has been monkey-facing my act behind my back." And Hoxie had been doing that. But had he been saying "Do not believe all of it" with his monkey-facing, or had he been saying "Do not believe any of it"?

"The third legend is that it is all pound-of-flesh gold," Hiram said. "This legend states that we sell pounds of flesh for the yearly bashes of the Extortioners' Guild and the Hatchet Makers' Guild and especially for that dread secret society Glomerule; and that we receive our gold for the pounds of flesh. Ah, there it is, Canute, all ready for you to take it: eighty-five thousand dollars' worth of gold. It's quite a bit over a hundred pounds. The young ladies will help you carry it."

"Which of the three legends is true, Hiram?" Canute asked softly.

"Oh, they're all a little bit true, but all together they would account for only a fraction of our gold."

"What accounts for the rest?"

"How can we tell you that? It's a secret. We know you are not so base a person as to want us to tell you the answer. You will have the pleasure of guessing it as the years go by, but we will not tell it to you. Ah, your gold is ready for you, Canute."

"We know you are not such a fink-dink as would like to be told," Effie said. "It took the last one about a thousand years to guess it, and you want to miss all that fun?"

"Who was the last one to guess it?" Canute asked.

"Me," said Hiram.

"We know you are not such a cheap-creep as would listen even if someone whispered the answer to you," Maharana Shortribs said. "We know you are better than that. My sister and I will help you carry the gold."

"You will not tell me where it comes from," Canute mused. "And you offer it to me so freely that there has to be a catch to it somewhere. What is the catch, Hiram? There's a hook in the bait, isn't there? It's logical that there would be a hook."

"Oh, sure, but it's so thin a hook that you'll hardly notice it. And believe me, the hook isn't a logical one."

"Hardly notice it, huh? That may be like saying that a knife is so thin that you'll hardly notice it when it goes in between your fifth and sixth ribs," Canute said doubtfully.

"Yes, exactly like," Effie Poorlode chimed in. "How did you know about the cut between the fifth and sixth ribs, Canute? It isn't one of the major cuts."

"Lose weight free in seven-minute process," a little boy chanted at Canute. "My father is king of all the weight-takers-off in Leptophlebo Street."

"Not right now," Canute said.

"Get your clothes rewoven free," another little boy chanted. "My father reweaves baggy too-big clothes for slim-trim limb."

"Not right now," Canute said. "Does the hook hurt, Hiram?"

"Only a little bit. Only for a minute. Take the gold, Canute, and go close your deal. Then come back here for certain entertainments and kindnesses that we will have scheduled for you. You'll really like them. And when you have experienced them, and the mark that goes with them, then you will be one of us and you may enjoy Leptophlebo Street as often as you like and for as long as you like. And you won't even notice the hook when it goes in."

"And afterwards? When I do notice it?"

"I told you that it hurts only a little bit, and for only a little while. We do want you to be one of us. We want you sincerely."

Canute Freeboard looked up and down the crooked length of Leptophlebo Street.

"Choose us, join with us," said that skinny young lady Regina Shortribs. "Have fun with us. And come back often." And Canute looked at the wonderfully bony form of Regina.

He looked at Hiram Poorlode's sign, which read "Nuts, Wholesale and Retail." He looked at the three sad grackle birds that were stuck to the top-of-the-head garden of Effie Poorlode, and at that other unstuck grackle that was flying around with a piece of looking-glass in its beak. He looked at Highfellow, Redbone, Roxie, and Hoxie, the solemn monkeys of the street.

Hoxie wrote a note and gave it to Canute. "Join with us. Stay with us. We like you," the note read. Effie Poorlode took the note from Canute to dissolve the ink off it. A tear ran down Canute's face, for he was genuinely moved by the friendship of the monkeys. The little boy Crispin Halfgram raced in and caught the falling tear in a special little cup before it hit the street.

"My mother can use it," Crispin said. "Each teardrop is a storehouse of balanced chemicals. The special salinity is quite prized."

"Analyze your dreams, analyze your dreams!" A little boy of the street was making a pitch. "My father makes fine dream analyses free. Lie down on the cobbles."

"How can your father make a living by analyzing dreams free?" Canute asked.

"Residuals," the little boy said. "He gets rich on the residuals."

"Choose us, join us," said that skinny young lady Maharana Shortribs. "Have fiesta with us and come back all the time. Hey, do you know what we do for the climax of one of our night-life go-it-alls?" Canute looked at the wonderfully bony throat of Maharana.

"I make my choice," he announced. "I swallow the bait, hook and all. I become a partisan of this street." (Even the lop-eared dogs of the place raised their ears and snouts in joy.) "I take the loan now in cash." (The people began to cheer.) "I will go and seize the once-in-a-lifetime opportunity." (Folks began to laugh and to tune musical instruments.) "And then I will come back here for the entertainments and kindnesses and the night life." (The monkeys were clapping their hands.)

There was real welcome in the wind, and somewhere near, there was the joyful whetting of knives. Canute and the Shortribs sisters picked up the gold bars and went with them and closed the deal. So Canute nailed down the once-in-a-lifetime opportunity, but he knew that it was small stuff compared to the mysterious opportunity of Leptophlebo Street itself.

They came back to Leptophlebo Street, and a "Gala and Welcome" banner was stretched clear across the street. So it was quite impossible to decline any of the activities. And who would want to? The trumpet was blowing a great blast, and the other instruments were joining in.

Canute was having his teeth cleaned, his head groomed, his appendix removed, his dreams analyzed, some other pleasant surgery done to him, and his clothes rewoven, all at one time. This was life at its most full, and the dazzle and confusion were to be expected.

"This is the first appendectomy since my father got his knife sharpened," Pat Thingruel sang happily in Canute's ear. "Oh, you are lucky! Listen now as I join the rowdy-dow band for you. I play eighth flute."

"And this is the first free seven-minute surgery since my father got *his* knives sharpened," another little boy was chirruping. "Listen when I join the band. I play fifth drum." Canute couldn't remember what the free seven-minute surgery was about, but it had to be good. He heard the eighth flute and the fifth drum join the band and it was rapturous music. His dreams were being analyzed, right on the glittering edge of his senses, and he could only guess what rich residuals they would leave. And a written note was placed shyly before his eyes.

"Listen now as I join the rang-dang band," it read in the handwriting of the monkey Hoxie. "I play third bagpipe." Canute passed the note to Effie Poorlode for processing and salvaging. Everything that was done on Leptophlebo Street contributed to the fortune of that famous place. With joy Canute heard the third bagpipe join the rang-dang band. He was in glowing confusion as he recovered from his surgeries (there had been several of them) and his cleanings and groomings and reweavings and other things. Oh, it all did make him feel light and lightheaded and slick-fit and trim-limbed and happy!

As Canute rose to his feet, with a little help, the band played on with flutes and drums and bagpipes and all the wonderful and skinny-sounding instruments. It was certainly fine just to be there between the two beautiful and meager Shortribs girls.

"I have swallowed the hook without noticing it," Canute said, "and it didn't hurt a bit. I wonder what distinguishing mark has been placed upon me? And my rewoven clothes fit me so trim! How is it possible that anything should be so trim?"

No man can have everything—but on Leptophlebo Street he sure can come close.

A BRILLIANT CURIOSITY

A glove implies a hand, a lock a key;
and a black girl—

Doris Piserchia

Plumbing the depths of the prejudice in my soul, I came upon an unpleasant piece of debris, like when I once stirred a cup of tea with my finger and picked up a stray leaf: I didn't know why I hated Blacky or, indeed, if I hated her at all.

I decided to enumerate the reasons in my mind: number one, two, three, and so forth.

Looking at her was one thing, but thinking about her was another. I would rather have done the former, as the latter made for a tight belly.

Without skin, Blacky would have been attractive. Hmm. There was that slight protruding of her rear. Some of them had odd hip structure. Too leggy. Bosom too high. Head elongated. Why? Genes, naturally.

That last conclusion brought me no satisfaction, reminded me of pants, inside which all sorrow resided. People ought to have been more fastidious about where they dropped their jeans/ genes.

I think maybe I'll die tomorrow.

Blacky's grin? She had good teeth, but I didn't care for pink-gray gums. The palms of her hands were all wrong. Off-shade. Another thing I never took to was the whites of her eyes, because they flashed red. You could spot colored right off that way, like for instance the famous movie star who said he was Mexican. His wicked eyes gave him away, with their streaks of red.

I didn't feel right when I called Blacky a nigger. It embarrassed me. She didn't deserve it. Nobody ever persecuted me for anything. I am—I was a Wasp: you know, one of those people who didn't know what they were and were proud of it. (Relieved?) A chunk of potato in a stew; a little fish in a big pond.

As for us rednecks, we're okay, we're more American than any of you foreigners. My folks brought me up to be a good little girl and never even told me what a Jew was. I grew and went around with a frown because people were so concerned with names. "Levy? You say Levy?" Berg-stein-wald, hell, I learned, but I still had to be hit over the head with a name before I recognized it as anything but homo sap. My talent, you realize, lay in the two big dark balls above my nose. I couldn't hear anything but homo sap, but I could spot an ape a mile away, whether he was peeling a banana or not.

I wish all those apes were around now. (Without an equal complement of rednecks? I don't know.)

Blacky opens her mouth and you can hear the collard greens squeezing through her teeth. Where in the hell did that godawful accent originate?

Did you know their sex organs were blue? S'fact. Whence comes this sacrilege? We don't need or want blue but in the sky. Human beings have this and that. Anything else is an added upon, and we question who did it.

I don't believe in God. Never did. Well, when I was little. They said, "Don't, give, sweat, give, suffer, give, cry, give, give, give." I stopped listening when I realized they were a carbon copy of the government, or vice versa.

Blacky, you and I, we are both lost. Will you cry tomorrow when I get killed? No, I imagine you'll do like the psychs used to say was normal and sensible and virtuous. You'll cower in a corner and be glad because it isn't you.

I ask you to analyze that bit of indecency: "Better her than me." Never mind God, or what price valor, or what does it profit a man if he . . .

At the time I thought all those things, I was curled around Blacky's back, keeping it warm, while she kept my front warm. It was chilly spring outside.

It isn't true that they stink. Blacky shivered and moved closer. My back was plastered against a wall colder than a witch's ninny. (I don't like vulgarity, but sometimes use it without thinking, as I'm a ridge runner who never ran fast enough to get away from it one hundred percent.)

Nigger, nigger on the wall, who's the fairest of the two of us? Which one of us represents humanity? Poor little lambs, we are victims of our archetypes. How deep does the blood have to run before the subconscious lets go of that old survival rope? A foot deep in low gutters? Don't ask me. I have a strong stomach. Ask the nigger in my arms. Sometimes I think she is almost all ape. Cry? As she laughs. All the time. How high is her IQ? Statistically speaking, that is, in comparison with mine, well, neither of us had the brains to find our way out of the maze, not for weeks. (You should be alive to try this dilly. Einstein would give up after a year.) My roomie and I took a stab at it every morning before breakfast. And who ever said "Straw for the ox and wheat for the man"? I ate straw, or anything else that didn't break my teeth. But every morning, Blacky and I were forced to run and climb and crawl, and we had lots of energy because we dined so well.

I got out of Blacky's clutches, climbed from the bed and prac-
ticed walking on my hands. It wouldn't do me any good, though,
because I'd made up my mind that today I was going to get
through the maze with no assistance and that it was going to be
the last day I acted like a clown.

Maze: Like a honeycomb, glittering white and yellow, glisten-
ing as a sticky surface will, a little like frozen crystals on ice cream.
The floor didn't feel sticky to my touch. My hands sank into it a
fraction and I experienced a sickening sensation. I didn't lose my
balance, but then I never did.

There were thousands of holes in the walls, each large enough
to accommodate a body, and each having no end, or so it seemed,
besides which, a person inside one of those holes could end up
getting eaten.

The single door in our wooden shack led into the maze, and
we couldn't dig our way out of the shack, having nothing but our
teeth and fingernails. Woman is a piece of meat. Note I didn't say
man. We, the nigger and I, may be the only men left, and what
would all you studs who are inseminating flowers have to say to
that? You let us down. You got yourselves slaughtered and who
have we to depend on now? As you depended upon bigger men
and men in positions of power, even so we women depended on
you. Everyone did it, it was no crime, for this was a symbiotic
universe and not even light traveled on its own ticket. We are,
were, together. You lost. I cry to think how you tried. You don't
know about Blacky and me. What would you do if you knew? I
mean, illogic, if drawn to infinite length, can make a mind go
bananas. That's it. What's the point of two girls surviving?

Don't interrupt, mind, I'm looking at that maze.

I tried crawling into a hole, any hole, got ten yards and the
thing reached out little yellow suckers and started tasting me. I
scrambled backward and got out of that hole and tried another.
How would you like getting tasted every day of your life, a dozen
times a day?

Every morning Blacky and I woke up to the noise of the maze, and talk about a thing getting ready for a meal, even the floor became active. Blacky and I hopped, were experts by then, and we continued to hop until we finally saw the one inactive hole in the entire joint, and in we dived, fighting to get there first, and we crawled like hell to the end of the hole, and we dropped out and there we were, on stage in the Council Chamber, and right away we began our acrobatic act, and that was why we didn't die. Because we had good balance.

So I was just spouting when I swore I'd get through the thing with no help and I was braying when I said I wouldn't be a clown anymore. I'd do anything to keep from getting killed.

What would you do if razors suddenly started raining from heaven one day? Likely you would get sliced up. Not just likely —you did get sliced up. I didn't. Talk about a mob, there must have been three hundred people on the block, gawking at the sky. When that many bodies began to fall apart, there wasn't much space left that could be described as unlittered.

I was in the middle of my act when it happened. Soap-box stuff. Fifth Avenue, standing on my hands on the sidewalk. More natural to me than being on my feet. Everybody started dying in a hurry. I froze solid, I did. My hands grew red to my wrists. I examined my environment with my crazy eyes while my body remained stationary.

They had good eyesight, spied me standing the wrong way, down on the ground, otherwise they would have showered me with spears, along with the others.

The red was nearly halfway to my elbows. Something closed around my ankle and I was hauled into the sky. I had me a slow, slow jaunt through the countryside of NYC. Above me hovered a white bug the size of a truck. Shiny streamers hung from it like Christmas ornaments, and one of these held me suspended.

Occasionally I raised my head to look at the sky. Over the Empire State Building a huge white bug drifted, and from its tubular rear poured a stream of eggs. They bounced when they hit the streets. They were white as they dropped but red when they bounced. The bug covered ten blocks with eggs, and after they stopped bouncing they lay and soaked in the inert nourishment. Over New York I flew, and witnessed my species being cut to ribbons for fodder.

Into the Council Chamber we two crawled every day, and the bugs loved us. Blacky said once in a while that they only loved our sweat, otherwise why did they carefully lick us clean after we tired ourselves out? It made me mad when she said that.

"You stupid nigger."

"That wasn't necessary."

"I beg your pardon."

"Up yours."

"The same to you and more of it."

I wished it was anyone but me getting licked. The queen was beautiful and big, and there is no need to mention that she was also terrifying. The tip of her tongue, just the tip, was longer than I am. I never knew when she would tire of tasting me and swallow me. But maybe they didn't eat meat, once they hatched.

The tongue slid down my back, making me shiver; it ran into my hair to play, fondly nuzzled my silky armpits, bored into my navel. I stayed balanced on my hands and tried to stop shivering; the tongue sucked my leg too hard and some hair went. I think she liked me. Not my taste. My soul. The thing God goofed while making.

"Blacky."

"Shut up. They can hear. And don't call me that."

"They can't hear," I said. "And they're stupid."

"Oh, yeah? Then why are we getting licked like a pair of lollipops? If they're dumb, why are they the bosses?"

"I don't think I can stand this much longer. There's such a thing as private—"

"Shut up and stand still."

Being a nigger, she was one up on me in obedience. Her black body shone like grease, unnaturally so, as if something was com-

ing off the queen's tongue and sticking to her. Jesus, maybe we
were being coated with a layer of egg seeds, and maybe the seeds
were sinking into our pores.

"Blacky."

"Don't be a jerk. She eats vegetables and that shine is oil. She
already laid her eggs. She brought them with her."

"From where?"

"God knows."

"He doesn't."

"Well, we know. They came out of the ground."

In our wooden shack, I grabbed Blacky around the belly and
tried to steal her warmth. It didn't matter if she froze, as long as
I didn't.

Where did everybody go? What happened, for instance, to the
horses that lived here ten thousand years ago? What became of
those other species that should have thrived but instead went
away in a hurry to oblivion?

Down under the ground lie the eggs of Valene. So flexible are
they that it takes a special kind of force to perforate them. They
can't be opened by, say, a section of earth shifting against them.
Valene's eggs flatten out and slide like fluid until they are free.
The very pressure assists them in their flight toward open space.
A rock falling on one of these eggs does no damage unless it stabs
with a sharp edge, and this rapidly, before the shell begins its
automatic cringing and sliding activity.

Say you dropped an egg in a field ten thousand years ago. A
caveman who had survived the period of your reign came upon
the egg and tried to destroy it. He was too demoralized to suc-
ceed and so he finally went away and left the egg in the field.
Eventually the thing became buried. Ten millennia went by,
while the egg lay like a lump of clay, moving not at all, except
away from pressure. But one day the egg behaves differently. It
swells a bit before a needle-sharp antenna penetrates it from the
inside. A child of Valene emerges and begins a patient journey

to the earth's surface. It can bore through almost anything, though it prefers the easy way, and so it will detour around solid rock rather than go through it. Water presents no obstacle to Valene's child. In fact, the innumerable underground wells and lakes are the reason so many of the monarch's offspring arrive topside so quickly.

A starving Valenian will leap upon the first moving thing it sees. Animal or vegetable, it matters not, provided the youngster is able to penetrate the organism with its teeth and thereafter swallow pieces of it. A meal is a meal, and a Valenian is omnivorous, and practically anything will make it smack its lips in satisfaction. Of course, if you happen to be either of a pair of little gals named Blacky and Whitey, the Valenian won't have a craving for your body except in an indirect sort of way.

Was that last part obscure? Well, the eyes of Valene's child are drawn like magnets to beauty, after which it experiences a visceral blast.

Still obscure? Hmm. Consider a creature that digs pleasure, trips the light fantastic as a way of life, sucks without reservation when it is rewarding, and defines "reward" as anything that feels good. Know anybody like that? Of course you do. We. Us. Valenians are like people—hedonists at heart.

Valene was a big bug-mammal whose fur was whiter than snow. She had the wings of a bird, tail of a bunny, belly of a porcupine, ears like a hound and head like a grasshopper. So short were her legs that she might as well not have had any. The reason why I called her a bug was because her body was in three segments and she also had six legs and four wings.

Long ago, Valene courted a partly mammalian creature, a maguma, who went by the name of Mattu. This was before there were any people on earth. Mattu was scared of his children because they hatched from eggs and were bigger than he. He tried to kill them and Valene. The babies killed him instead, and Valene gathered all magumas into an open pen and slaughtered them, except for the handsomest male. She kept him as a lover.

His name was also Mattu. He had a furry white coat, long tail, padded feet, short legs, long snout and ears. A healthy stud, he was easily domesticated and all went well until dying time for the Valenians approached. Because Valene loved Mattu, and for a few other reasons, she commanded that he be treated with chemicals so that he would never die. As for herself, she would go the way of all flesh. Though she winced at the thought of another Valene having her lover, she needed to answer the call of her kind and go down into the grave with her comrades.

Mattu was given special transfusions that made his pituitary halt its normal processes and lie dormant in preparation for regeneration. He looked as if he were dying. His body shrank to a fraction of its former size, his eyes turned rheumy, he became senile and foolish. His body servants stuffed him into an egg sac, poked a feeding tube down his throat, laced the opening securely and transported the egg out over the ocean, where it was dropped. The tube in Mattu's throat fed him a solution that placed him in suspended animation. At the end of ten thousand years, the call of the wild reached his ears. His pituitary flickered to life and so did all of him.

The next generation of Valenians was pleased with Mattu. He was a good lover to the new Valene. However, being mortal, he needed to die at the end of his normal life span, which had been considerably shortened by the treatment. The alteration of such an essential part of his existence made him extremely argumentative and he turned out to be a far more earnest griper than his ancestor.

In this dispensation of time, the President of the United States was the first human to be killed by a Valenian. It wasn't part of any plan of Valene's to have such an important person killed first. To her he didn't even exist. It simply happened that way. She wasn't responsible for the places where the children of her predecessor chose to surface after their long sleep.

The President was walking his dog on the White House

grounds, and the dog attacked something in a clump of shrub-
bery. The something was a Valenian, still groggy, sore from
having crawled upward through a mile or so of clay, and hungry.
The thing ate the dog, the President and a bodyguard who
rushed across the yard when he heard their cries.

Most of the Valenians surfaced on the North American continent. They always would as long as the queen-egg was secreted
in Old Faithful. The heat didn't bother it, and it had sunk too
deeply into the mud bottom to be belched out.

Ten thousand years ago, the world's medicine men were called
upon to get rid of the Valenians with magic. This time, in the
twentieth century, scientists were handed the task. They did as
well or as poorly as their counterparts of old.

Many people provided meals for the furry giants, but so did a
large number of cows, horses, sheep, et cetera. In the meantime,
the armies of the world plotted. How could they kill an enemy
who was in every city?

The egg in which the nest resided finally hatched in Rockefeller
Center, and the world thought victory was at last in sight. They
believed the Valenians were like bees and that the nest was necessary for the bugs' survival.

While the governments planned their strategy for dropping an
atom bomb on the nest, Queen Valene was making love to Mattu
and growing more pregnant hourly.

Man was too slow in making up his mind. Time ran out. Valene
prepared to lay her eggs. The first was carefully dropped into Old
Faithful, and it was the largest of all. In ten millennia it would
produce the new Valene.

From the geyser, Valene flew to a heavily populated area,
which happened to be New York City. Her eggs flowed from her
in a deluge. No more would the Valenians eat human flesh. Only
the eggs would grow fat on such nourishment. From now on, the
Valenians would be strict vegetarians.

Dalia was the second-born of the old Valene, a sweet-natured specimen who never let me out of her sight, except when I was sleeping. She had a deep concavity in her skull where it connected with her backbone, and every day after Blacky and I went through our acrobatic act for the queen's entertainment, I climbed up Dalia's side and seated myself in the depression in her head.

She crawled from the nest, spread her wings and flew over the countryside of NYC. I beat her with my fists whenever I wanted her to do something.

We were on the hunt for survivors, and this time we intended to go a far distance. Dalia was always hungry, like me, so whenever she spied an orchard or a garden, she grounded and we had a snack.

It took us twenty hours to get to Africa, and we made two stops to eat. At last we parked on a mountain ridge above a campsite of jungle bunnies and slept until morning.

The natives were restless at sunup. For a thousand years Whitey had been after them to join civilization. They weren't supposed to hunt with spears or live like savages. Of course, what happened as a result of this was that the niggers didn't really live at all but were spectators to Whitey's life. In the meantime, they lost their spears and ate what Whitey tossed them.

At any rate, this morning, civilization was gone. Valene and her slaves had demolished the status quo. This bunch of niggers that Dalia and I watched were restless because their stomachs hurt.

They had the oldest member of the tribe for breakfast, after which they griped because he had made tough chewing. These were educated niggers, spoke English and had up-to-date catalogs in their outhouses. During the gab session, some old buck suggested that a virgin be on the menu from then on. He put up a good argument, concluded by pointing out that a virgin was like a tasty dessert, you could have it and eat it too. This served as a reminder to all that they hadn't had any dessert after breakfast, so every girl in the group started running. The last Dalia and I saw of the tribe, they were hauling down on some young critter.

My people were doing the same thing in NYC. On top of buildings, in alleys, in offices. With no fire, more times than not. They ate a lot of black meat. I saw them eating rats, too, but they didn't care what color they were.

I saw a crippled man walking down the street. So did a fellow on top of a building. He slid down a rope and, knife in hand, approached the crippled man. From the buildings poured a horde of hungries. They took the fellow's knife from him and used it to parcel him out.

I saw a child walking down the street. It was the same story. This time three men tried to jump her. The meal was three times more substantial.

Didn't anybody eat vegetables? Well, where in NYC were any? A human didn't dare go in a food store, for there was likely to be a Valenian dining in it.

I saw a horse running down the street, a pack of human savages chasing it with a net. I gave Dalia a whack on the head to gain her attention, squeezed her neck with my legs and guided her to a spot over the savages.

"Let 'em have it," I told her, and she did.

Her belly sent an avalanche of spears to the ground. By and by the horse came back and ate half of somebody. Pretty soon he got sick and died. I had Dalia let go with a circle of spears around his body. No one bothered that horse, not that day or any other.

I was no longer afraid of the Valenians or the nest or anything else. Blacky and I didn't sleep in the shack; now we slept in a hole in the nest. The Council Chamber held no terror for us. It was simply a room in the nest, a big hollow area where Valene and her Council rested most of the time.

Mattu was a gorgeous creature. An orator by nature, he could spout for hours, and after I learned the language, I argued with him.

"Our life span is so short and we have killed so many."

"Doesn't matter," I said. "You aren't abstract enough."

"Should I try to pretend that it hasn't happened?" he said, a bitter light in his eyes.

"That isn't a bad idea."

The rulers in the Chamber stirred, stood on their short legs.

"Come before me," said Valene.

I hopped onto my hands and she had fun licking me all over.

"Mama, don't do too much. Leave some of her for me." This was Dalia speaking.

"You love her?" said Foster-mama Valene.

"Very much."

"You would take my pleasure?" said Monarch Valene.

"Never."

"Very well, you can have a lick."

While this went on, Blacky crouched in a corner and whimpered.

"Get the hell over here," I said. "You think I can take this much goosing all the time?"

"Don't kid me," she sniveled, "you love it."

"What's wrong with being a hedonist? There's no God. If there's no best, there's no worst."

"You been getting Dalia to kill people. How many do you think are left?"

"What does it matter?"

"Nothing, except that you're human."

"Pooh-pooh. I'm here, they're there. Where's the resemblance?"

"You lousy atheist."

I laughed. "With those words you explained reality. I can't see why there was ever a fuss made about it. No good, no bad, no great, no small, nothing, no nothing other than what I do, do, do, do, do—"

"Shut up!"

"Mattu, why do you want to die?" I said.

"It isn't a matter of desire. From the beginning, it was the pattern."

"Do you think you have a circle built into your brain?"

"Perhaps."

"Well, you haven't. Your brain is like mine. It is a thing. It doesn't travel the same course as your father's. He didn't see or want what you do. In other words, you were a tabula rasa at birth."

"Prove it."

"Dang bug."

"Sticks and stones."

"Remember you love me."

"I remember. As did my father."

"Whom I never met," I said with scorn.

"In myself are all magumas."

"You're more Valenian than maguma."

Said Mattu, "Valenian, maguma, human, horse or mosquito, we are all one."

"The universal id?"

"Soul," he said. "In the beginning, it existed, and like the amoeba, it began to divide. Fly to the terminal and see the myriad faces of the One. Tell them they are individuals, hear them agree, see them support or turn against each other. What they do or claim changes nothing. You and I wish to be distinct, but we are part of the One."

"My God, what's the use of living, if that's the case?"

Mattu's eyes held amusement. "Haven't I been asking that all along?"

"Tell me something. Just what the hell are you?"

"The Devil's Adversary."

"What you need is an opponent. I wish I could be it."

Ha, ha, ha! All the rulers laughed with pleasure.

"Don't you care that you're killing people?" This was what Blacky said to me. We were in the nest, and I was wishing Dalia was there so I could share my comfort with her.

"You have it backwards, as usual," I said. "I don't kill anyone. Dalia does it."

"At your urging."

"The Council doesn't object, so why should I worry? Besides, why should they care about people?"

"You sound like you're talking about ants or something. What do you call me? Am I a person?"

"You're a visual effect," I said, and she took a fit, started yelling and kicking the wall of the nest. "At least you could show some gratitude," I said, loud enough to be heard above the din. "When they look at you they get a terrific kick where it counts, and you ought to be glad since that's the only reason you're alive."

There are four castes in Valenian society. First there is Valene. Nobody dictates to her. She is the boss and the rest are underlings. Insulted I suppose she can be by someone, but it's probably nicer if she doesn't feel insulted. The second caste is the Ruling Council. They discuss regulations and curiosities. In the Council are the five first-born, after the queen. Dalia is top dog in this group. In a class all by himself is the Devil's Adversary, Mattu, but since he never challenges the higher echelons, it isn't clear to me how much power he has. The fourth group encompasses every other Valenian, and they are happy slaves. Actually, there may be a fifth class, the honeycomb or nest, though I'm not certain about this, as I can't absolutely claim the nest is alive and breathing. That is, it's surely alive, but it may not have a soul. I ask myself if it has a brain. It seems to have. Every morning it wakes Blacky and me, as I said before. That makes it sound like a clock. It coaxes us to crawl through our sleeping tunnel, which seems to indicate that it possesses motive. It doesn't hurt us, even appears to enjoy tasting us, and doesn't this mean it obtains satisfaction? The Valenians feed it—at least I think this is what they're doing when they fill the holes at each end with hay and grass and occasionally a bundle of bugs. That the nest eats these offerings is obvious. Blacky and I listen to it chomping away at night. So there are either four or five castes in Valenian society.

Yes, the nest is definitely a class by itself. Dalia told me so.

When the life cycle draws to a close, the nest experiences the same alterations as the Devil's Adversary. It atrophies, is sewn into an egg sac, is buried in a safe spot, et cetera.

The ancient Valene found the nest. Symbiote is its generic name. It was the only one of its kind that she located. Give it something, it will give you something. Think loving thoughts while you're in it and it will love you and kiss you and lick you and put strange juices into your skin. It will provide you with intraporous feeding if you can't find anything to eat, provide you with heat, softness, euphoria. In fact, lying in the nest is such a pleasant pastime that Valene has to make it off limits to her people, except when they are suffering from depression.

I saw a man agitate in the street. He stood on a box, and having drawn a sizable crowd around him, he yelled that humanity would not survive unless the nest was destroyed. He didn't understand the nature of the nest. But the mob invaded a missile site outside NYC and fired off a couple of rockets. I don't know where the rockets went. No one in the crowd knew a guidance system from a street sign.

Hitting the nest ought to have been easy. As big as a mountain, it sits in Rockefeller Center, a sweet-smelling pink box-thing which we all love with a fierce heat. From the air it resembles a soft slug. Its surface undulates, as do its sides. No openings are visible. Dalia flies toward it and suddenly there is a large tunnel with its mouth agape, always a different one, and this is how we go into the nest and say hello after our daily sojourns into the countryside.

Devil's Adversary: "Mattu is my name. Beloved Friends is your name. Together we reason. Then why don't we? Tell me, one of you, why the Valenians should continue."

"To do what?" said I, standing on my hands and walking around the center of the circle which Valene and the Council created with their white, sleek, crouching bodies.

"To live," said Mattu. "To come again. To experience another season when the ten thousand years are ended."

"Why do you usually begin a sentence with why?" said I.

"Shut your mouth, Wasp," said Blacky. She didn't walk around the circle, merely stood still on flat palms. Her head was tilted upward and the sheen of sweat on her face glittered.

I ignored her and spoke to Mattu. "Some truths are self-evident. A living organism continues because it wants to."

"Not so," said Mattu.

He doesn't look exactly like a Valenian. He is white and beautiful, aye, but his tail is long, slender, curled at the tip. His legs are furry pipes, his head is shaped like a horse's. He has no wings. Poor Mattu can't chase the wind. I think he speaks in ignorance.

He went on. "The Valenians do not wish to continue, nor do they wish to discontinue. Since theirs is a state of noncommitment, I repeat the question. Why do we maintain the status quo?"

"I fail to understand why you ask it in the first place." I said this at the top of my lungs.

"Because of external circumstances."

"Such as?"

"I am an abstract thinker, a philosopher if you will, which is why I have been preserved since the beginning. The Valenians are and have always been wishy-washy. This was why they wanted me to accompany them to the terminal, which is the end of eternity. As each new life span springs into existence, the Valenians forget a bit of the past. Mattu never forgets. I am the Reminder."

"You're the Devil's Adversary," I said.

"One and the same, speaking in the abstract. The Devil is a symbol of illogic. I am his enemy. Since the Valenians are wishy-washy and can't decide whether or not they desire to experience the next life span, and since they can't leave the decision to the eggs who aren't alive yet, the decision must be my responsibility."

"Which is where I come in, by golly," I said. The floor of the nest beneath my hands kissed me. "Not now," I whispered. It subsided, touched me ever so delicately with a hundred tiny mouths but never once tickled.

I went on and on. "What you say smacks of genocide, and I'm educated on the subject. It doesn't matter if the Valenians don't care whether or not the eggs hatch."

"So long as they do hatch?" said Mattu, an intolerable light in his huge pink eyes.

"Somebody has to care. Valene cares."

"She does not," said the D.A. (Dumb Ass.) "The members of the Ruling Council bring me reports of the humans who dominate this planet. Every ten millennia, the Valenians come up and destroy billions. This life span has showed us humanity beyond his pubescence. Man has cities, a struggling culture, and he reaches for the stars. Man cares about life and death. He wishes to continue. The Valenians don't care. There, Beloved Friends, is the situation."

Valene made a few short comments. "Surely there is more, Mattu. Your argument is rational to a point. I seek to see beyond it."

"Then hear my next words," said Mattu in sonorous tones. "The life span of the Valenians is twelve Earth months. The life span of mankind is seventy Earth years."

"I fail—" said Valene.

"The love of life is a thing," said Mattu.

"It exists?"

"Beloved Queen and Lover, it does, outside of us."

"Uncanny."

"Think deeply."

"I'm trying."

"Mama, Mama, see me, love me," I cried. "All groups are minorities. Integration is possible only for Valenians. I don't want to die."

"What is this?" The peaceful eyes of Valene rested on Mattu.

"The Devil's Advocate isn't wishy-washy." Mattu's throat

might have been rusty, so creaky were the noises it created. "That's me, that's me, a Devil's Advocate," I said. "Mama, do you love Blacky and me?"

"Valene loves you."

"Shut up, Wasp," said Blacky.

"Tell her, Mama," I said. Walking on my hands to Valene, I paused and allowed my bare soles to rest on the fur of her breast. "She's trying to kill me with conscience, Mama. Once and for all, put her in her place. She is a curiosity, only that. Remember the day you and your slave squadron first flew in the sky during this life span? On that day, you spied a curiosity down below on the ground. The Valenians love brilliant curiosities. The brain of the Valenian inspires the body to know pleasure. Tell this black nigger why your slaves didn't spear her along with the other humans on the street below."

"Shut up," screeched Blacky.

"Tell her, please, Mama."

"Very well." Valene looked sleek and peaceful and satiated. "I am attracted to vividness. That day I soared above man's city. My slaves dropped spears wherever I commanded. My favorite color is a combination of blue and black, or rather, I love that which is in contrast to my own pristine colorlessness. On that day, I saw a stunning sight. My beloved color could not be hidden. It was down there on the street."

Blacky was blubbering. "Don't say it, don't, don't."

"She spared you because you're a nigger," I yelled.

"The sun glistened on your body," said Valene.

Said I, "You were mother-naked and sweating up a storm in the hot sun. Remember how the crowd hollered for you to spread your legs so they could feed you peanuts. You're nothing but a peanut-grabbing little nigger."

Blacky screamed, leaped, spat. She hunched on her ass and cried. "It ain't justice, Mama. All my life, my being a nigger was the Reason."

"Amen," I said.

I held Blacky close and talked.

"You ever had a boy?"

She said no.

"Me either. You think we missed anything?"

She said yes.

"My mama loved me even though I had two incurable deficien-
cies," she added, after a while. "I was black and I was a girl."

"Aw, that doesn't matter," I said. "Everybody is a girl."

"Funny, but you're right. Underneath, we're all girls. Except
I never made love and I never made sex."

"You were too little."

"Which reminds me of the third deficiency."

"You mean your being a midget?" I said.

Shoving her back against me, she whispered, "Did you ever in
all your born days meet up with anybody freakier?"

"Old Mattu would say none of those three things are deficien-
cies."

"That's why I like him," she said. "He's tolerant."

"No, he isn't. He starts from a whole new premise. Tolerance
is a dirty word, and he knows it."

Blacky took my hand and kissed it. "I want you to do me a
favor. I'd do it myself if I wasn't scared to ride one of the bugs.
What I want you to do is take Dalia on a crusade. I want you to
kill every white person you see."

"God!"

"I wish I was a Valenian. In a few months they'll all be dead,
except for Mattu, and he'll be gone, too. Only the eggs will be
left. Wish I could go with them eggs. This world is shit. I want
you to kill Whitey and then the nest life span will be easy for the
new Valene and her people. Nigger won't build anything up. In
ten millenniums, Nigger will still be eating bananas for dessert
after he's had his cousin as a first course."

"I have no objections to slaughtering anyone who eats with ten
fingers. I'm hard, I guess."

Dalia and I cleaned out NYC. Whitey lay everywhere. Boats in the harbors left daily, but that made it easier to pick off those mothers.

We extended our reach and cleared the continent in a few weeks. Blacky had unleashed a tiger. The first day out, Dalia and I took along a squadron of slaves. We thought we would need that many spears. We were overestimating the enemy. It made me wonder if all victims of a genocidal ploy became so demoralized that they turned into lame-brained sheep. Perhaps simply knowing someone loathed your meat so much that he wanted to stuff every atom of it into the grinder created a psychic shock that traveled from limb to limb, or person to person, and numbed the entire carcass or race.

I wondered what the human reaction would have been had they known the Valenians didn't hate them, or, in fact, seldom thought of them. One good lawyer, bending Valene's ear for a while, could have saved homo sap a deal of agony.

Dalia had a few hundred spears in her arsenal. They were stiff feathers that grew on her stomach. A feather could grow back in a few days. The smaller ones were about five feet in length, hollow toward their base, but very tough and pointed at the tips. Their lethalness lay in the force and accuracy of Dalia's toss. Her big eyes could spot a snake from a quarter-mile up, and so in control of her body was she that she could erect a pore and pop a spear into the snake's head before it crawled twelve inches.

Did I love Blacky, after all? Why else would I do such a thing for her? More likely, doing her bidding satisfied an inner craving of my own. Man of my flesh, you were such a sniveling sinner. Your thievery caused starvation and pain. There was more than enough money to conquer all our enemies, but you siphoned it away before it could be used for that. Pollution, poverty, disease and the stars were what we wanted, needed, to conquer, and we could have succeeded if you thieves hadn't stolen our blood. You, I mean you, who ripped off the box of pencils, the tractor, or ten percent of the till you were supposed to protect. Every little bit hurt.

The men of my flesh ran like rats as the squadron shadowed the sun, those days. But they were bigger than rats and easier to stab. I was merciful and directed my pilots to aim for the head. Besides, it made the slaves more enthusiastic. Going for a target made better sport than just dumping a load.

"Did you do it?" said Blacky.

"I did."

"Do you feel guilty?"

"Why should I?"

"Well, considering that you put down every Whitey in the country—"

"Nobody will ever do that," I said. "Some personalities are basically slime and spread out over the woodwork like a coat of paint. You can't spot them and they survive. They'll always continue. There are plenty of them left."

"I told you to kill them all."

"I did."

"But you just said—"

"Let's keep illogic logical, okay? I'm not omnipotent. I killed everybody who lost his head. Hey. Ha ha ha! Anyhow, you can't expect me to personally rout them from their holes. They might catch me. And then they'd do me like Mussolini."

"They're too desperate to think of revenge."

"Don't kid yourself," I said. "Homo sap is never that desperate."

MATTU: "I ask the question, my queen. Why shall the Valenians continue?"

VALENE: "The question is important?"

BLACKY: "It is."

VALENE: "Elaborate, Mattu."

MATTU: "It is all in desire. Man wants to live. The horse, the cow, the creature that moves on his belly, the one who lurks in his lair desires to remain living. Every living thing on Earth desires this, save for the Valenians."

BLACKY: "Does Mattu want to live?"

MATTU: "What price glory? I am not pure Valenian, which is why the ancient queen preserved me. I provide the piece of soul found lacking in Valene. I have a conscience. For this reason, my life needs a reason."

BLACKY: "Queen Valene, Mattu is like man. Long ago he suckled his young. Maybe this is the creator of conscience in all creatures who possess it."

VALENE: "How so?"

BLACKY: "The sharing of self is always by choice. Once made and done with, it is irrevocable. Do we automatically love that which takes a portion of us with our blessing? And if we love, doesn't that put our feet on the dual road of morality? If we never love, the question of good or evil doesn't concern us."

MATTU: "The Valenians love, but the question of good is not in their heads."

BLACKY: "The Valenians don't love. They want. There is a difference. Any hedonist is well acquainted with it."

VALENE: "Hedonism, then, is the epitome of evil?"

BLACKY: "The epitome of evil is heedlessness."

MATTU: "We digress. The option for the Valenians can be death, for we don't care. Everyone cares but us."

VALENE: "Care is the epitome of good?"

BLACKY: "You will sacrifice me on an altar if I say yes. If care is the highest good and the Valenians don't care, then the Valenians represent the lowest evil."

MATTU: "You forget that they don't care."

BLACKY: "I could go mad with this conversation. It isn't sensible that an insult isn't always an insult. I can call the Valenians bastards and they take no offense and lick my beautiful black body because the sight of my blackness gives them a charge. Mattu, what do you feel when you look at my opaque hide?"

MATTU: "I am half and half. I like in many ways. First, my teeth itch. Long ago I was pure carnivore. Second, my id stirs. Your brilliance is in contrast to my whiteness. You are so black. Come, let me lick your face."

BLACKY: "Watch the teeth."

MATTU: "Why stand on your hands in our presence? It is not the way of your kind."

BLACKY: "Yes, it is. It's called rationalization. You can't possibly love me for my goddamn color, therefore you love me for my acrobatic ability."

MATTU: "Having a conscience, I know a smell when I smell one. You are on the road to insanity, mad with a great madness."

BLACKY: "Hell, honey, I've been on that road since the day my mama dropped me among the boll weevils."

THE GREAT I: "On your pointy head."

A thought came and went in my mind, came and went, came and flew, came and crawled away, came and reeled before me, staggered, fell. I made it mine. It was evil and treacherous and absolutely essential for my survival.

Dalia and I went to Africa and chased jungle bunnies. That tribe we had watched a few weeks ago, they were fresh out of girls. Being a girl myself, it teed me off. Why the hell do men hunger for the taste of woman? You frail mice, you just want somebody you can take advantage of. That way you don't have to apologize for your poor performance.

I once knew a woman who was so scared of getting pregnant that she spent years running from her old man. Finally he got sick and tired of it and had a vasectomy. After about a year of puzzling it all out, the wife got it into her head that she didn't have to be afraid of anything anymore. She went after that man of hers with a vengeance. You know what? He went limp as custard. Permanently.

Now that the women were gone, the tribe of natives were using up each other. They drew straws that day, and the loser of the duel furnished dinner to the rest.

I waited until they were all fed and then I killed them and I cried as I did it.

MATTU: "The Valenians existed before man. Perhaps this means we have rights above man. Yes. Squatters' rights. But rights mean nothing to us, which places us back where I started. Desire is the purpose."

BLACKY: "Listen to him, Queen Valene. Mattu is good and sensible and full of peace."

The Council Chamber was empty when I killed her. I had brought a rock with me from my last trip with Dalia, and I took it and held it behind me and sneaked up on her. She turned and saw me.

"Mama mama mama mama—"

"Why call her?" I cried. "She can't help you. She's been dead for years."

"You remember her."

"So?"

"She'd look at you with her fierce eyes and you'd go hide in a corner."

"I'm sorry I have to do this," I said. "Lay down and don't fight. Make it easy for me."

"I'll come back to haunt you. I'll never let you rest."

"Like hell."

I brained her. I knocked Blacky with that rock. It was because of her big mouth. She should have been on my side.

There were about two million people still alive, was my guess. I wouldn't kill any more, as there was a need for them to build up their numbers again. In ten thousand years, the children of Valene would need food. Man would make his old societies new, he'd commit self-rape, and when Valene came she would win again. I hoped I did it right. All my teachers had told me the blacks were intellectually inferior, so I left mostly blacks alive.

The brains were all gone. I hoped those niggers wouldn't be waiting for Valene with a pack of superweapons, come the resurrection.

I couldn't find Blacky. I hunted for her.

"Nigger, where are you?"

Everyone who has ever lived leaves a footprint somewhere.

"Nigger, you're around, I know."

Maybe her mealy mouth had deposited an echo in a crevice.

"I can't hear you, nigger.

"Are you good and dead?

"Did I really get rid of you?

"Hey, collard greens, I cut the mustard this time, didn't I?"

A mattress sinks and stays sunk after a body lies on it for a time. Blacky didn't weigh much and had left no indentation. Clothes? She wore none, but I hunted anyway. No jewelry of Blacky's lay in the shack. No shred of her body was stuck on the furniture. No hair was caught in the nest; I know because I crawled through every one of the holes. Talk about getting sucked! That sucking was finally taking hold. My skin was a fraction of an inch thicker. The nest was prepping me, coating me for the big trip halfway to yonder.

"Have you seen Blacky?" I said to Mattu. "And I just want a simple answer without a lot of philosophy wrapped around it."

"How can I have seen her when you murdered her?"

"I'm glad Valenians don't care. If they saw her, they'd want her, but they can't see her and they won't hold it against me."

"I'm a Valenian and I care."

"Don't kid me. You couldn't care less what I did to Blacky."

"Well, at least remotely. Immortality begs for diversion and you provide me with such."

"Do you love me, Mattu?"

"Do you care one way or the other?"

"Hell, no!"

"You are going to be a Valenian with a difference," he said.

"Same as you?"

"Opposite of me."

I said, "Devil's Adversary, meet the genuine, already crowned Devil's Advocate. From now on, I will be the Valenians' lawyer, and I intend to see that they survive."

"You have been chosen by the Council?"

"Signed, sealed and practically delivered."

"Before you go to the nest, approach me for a last farewell. Look me in the eye and see a brilliant curiosity."

He tilted his head toward me, and the outer portion of his eye nearest me acted as a mirror and revealed the Chamber and its contents. Before I turned away from him, I caught a glimpse of the last human being I would see for a long time. It was a tiny nigger gal with blue-black body and crazy eyes. A brilliant curiosity.

The nest is the laboratory. It preps oddities, like, say, Valenians who are unusually large, or the Devil's Adversary, or the Devil's Advocate, or anybody different for whom the Valenians form an affection. To them, life forms are all the same. They don't care at all.

The nest sucks. Not out, but in. Into me went the chemicals necessary for my preservation. I felt bloated and well sucked by the time the nest finished with me.

A bit shrunken in size, but not much because I was small to start with, I was lifted by Dalia and kissed good-bye.

"We had a good time," I said. "Love you."

"I'll see you after a short sleep."

"It won't be you. You're going to die and I'll be playing with another Dalia when the nest life span comes."

"What's the difference?" she said, and of course she was right.

The egg sac was warm and cozy. The tube was stiff when Dalia placed it in my throat. Immediately reality became fuzzy.

"Mattu, do you think the nest can give me a nice fur coat, next life span?" I said.

"It is a very capable organism. If you desire to grow fur—"

"Will it be shiny white like yours?"

Oh, how the gleam in his eyes pierced me. "Little girl, didn't anyone ever warn you about wishing for the moon?"

I settled back, disgruntled, but not too much. "Mattu, you're my friendly enemy and I'll get you next time around." It was the last thing I said.

I was aware of the sac's contents pressing at me from all sides. My knees touched my chest, my chin touched my knees, my arms hugged my legs, I felt more comfortable than I had in my mother's womb. If she were alive, she would understand. She gave me life, which, as I said before, was a mound of crap. Anyone would do the same as I was doing.

I heard Dalia close the sac. I sucked on the tube. It softened in my mouth. Sweet nectar slid and dropped and beckoned sleep. I was still aware as Dalia flew me to my resting place, scarcely felt it when I hit the ocean and sank.

In a minute I'll take the deep nap. In the meantime, I think of the future. I am happy. Come the resurrection, I'll live again. I am the Devil's Advocate. As for you who are going to be around when I wake up, you mothers had better watch it. Blacky, my better half, my conscience, is dead. I killed her. Now there is only myself, and it is a thing you created. Here's to an everlasting vacation in Hades.

PHOENIX HOUSE

It came across the desert, in a jeep nobody was
driving, and its message was Hate.

Jesse Miller

Easterly, Nevada, 2016. In all the world, one of the few things
remaining unchanged was the wind. It never ceased whistling
sand in from the desert, where there was no one to be stung. The
sand hissed against the porcelain flanks of the ghost town's Car-
vel. It duned and piled in strange, eddy-chosen places.

Across the earth, over broken porches, banging shutters, howling unimpeded, whistled the wind. Through rusted streets,
against crumbling buildings, currents of air flowed like water.

In New York, the Verrazano Bridge began its sweep whole
from the Staten Island side, ending in the middle of nowhere.
Halfway out over the Narrows, cables blew dangling like the
ragged hem of a woman's skirt.

Perhaps a hundred survivors led nomadic lives, scattered
throughout the world. A few had settled, briefly, and children
had come again to the earth. That was better; the children
remembered nothing but their own lives. The remnants of men

wandered, after fourteen years they wandered yet, as if in a dream.

Jake had been by himself for so long he had forgotten what it was like to be anyplace other than the desert. He was a hermit; he had learned desert ways, and he acted so wise and steady, there was a sort of crust about him.

It was not that he deliberately shunned contact with people, or that he hated civilization. What he remembered of humanity was heaven, and he wrote almost every day in his notebooks about the people he recalled.

"The blowup," he printed neatly, "was an act of nature." He looked up, out through the open door to the mountains, always on the horizon. Laying his palm against his forehead, he returned to the diary. "Our technology proved itself to be no more than dust. Our planet was simply too crowded. There wasn't enough of anything to go around.

"Now, in her wisdom, Nature has the few humans left struggling with the mutants. We are natural enemies." Jake put down his pen, thinking for a moment about the little graveyard behind the shack. "May the best man win," he added finally, slapping the thick diary closed.

The mutants had shown no more evidence of trying to stick together than the humans. They too led a solitary and nomadic life, scattered about the world. The mutants displayed a ferocious curiosity, and they examined whatever interested them in a way that could only be described as brutal. To be trapped by a curious mutant, young and eager to learn, often meant mutilation, sometimes death.

At Jake's desert outpost there was an occasional human visitor. He called these migrants "pilgrims" in his notes. They all had stories which varied only in degree of horror.

There was a sweet well in the hermit's yard. All who came through stopped for at least a day, and tales were exchanged into the starriest parts of the night. Jake was happy then: he felt important and vital.

Many pilgrims came to the shack injured, and a few died there.

There had been a girl, a few months ago. Jake recalled her now as he drew water from the well. She was covered with burns, and she walked stiffly. She saw Jake and did not see him.

The desert man interposed himself in her path, and she collapsed in his arms. Jake dragged her to a cool place and went to the well. When he returned, cradled her head and dabbed her lips with water, she opened her eyes, and they were lackluster.

Jake buried her with the others, but he remained haunted. He felt, more and more each season, that time was passing him, and he told himself as he filled his books that he was essential to the continuance of the human race.

"There will be others," he wrote.

On one of his two-day treks to Easterly, he had found a tin placard, hot with the sun. It was yellow, and in blue letters it bore the legend "Yoo Hoo, America's Favorite Chocolate Drink." Smiling ruefully, Jake had stooped and turned the sign over. The blank side was covered with white, and in sun-faded red paint there were two words: "Phoenix House." He nailed the sign to the side of his shack, and it looked just right.

In his notes, he wrote more and more about the methods of nature, and he began to think of himself as wiser than he really was. After his evening meal he stood out in the yard and watched the sun go down behind the shack, tinting the big metal mountains pink.

His favorite time of all was when a storm came and he could watch it from the moment it was conceived, against the mountain slopes, until it was fully upon him, battering all that he owned, and scaring him out of his senses. He thought of these shows as a gift of nature.

It was his habit to lean against the doorjamb, a piece of grass between his teeth, and watch the turbulence brewing. First there was always the feeling of hot disturbance and conflict. A midday chill suddenly passed through the air. Then the hermit looked up and out, and he saw darkening streaks, like smoke, tossing and swirling out over the desert. He saw far-off bright flashes, followed by great slow rolls of mumbling thunder.

It quickly darkened then, and Jake trembled with anticipation. It wasn't because he was a novice, but because he had gone through storms before that he became so nervous as the wind grew and the dark thickened.

Sand and debris came flying in off the desert and thunked into the sides of Phoenix House. The shack creaked and slapped like an old ship, and the hermit lit his Coleman lantern.

During the most savage parts of the storm, Jake frequently felt overcome with the sensation that his dry house was on the verge of flying apart around him. He grew certain he would be left naked, clutching his lantern and grinning, grinning insanely with terror into the raging wind and the howling dark.

Pulling the log nearer, he crouched over the crinkled pages and scribbled notes at the height of the storm, so that he could see later how frightened he had been, how full of repentance and promises, and he would be reminded of how glad he should be just to be alive. "Life," he wrote, "is free for no man."

When the turbulence had passed, the sky rapidly cleared and filled with stars, and the hermit, like the desert, was glad and refreshed, and they slept together.

"Convulsions," he observed, "are natural, and renew my confidence."

On an afternoon three months after the girl had appeared and died, the hermit stood in his doorway looking out over the plain. He saw the air at the edge of his vision fairly congeal with the weight of an impending storm.

There was something slightly wrong, a little too powerful about the way the dark rain clouds were swirling. The charcoal-colored turbulence was high and piley; the air around the shack cooled more rapidly than it had ever done, as far back as Jake could recall.

Nature brewed all her storms in pretty much the same way, step by step, so that by the time the storm was upon you, you would be ready to believe the weather had always been the way it was at present. But on this afternoon it was as though certain phases of the buildup were missing. Jake was puzzled. Out there, in the center of the growing turmoil, he could see a curious light.

The more he concentrated on that point of artificial brightness, the more he could tell about it. After a moment he saw that the light was coming toward him; then he could see that it was moving very fast before the storm, and at last, there was that huge rooster-tail of dust kicked up by fast-moving vehicles in the sand.

Whoever it was had a long way to go before he arrived at the shack. Jake wasn't sure there was time to get here before the storm. In his excitement, he ran out into the yard and jumped up and down, waving his arms and yelling. The prospect of having company during a storm filled him with glee.

Then something happened. The purpling boiling clouds towered high behind the onrushing vehicle, and suddenly Jake could see what was happening out there as though he were standing a few yards away. He saw that the vehicle was a jeep. Then he saw there was no one behind the wheel. In the back a woman sat upright, her hair long and blowing behind her, and she was beautiful. But where her eyes should have been there were only hard orbs of electric sparkle. Greenish, now blue . . . she was a mutant.

The vision could only be coming from a telepathic contact with the mutant. "She knows I'm here," Jake said aloud, and he began to think about a place to hide.

She was pushing at him even now. He could feel her power in her message. She was broadcasting her name, "Ta Chaunce, Ta Chaunce . . ." It seemed to Jake that his brain was beginning to burn around the edges. He fought to shut her out, but he was battered and stunned by the unearthly light, growing and spreading in conjunction with the storm, like some malignancy radiating from the woman in the driverless jeep. He felt the first traces of the nausea that comes with unacceptable telepathic contact.

The jeep had swept closer, and now Jake could hear a faint buzzing. The awful light shifted from a pastel flickering to a harder, Day-Glow orange. It flashed and sputtered like a high-voltage wire. Behind the flashing there was a random snapping of white-hot lightning, big thick electric branches appearing for seconds at a time before the crash of thunder.

The young presence in the jeep sent out waves of malevolence, and Jake fought to free his mind from hers. His hands found the Coleman lantern, and he began to pump it up.

Ta Chaunce had been drawn to Jake's area by the feeling of age and solitude she had picked up from his shack. She felt the desert wisdom of the hermit, inert and crinkly, waiting to be ripped and probed. For probing and ripping was her way, even with herself, although she never meant to hurt anyone or anything.

Jake could feel in Ta Chaunce a mixture of pride and confidence, with undercurrents of wonder and the careless freedom of unchallenged power. The images of Ta Chaunce crowded into him; involuntarily, his hands went up to cover his ears.

"Roll," Ta Chaunce thought. "Faster." The driverless jeep responded, careening across the desert. The mutant perched in the back with her dark hair shining and blowing, idly perceiving the hermit's desperation.

When she arrived, screeching and bouncing, Ta Chaunce caused the jeep to slow and cruise around the shack. Chewing gum, she sniffed the air as the jeep circled, jouncing in ruts, investigating.

"Cease," she thought, and the jeep came to a halt behind the shack, by the graves. Ta Chaunce silently got down and stood tall beside the hermit's cemetery. The tumultuous air whirled around the spot like a funnel.

When their eyes met, fear overwhelmed the hermit. Ta Chaunce walked purposefully toward him, and he dropped his lantern and ran.

She did not watch him go. Her immediate purpose was to examine the shack: she could study the hermit later. Once she had discovered the secret of the shack, she need never again be puzzled by such things. And later, when she had examined the hermit, she would know this type too; and from the study of one she would learn the weaknesses and strengths of many.

She paused in the entrance of Phoenix House. The air was suddenly thick and cold, and Jake stopped, quivering in the sudden, ethereal quiet. Ta Chaunce's boots were loud on the floor. She could smell time working in the house, and she was careful where she stepped.

"What do you want?" Jake's voice quavered.

She turned and regarded him through the doorway, but made no sound except for the hissing and fizzing of her horrible sparkling eyes. Then her thoughts began to bombard his senses. Jake squeezed his eyes shut and pressed the sides of his head with his hands, as if he could force her images from his brain.

The shack was glowing with her power. Her mind was smoking here, touching there, passing up some things for later examination. What she touched unfolded, like a flower, then dropped, burned out and dead.

Jake felt her turning to the old piece of flypaper dangling from the center of the ceiling. It was a brittle strip of yellow paper, and the hermit could feel the mutant comparing it to the tattered windowshade, and then to himself.

Abruptly her mind went deeper into his. Revelation and irrelevance together assailed the hermit's overloaded senses. He was torn between his drive to comprehend a little, and the need to survive whole. But his desire far outpaced his ability, and he buckled under the pressure of insistent unwanted visions. Jake's eyes watered and he gasped for breath. His hands appeared in the sand before him, his throat caught, and he began to vomit.

Together the desert man and the mutant felt the sun, in days and days gone by, moving across the floor of Phoenix House with slow warming strokes. Ta Chaunce probed. She put the shack and the hermit through time past. There were nights of the shack groaning and ticking as the cold swept down from the mountains

and the day's heat rushed out to the open desert sky with nothing
to retain it. The void above filled and refilled with stars, year after
year.

Jake felt his brain slip the way a pail full of water sometimes
slipped a foot or two in the well. He shook and wept while his
head pulsed with the imagery of the mutant. Jake went down on
his side, curling into the fetal position.

In the shack, Ta Chaunce felt the hermit fall, but she was not
disturbed. Human emotion was not hers; compassion was a thing
alien to her. She was equipped marvelously to explore and
wander in a broken world. Now she was tuning in on an anonymous voice from some time far away. As she focused on that
distant calling, her hooded eyes opened fully and the shack
blazed as though it were filled with flares. Outside, Jake groaned
and writhed; he squeezed his eyes shut.

The voice Ta Chaunce had picked up was located before even
the arrival of the hermit. The speaker had been staring at the
starry sky of the desert and had said, full of awe: "The more you
look, the more you see . . ." It was this man who had painted the
sign "Phoenix House."

The mutant focused on an empty bean can on the table. Together she and the hermit saw rust working as a retarded fire, the
shack holding the flaking, reddening can on the altar of the table,
fresh, good-smelling wood going dryer than paper. The hermit
became aware of his bones.

There were shelves falling and shades slowly tearing, time
passing rhythmically, until the day Jake himself slowly walked in
from the outer desert with a pack on his back.

"Time," the mutant whirred and clicked. She walked out of the
shack, her closed lids diffusing the solar luster of her eyes to a
cold blue glow.

Jake didn't have to look to know she was coming out. He felt
her desire to leave a marker, something time could not affect. It
came to him that she was about to burn the shack.

A small tongue of flame appeared, dancing and pale in the

cloudy gray light. Then there were others, and Jake could feel the mutant carefully watching.

Filled with sudden rage, the hermit lowered his head and ran at the mutant. He caught her around the waist, knocked her back through the open doorway so that she tripped and stumbled backward over the step just as the little house erupted, belching dry crackling heat.

Ta Chaunce lay on her back a moment. She pulled herself up to a sitting position, slowly, as if stunned.

There was a vacuous sensation, and Jake knew she was bottling her rage, preparing to release it in one terrible bolt. He started to run, but stopped, feeling suddenly free. There was no sense of danger, no feeling of impending disaster.

He turned cautiously. The shack was filled with fire. Cinders and thick crumbly ashes were dancing in the shimmering air above the inferno. At the center of the fire Jake could see the dark silhouette of the mutant. She was standing erect now, trapped in the center of the blaze. Jake approached as close as he dared. He saw the mutant turning toward him. He saw, or sensed, her eye-lids opening, and suddenly it was as though he had entered the fire. The heat was so intense it was like the burn of liquid gas. It seared his skin and he knew he was blistering. His face seemed to be hardening, and when he tried to touch it, his arms were stiff and his skin cracked, dry and crisping.

Then it was over. Jake was standing alone again in relative coolness, watching a fellow creature burn. He recalled the girl who had died in his arms, and he knew what he had to do. He turned, ran to the well, began to pull up the bucket.

Jake's notebooks had been lost in the fire. He had started a new one, but between repairing the house and nursing the badly burned mutant, he had had very little time to make entries in it. The mutant seemed to be gaining strength, but she was dehy-drated. Jake spent hours dabbing a wet cloth to her lips.

He knew she was improving because she lay very still. Through her closed eyes there was a tiny glimmer of light, and that light grew stronger day by day.

He had a large supply of white gas for his Coleman lantern. When he poured a few gallons into the jeep, to his delight it started. The trek to Easterly had taken him more than a day on foot. In the mutant's jeep, it took less than an hour. He had never wanted a vehicle before, but now, with two people to care for, he needed it to haul extra supplies.

In the remains of Phoenix House, Ta Chaunce was coming out of hibernation. Her breathing remained shallow, her features changed not at all, yet she was fully recovered. She perceived the hermit, away in Easterly, and saw that he was open and defense-less. She saw him on the road, felt his presence nearing, and she strode out into the yard.

Jake hopped from the jeep and walked quickly to her side. Ta Chaunce was facing the mountains. When she felt him beside her, she turned to confront him.

Jake recoiled. Her eyes were not eyes, but bright points of shining energy. She was in his brain again, marveling at his con-stant amazement. He wondered briefly how they could stay to-gether if he could never look her in the face.

Immediately there was a picture in his mind of the two of them, together at night, and the light radiating from her eyes was strong and bright enough to read by. Jake shook his head to clear it, but the image lingered, and Ta Chaunce turned away from him again, looking out at the horizon.

She seemed to be telling him he would just have to get used to it.

"I can't see your eyes," Jake sputtered.

The mutant was aware that Jake didn't understand. But she was also aware that he had made a beginning. How to tell him she had no sight? How to tell him the power of speech was not hers?

She knew there was plenty of time. Life was suddenly full of promise. When the hermit became adjusted, there were many things she could teach him, and she would learn compassion, and for the children . . . nesting.

JACK AND BETTY

What would the reciprocal of this story be like—
that is, what if the author had put in what he left
out, and vice versa?

Robert Thurston

The room was all Jack knew. He had been other places but he
could no longer remember them. He stood still, concentrating on
his peripheral vision. To his left the room seemed to have
blurred, then faded. He turned quickly. For a split second the
other side of the room was not there. Then it reappeared, mud-
colored and barren.

Betty was long in coming this time.

He paced the mud-colored floor. Floorboards sank beneath his
feet like the springs of a hard, lumpy mattress. He sat on the
mud-colored divan.

Whatever Betty did when she was away, this time she was a long
time doing it.

He played breathing games. Long inhale, long exhale. Short
inhale, short exhale. Long inhale, short exhale. Short inhale, long
exhale. Rhythmic breathing where the breaths imitate the drum

accompaniment to a song played by full orchestra in the mind. He concentrated on the orchestra itself, placing the bass fiddle section right by his left ear. Second bass fiddle was an orange-haired girl with a freckled face. She leaned over the instrument as if she were having an argument with it.

A long time this time, Betty.

As soon as she materialized, Betty realized that Jack always broke into a grin when she returned. What's he got to grin about? I must be ten pounds heavier this time. Stupid. I feel shitty. I feel shitty and witty and wise. Dumb fat-girl dress, daisies all over it. Why would I ever buy such an atrocity? At least it's colorful, something better than the faded-lace color of this room.

"You remember, this time?" Jack said, as Betty sat down beside him.

"Not a goddamned thing. One second I'm sitting here, deciding to let your hand sneak into my cheerleader's sweater, the next I'm standing over there in a party dress. But I've been someplace. I can almost remember where. It's like waking up from a dream, it's gone now."

"Like that for me, too."

Jack's face was heavier, a suggestion of jowls. His eyes looked as if they'd been smeared with coal dust.

"What do I look like?" she asked.

"Cotton candy."

"Is that complimentary?"

"I doubt it."

Jack held up his right leg and pointed to his trousers. Betty saw droppings of what might be dried paint—bits of purple, black, and brown.

"You think maybe you're a painter?"

"Yeah."

Jack put his leg down. Delicately, so as not to dislodge the drops of paint.

"House or canvas?"

"Looks like oils to me."

"You should be happy then. A clue to your identity and all. Why aren't you happy?"

"What if I'm not good at it? How do I get any satisfaction out of knowing I'm an artist if I can't see the fruits of my labor?"

"In an automated society the majority do not see the fruits of their labor. Many people don't know what their labors are."

"I've got to know."

"Well, then, you may possess some talent, a dabbler's maybe, an alien corn's. But yours is not the artistic temperament."

"Pompous bitch."

"Yes, isn't it worthwhile?"

Betty disliked the way her skirt slid farther upward each time she shifted position on the divan. Each movement revealed a little more of her meaty thighs. She stood up, knowing that the perspective suited her figure better. De-emphasized were the big stomach, the upper-arm fleshiness, and the awesome thighs. She felt her muscles strain holding so much of her in place.

Jack disappeared, which was something of a relief.

Betty spent the next few hours relaxing, letting her flesh fall where it might. She wondered if Jack was worth all the trouble. Putting up with his curtness, listening to his egomaniacal self-pity, trying to keep her witty remarks down to his level, watching his baldness run from his temples upward in a pair of flying wedges—all because he was the only game in town.

Jack returned. He was dressed quite conservatively, like a stockbroker or banker, and now had a slight paunch and a mustache. Betty laughed at the mustache. Touching it, feeling its strangeness, he said, "Does it look good at all?"

"Want an honest answer?"

"If the honest answer is yes, I want it. If it's no, I don't want it and I want you to tell me yes anyway."

"Okay. Yes. It looks just marvelous."

"Really?"

"Honest or dishonest answer?"

"Forget it."

He sat beside Betty and held her. She looked quite sexy in the daisy-flowered dress. Staring at the low scoop of its neckline, he felt desire for her. Betty kept touching his mustache and giggling. He kissed her, which initiated a giggling fit. Later, when the kissing became more intense, she appeared to enjoy the mustache. At the moment of her disappearance, he was beginning an affectionate hug. One hand slammed against his chest as his arms crossed where she had been.

Jack discovered some marijuana in his suit-coat pocket, along with a packet of Zig-Zags. He rolled and smoked the first joint, then looked slowly around the room. There was nothing for heightened perception to fix on. The mud-colored room just became more mud-colored. No kick in that. Betty better make it back quicker this time. Betty better. The second joint worked.

Betty came back pregnant. She almost fell flat on her face because of the sudden abdominal weight. She looked to Jack for help. Through the smokescreen that surrounded him.

"My God, what a time for you to be stoned! You always know, don't you? What do you have, advance information?"

"Bug off. Any time you want to is a good time to be stoned."

"But not now, stupid."

"Why not now?"

Betty stood sideways. "I'm pregnant, God damn it! Knocked up. *Enceinte.* In the family way. Preggers. Unexpectedly with child."

"I gave at the office."

"Help me or something!"

"Here, you should sit down. Sit down here. Mustn't exert yourself. That's what all new fathers-to-be say."

"I strongly doubt that you're the new father-to-be, my friend."

"Well, sit down anyway! What the hell do I care whose kid the bastard is?"

Betty sat at the end of the couch. With some difficulty, because her pregnancy prevented graceful movement and because the battered slope of the couch made it tricky to sit as far away from Jack as she wanted.

"What I hate most," Jack mumbled, "is people who continually give you stage directions for the roles you play."

The pot smoke dissipated slowly. Jack stared straight ahead, his lips working steadily on unheard mutterings. Bored, Betty fell asleep. Bored Betty. Baby-kicks awoke her twice. The second time Jack was gone.

She wondered what to do if the kid decided to get born here, *here*, before Jack came back. She wondered what use he'd be anyway.

Jack's return coincided with a labor pain. He was put on edge both by her scream and the rage in her eyes.

"What can I do?"

"Pray."

In between pains her whole body went slack. Her arms hung over the edge of the divan. Her face looked puffy.

"God, you're bald!"

He felt his head. It was true, his hairline had receded further. Only a few strands crossed the forelock area. Still a lot of hair above the timber line, though. A cold breeze blew across the barren slopes and made him tremble.

Without dignity Betty endured another labor pain. Afterward she said, "Have you read *A Farewell to Arms?*"

"No."

"I think I have, God damn it!"

Jack felt he must do something, concoct a heroic act, make a civilized gesture, accomplish something worthwhile before he lost all his hair. What *could* he do? Talk to her, offer her encouragement? "Go to it, Beth old girl . . . Another heave and it'll be all over . . . Open wide, it won't hurt."

Her pains came with more frequency. He held her, first for affection, then to pin her down.

"Boy, if I ever come across the guy that did this, my impregnator, I'm going to—Jesus!—it's coming now. I can feel it. It's coming, God damn it! Help me, please. I can feel it. It's coming. Jack, do something, do something, do something!"

He could not move. Betty's words dissolved into a long-drawn-out shriek, the sound of which ended sharply as she disappeared, leaving a broad, deep gully in the divan, which slowly inflated to its regular shape.

Inspecting himself with a hand, Jack stroked his baldness, detected a new graininess around his eyes, a bit more weight in his chin and waist, and an operation scar. There was added congestion in the nasal passages.

What accusations would Betty throw at him upon her return? Too many. That's what you get when you make your mistakes out in the open. He was furious with her, anyway. Somehow she was no longer his, the stupid bitch. She belonged to somebody outside the mud-colored room. He would never know his rival, or even know if there was a rival. Maybe, when they disappeared, they went to another room like this one. And there they met each other again. No, they could not meet each other, they never disappeared together. Maybe they met antitheses of themselves. When Betty went, she rendezvoused with anti-Jack, a guy just the opposite in manner, abilities, and ideas. Gregarious, optimistic, loving, possessed of brilliant moral strength. Anti-Jack would be everything that Jack was not. With him she would get what she wanted, which was why she often returned so happy. But, then, how in hell could *he* put up with her, if he was so goddamned perfect? She'd drive him out of his head.

Betty came back short of breath, fatter. She seemed to have gained weight everywhere. The loose faded-print dress she now wore didn't help either, it seemed to touch her body only where it could not avoid it. She felt her hair, which was now dry and brittle. I must look like hell.

"You look like hell," Jack said.

"You *go* to hell," she said, and began to cry.

Jack just stared ahead. Brushing away tears with the back of her hand, she felt a leathery coarseness in her cheeks. I should kill the smug bastard, tie it up in a sloppy little knot. But what if I killed him and *still* kept coming back here?

"Do you think we can save our relationship?" she said.

"Save it for what?"

"For five and a half percent interest! You . . . you would destroy everything that's beautiful between us."

"What's so beautiful between us?"

"Between us, nothing. I only want you should pretend, to take up the time."

Jack sighed.

"Please don't do that."

Jack sighed again.

Betty sighed as long as she could, with some shrillness in her voice.

Jack sighed in sincere despair.

Betty sighed *The Carousel Waltz.* Look at him, pouting like a kid when somebody's taken away his toys. I'll take away his toys. I'll take away his balls.

"Want to make out?" she asked.

"Bug off."

"I'll bestow upon you the ultimate gift."

"You couldn't give that away if you took out a want ad under merchandise, used."

"Prude!"

She tried to control her temper. "What do I look like? In metaphor."

"Betty, I don't know. Leave me alone."

"Tell me."

"Beauty seen through a shard of Coke bottle that's been beaten by the sea and aged by the sun."

"I don't know *what* to do with that."

"Shove it in your glass eye."

"I don't have a glass eye."

"Well, find somewhere else."

Betty tried to strike an adamant pose, but she could not make her arms work right. Extra flesh slapped against extra flesh. She had trouble fitting her left hand into her right armpit. Only the fingertips of her right hand touched the flabby muscle of her left arm.

"I think we should split," she said.

"Gladly."

"Agreed then?"

"A-greed."

Each sat motionless, waiting for the other to move.

"Well?" Betty said.

"Well what?"

"In every separation somebody has to go. You!"

"Go? Where'll I go?"

"Out there." She waved a hand at the mud-colored door.

"Now wait a minute. One thing I do not do is go out there."

"Coward!"

"Intimidator!"

"Well, *I'm* not going. It's not the girl's place to challenge the unknown."

Jack stood up, began to pace.

"At your age afraid of dragons!" Betty said sardonically. "Remember when we looked out the door and saw only a hallway with dark at the end? Quite conventional-looking if you ask me, just a quaint drab corridor, nothing to be terrified of. You just walk on down it, all you'll probably encounter is a minotaur or two."

"I won't go. I can't."

"Bloodless. Spineless. Shrinking violet. Drooping lily. Chicken. Faint of heart, cold of feet."

Betty spoke tonelessly, leaving a precise two-second pause after each insult.

"Poltroon. Dastard. Jelly-testicled. Churning-stomached. Trembling-lipped. Scaredy-cat. Shadow-terrified. Pusillanimous. Sissy. Effeminate. Milksop. Lacker of the essential juices. Slacker. Dodger. Abdicator of responsibility. Limp-wristed. Eye-flincher. Pigeon-hearted. Spermless."

"Are you going to keep this up?"

"Impotent. Weak-kneed. Worry-wart."

"Stop it, please."

"Terror-struck. Blench-faced. Bulgy-eyed. Panic-stricken."

"Okay. Second chance. We'll try harder."

"Number two. Cold running blood. Goosefleshed. Tremoring cowerer."

"Betty!"

"Cold-sweated. Ball-less. Yellow-streaked a mile wide. Duty-shrinker. Quisling. Benedict—"

"All right, I'll go."

He opened the door a little way, slipped through the narrow space. The door clicked shut hollowly. She listened to his steps going down the hallway. Tentatively. He seemed to pause near the end. Betty grunted, she expected now to hear him return. When the sound of steps resumed, the footfalls came quickly, resolutely. Their sound diminished gradually until Betty realized that she had imagined the sound of the last few steps. The faint scream seemed to come also from her imagination.

Although she had been alone in the room before, this time she felt stimulated about it. There was that chance that he would not come back. She listened for his footsteps.

He won't get far. He'll be like the first one to test the water on the first good swimming day. He'll test the surface with his toes, let the good chill run up his legs, venture out to knee level maybe, then race back to the beach, heedlessly splashing water behind him. Unless he's dead or something. Eaten up by the minotaur, bad-breathed by the dragon. Strongest odds are that there's nothing out there but more of this. He's probably lost in a maze of hallways. Or maybe he's outside the cave, foraging for food. He'll come back a naked ape. A welcome change.

She stretched out on the divan and tried to go to sleep. At first she was disturbed by worries. Maybe something *had* happened to Jack. What about the scream? If that's what it was. Too far away to be sure. He probably just saw his own shadow or something.

Gradually she dozed off.

She could not keep track of the number of times she awoke groggily. At these moments she would not allow herself to come to full consciousness, at least not to a consciousness where she might have to reflect upon anything serious. Enough to notice a change of dress and return to sleep. On some awakenings she would look around the room to see if Jack had returned. When she did not see him, she shrugged and resumed the napping position.

Abruptly she was aware of herself lying awake, staring at the faded-lace ceiling. Her body felt stiff. Gripping the back of the divan with both hands, she pulled herself up, muscles straining at the effort. Sharp pains ran between her elbow and wrist.

Reluctantly, she examined herself. She looked like a mountain. Breasts like elongated watermelons, resting on the ample field of her stomach. Thighs like overfilled sacks, so thick she could not make her knees touch. Below them, parts of her body she might never see again. She wore an old lady's dress, basic brown with miles of grainy lace, fading.

Jack had not returned. Or else he'd come back while she slept, seen her grown fat and lumpy, and had left again.

She let her fingers journey over her face. Trenches and pits, loose coarse skin, eyelids like thin lampshade paper.

I can't stay in this room anymore. I should never have let him go. Retribution like that takes the juice out of victory. Well, who the hell likes victory juice anyway? I'll go out there. Anything'll be better. I'll step tippy-toe into the mouth of the nearest dragon.

She stood up. Unbearable pain rode up from her calves and thighs. She sat down again. Eyes shut, concentrating, she tried to separate herself from the fat, as if the fat were pasted to her thin body and could be ripped off at any time. She felt it as discrete and alien matter. She inhaled and *it* rose, pushed up by her breathing. She shifted position on the divan and *it* moved with her. Silly to get hysterical about it. I should relax. Contemplate my navel. If it is physiologically possible to locate my navel.

Hours later she heard a shuffling sound, somebody walking in the hall. The echo of the steps seemed awesome, threatening. She pictured, in a quick series of flash-card images, hundreds of monsters in a variety running from reconstituted human crea-

tures to the ugliest possible sentient collages. The steps stopped
in front of the door. Betty wished she could disappear at will. The
doorknob began turning.

"Who is it?" she shouted.

The doorknob's movement stopped.

"Is it you, Jack? Is that you?"

An answering mumble. He slowly opened the door, slid in
sideways, a little of him at a time. A withered old hand, sharp-
pointed and lace-colored. Glimpses of an emaciated arm beneath
a tattered shirtsleeve. Half of a dirty shirt and trousers, half of a
wrinkled bearded face. The entire head came into full view: skin
yellowed and spotted, completely bald, lines running into lines,
sparse and speckled whiskers. The creature seemed to be Jack. It
must be. But Jack as if his face had been made of candlewax which
was now half melted. He stood before her, tottering on trembling
legs. Shakily his hand rose in a hello salute. It was almost the wave
of a returning hero.

Struggling to control her nervousness, Betty spoke in a
guarded and toneless voice. "Where've you been?"

He shrugged a long, quaking shrug. "I have some memories,
but dim and growing dimmer as I think of them. Broken side-
walks, thick forests, a strange city that left me messages, rocks
falling from the sky. There *was* a dragon, I think. But I can't
concentrate, synthesize."

He could hardly see her. His vision was impaired by glaze and
other matter. She looked big now. She looked very big.

She beckoned to him and patted a cushion beside her. Without
speaking, she kept patting it. His feet sliding along the floor, he
walked toward her. It seemed a long way. She extended her hand,
took his, and guided him onto the divan. Her hand remained in
his. The skin of their hands had the texture of wood, of old
boards; if one altered the grip, the other would get splinters.

"How do you feel?" Betty asked. "You feel okay?"

"No, don't feel so good. Don't feel okay."

He looked at her with eyes so dark they reminded her of tarnished coins. She touched his grizzled beard, with the tips of her fingers wiped away some wetness by his mouth.

"You know," she said, "I have this funny feeling that any minute now somebody is going to scream 'Cut it and print it,' and the walls are going to be struck, and the makeup men are going to stride in and tear off the plastic that's our makeup and rip out the pillows from inside my costume and compliment us for a good job well done and escort us to our limousines, and you can say to me, 'Nice working with you,' and I can say to you, 'Nice working with you,' and we can bid farewell against a setting sun and drive off in highly polished Cord automobiles. Something like that could happen, couldn't it?"

"Not bloody likely."

She rested her head on his shoulder, felt herself drifting off to another nap. "My legs hurt like hell," she muttered.

PRISON OF CLAY,
PRISON OF STEEL

The tale of a little man who threw himself over a
cliff; a dynasty of sick princes; and a captive sun . . .

Henry-Luc Planchat

I was a sun, and they made me their slave.

And I am here, alone, a prisoner in this body of steel, between
these cold walls.

In this block of clay that imprisons my soul.

GOLEM

> Made of sun and clay
> Powerless, with this punched card
> That holds me like a chain
> Son of Heaven and the Machine

GOLEM

I was a sun, and they made me their slave.

They drew my soul into this block of clay and shut me up in

153

this prison of steel, of integrated circuits, and they locked away my freedom with this punched card. They, the merchants, they bought my life and the lives of those I created.

He threw himself down from the top of the cliff, the one who sold me, but that did not set me free. And they, the merchants, they keep me here, in this machine, to watch over their city.

Watchman at their gates.

GOLEM

But I must love or die.

And they have taken away my love and condemned me to life.

They have mastered me—me, a sun. And they say:

"Here are the data, Golem!"

And I record them.

And they say: "Destroy our enemies!"

And I, who was drunk with love, must kill. And I cannot rebel against these bonds which hold me, from beyond space and time, in this block of clay. Then I wait (and time is no more than a hope) for them to need me again.

While the beings that I created are dying, far from me, in the glacial cold of space that overcomes them little by little, and while my body of energy and light, their only protection, so far away, is going out.

Oh, when will I rekindle the star-fire!

GOLEM

The city is called Pharès. For thousands of years it has been the greatest port of the Northern Ocean, and its ships go in search of precious cargoes even beyond the Mountains on the Rim of the Abyss. Its caravans cross the Great Plain to bring back goods found only in the most remote countries of the Old Continent. Pharès is famed for its great wealth, but famed also for being a city it is best not to attack, and all who have tried it have failed, for the City of Merchants is protected by Emidhin, the slave-sun, the chained god, the Golem.

Hyersios, the Prince of Pharès, opened the sanctuary door by means of the retractable key embedded in his left forefinger.

Hyersios, the seventeenth of the Sick Princes, was dressed as usual in a wide toga of green silk which brushed the floor, and his face and arms were painted with the blue insignia of his rank.

Hyersios, the Jailer of God, had a somber visage, and the lines traced by illness on his forehead made his expression even darker.

Hyersios, the Master of the West Provinces, was soon to die.

And he knew it. He closed the door quietly behind him. Here he was in the presence of Emidhin.

Or rather of Emidhin's organs of communication, for the soul of the star was imprisoned in a block of clay behind twenty meters of metal. The sanctuary. A little room. Walls painted green. On the floor, white tiles. At the rear, metal. A few buttons and handles. A little loudspeaker, the voice of the sun. A little mobile camera, the eye of the sun.

Cold.
Hold me tighter, child.
The wind. Cold.
Take my coat, child, I don't need it.
The dark . . .
Don't be afraid, child, I am here, close to you. Sleep now. Tomorrow it will be light and we will go to the dune.

"Good morning, Emidhin," said Hyersios, advancing toward the wall of metal.

"Greeting, Hyersios the Prince," answered the prisoner.

Hyersios seated himself delicately on the only chair in the sanctuary. The pain in his back made him grimace slightly. The corner of his mouth rose a little, pressing his right cheek upward. The eye half-closed. A silent rictus. A contortion of pain and a resigned smile, mocking that illness that had fastened its claws in the dynasty of the Princes of Pharès. He leaned gently against the wooden back of the chair and for a moment had the illusion that it eased him. But the pain returned, stronger than before. He closed his eyes and slowly passed his hand over his forehead, rubbing the lines as if to make them disappear. The camera, motionless, gazed at him.

The Prince of Pharès opened his eyes again and breathed deeply. The green silk sleeve had slid back along his arm, revealing the blue marks that Freeyn had tattooed there when he had received his title, seven years before. The marks said things known to him alone, and sometimes he had an almost irresistible impulse to tell them to someone. To Emidhin, to a beggar in the North Quarter, to anyone. His hand fell slowly and rested on the punched cards which he held in the other hand, the left, the one that contained the key to the sanctuary. His fingers slid over the edges of the cards, then held them tightly. Hyersios leaned forward to place the little pile of cards on the cold tiles. The pain seized its opportunity. It gripped the right hand as it moved toward the floor, then climbed along the arm, turned around the shoulder and sprang onto his back, between the shoulder blades. Hyersios grimaced again, then straightened. He had thrown down the gauntlet to the illness that tormented him, and it had accepted the challenge. They understood each other very well. Each was lying in wait for the other. But the Prince of Pharès already knew the end of this silent duel. He straightened again and leaned against the back of the chair.

"I'm going to need you, Emidhin," he said at last.

The little man had said simply there it is, and had left the sanctuary. Prince Greter, President Tremis and the other high dignitaries of the city followed him for a moment with their eyes, then turned back to the wall of metal. The Prince activated the

prisoner's organs of communication. At once a murmur, almost
a moan, was heard:

"Aaaaah! Aaaaah!"

Then they told him that he was their slave.

He replied that he was a sun.

They told him that he must obey them.

He asked them to set him free so that he might continue to
protect his planets.

They repeated that he was their slave.

He told them that, without him, his planets would die.

They explained to him that if he did not obey them, they would
kill him and that in this case his planets would be lost forever.

He began to howl, and they lowered the volume of the loudspeaker.

The next day, the body of the little man was found at the base
of the cliff that overhangs the Northern Ocean.

Is that better, child?

Yes.

*Dawn has come, child. It is cold and the sun is very red, but we'll be able
to start moving.*

The dune?

Yes, child, we must reach the dune.

A man was working in his field when he saw them. They were
moving along the road, a little farther away. He was a brave man,
but he felt the sweat chill his back under the shirt. He wondered
if it was their footsteps that reverberated or the earth that
groaned at their passing.

A traveler from one of the worlds of the Great Star asked who
they were, and a scowling woman replied: "It's the Golem." He
said nothing and went on his way, but he stopped singing.

A girl named Minia went to her window and listened to the
noise in the village street. All the Enashins, at the same instant,
turned their heads in her direction, and she saw among them the

face of Yeni. Minia and Yeni were to have been married the previous autumn, according to an old custom still followed in the countries of the west. Yeni was a fisherman. One day his small boat was overtaken by a storm far out at sea. A week later, some other fishermen found his body, still alive, clinging to a piece of wreckage, but his mind was gone forever. The Enashins passed and the sound of their footsteps faded behind them. Minia was still crying when darkness fell.

Far away, elsewhere, in a country called Perihel, an old man sits at a table, close to the fire, in the Starhauler Tavern.

"I've seen many things, oh, I've seen many things!" says he to the yellow-haired stranger across the table. "I've seen the blue lakes of Samoth, I've crossed the Haeschenischen Channel, where there's traps that can pull you into another universe, a dream, or maybe another level, who knows. I've shared a meal with the pilgrims of the Green Galaxy and I've even fought the Enashins of Emidhin, the imprisoned god, the Golem. Ah! I was young then, and a little crazy. You have to be a little crazy to fight the Enashins. That was on my home world, Shangui-H'e, a good world, yes, a good world. I was working with my brother Elllis at the time. We had a few fields of myi and they enabled us to live in comfort. Myi is a plant that only grows on Shangui-H'e, at least as far as I know. It's very nourishing and much wanted by us humans, the descendants of the Emigrants, but also it's very hard to grow. At harvest time you've got to be very clever. The only death the myi will accept is suicide. If it realizes you're about to kill it, it commits suicide by releasing a virulent poison into its sap, and the whole crop may be lost. To keep it from doing that, you hypnotize it by making it listen to the song of a crazy bird called the ayetl, but that bird doesn't live in Essenin, the province where I was born, or in any other western province, either. So to reap the myi we needed the help of a Diatshin who had to imitate the song of the ayetl bird for hours and hours, until the myi was completely hypnotized and would let itself be reaped. But it's a demanding song; one false note and you're out of luck. Not only that, but after a while the song also hypnotizes people and can drive the singer crazy. We put wax plugs in our ears, but a Diatshin's endurance has its limits, and of course you can only harvest a crop once.

"Yes, yes, the Enashins, I'm coming to them. Anyhow, my brother and I had a few fields of myi and we knew how to work them. Myi is a valuable commodity and we were doing quite well. Very well, in fact; but Essenin is a province that depends more or less on the city of Pharès, anyhow I won't go into all the details, but we had to pay tribute to them every year. This tribute had been getting steadily bigger for some time because of the Merchants' Guild of Pharès—they're as powerful as the Prince of the city, or more so, and they always wanted more ships, wagons, spaceships. They were burning with thirst for power and wealth and they were getting harder and harder to satisfy. One year, Essenin didn't pay all its tribute and the Merchants threatened to withhold their goods from us. Then, when we still couldn't pay, they forbade the Diatshins to work for us. That was hard. Poverty, famine. Finally, we peaceful farmers took up arms, we banded together into a little army, oh, nothing much, two or three thousand young men, inexperienced and a little crazy, and started to march toward the province of Pharès, more than five hundred kilometers north of Essenin, to bring back the food we needed. Oh, of course, we had heard of the Enashins, but to us they were more like a legend, and we even joked about them. Yes, well, they weren't a legend. We met them on a hill, near a little town in the south of the province of Pharès. Yes, I'll never forget that scene. We were climbing the hill and we saw them appear on top. We all stopped and they kept on coming toward us. At first, we couldn't make out their faces, but I remember that the wind moved their hair in a strange way. Finally they stopped not more than fifty paces off and we could count them. Two hundred Enashins. Two hundred creatures, most of them human, but there were also some foreigners from nonhuman planets, as well as some metal humanoids. (And two or three arkel birds that circled above us must have been Enashins too.) Some were in rags, others in the uniform of the guardsmen of Pharès, some were dressed like fishermen, others like peasants, still others like lenyates. And I noticed that the humans' eyes were like those of madmen, gray and staring, not really seeing us. And each one carried a double-bitted ax in the same manner over his shoulder. Then they began to talk, and I still remember those first words. Imagine it, two hundred creatures speaking the same words all together, at the same instant, and with the same voice. They said: 'I am Emidhin, the keeper of the gates of Pharès. Go home, brothers. I beg you.' Then some of us tried to argue, but the Enashins only repeated in their one voice: 'Go home, brothers. I wish you no harm, but I must obey the orders of the Prince of Pharès. I beg you, go home.'

"At that point, a few of us, no doubt a little crazier than the rest, moved toward the Enashins saying that we couldn't retreat any more, and the rest followed. Then, of course, the fighting began. Oh, it didn't last long. I can still see the blood that spurted. The Enashins seemed to be able to look in every direction at once, they were like the tentacles of a gigantic octopus, and they were amazingly strong. They raised their axes in both hands like woodcutters and brought them slashing down through our ranks. And they kept shouting, 'Forgive me, brothers! Forgive me! Forgive me!' After that, I don't remember much. I'd had my right hand lopped off by an Enashin and I was lying on the ground thinking, 'I must be dreaming, I must really be dreaming, this isn't possible.' My brother found me after the fight and brought me home. Not long afterward we left Shangui-H'e aboard a spaceship bound for the Blue–Blue–Yellow Galaxy. I had another hand made for me, and it works very well, but I'd rather have the first one. It was a good hand, yes, a good hand. Oh, I've seen many things, I've seen many things! I've been to a place called Roquebrune . . ."

Exhaustion.

Yes, child, we'll stop and sleep here. You see, the dune isn't far away now. Tomorrow.

Yes, tomorrow we'll reach the dune, child. Tomorrow.

The Prince Hyersios died.

The Prince Herdunt succeeded him, and the Prince Blillil succeeded the Prince Herdunt. And the dynasty endured a long time.

And the centuries passed, and still more centuries.

Pharès was still the principal port of the Northern Ocean, but that no longer mattered very much. On Shangui-H'e, the human race was coming to the end of its term. The planet had lost most of its inhabitants at the time of the New Emigration and man was disappearing little by little, giving place to others. So it goes, and so it should go.

The last Prince of Pharès was called Moyann. He was master of nothing but a few old farmers and an immense city falling into ruin, almost deserted. But that did not matter very much.

When the Prince Moyann felt his approaching death, the same that had struck down his ancestors and that was about to strike now for the last time, he went to the sanctuary. There he was in the presence of Emidhin.

"Greeting, Emidhin." The Prince Moyann advanced slowly toward the wall. His left leg dragged behind him, and that was almost a blessing, for the paralysis was winning out over his pain.

"Greeting, Moyann the Prince." The little camera stared at the Master of Pharès.

Moyann, with that little grimace which the Princes of Pharès had made for so many generations, sat down on the only chair in the sanctuary. The pain subsided a little.

"My race has done you much harm, Emidhin." He shook his head slowly and closed his tired eyes a moment.

"You are not responsible."

The Prince noticed that the paint on the wall was flaking more and more, leaving tiny green spots on the dusty tiles.

"Yes, in a way, I am responsible." Moyann was almost whispering. It was becoming difficult to speak.

"What do you want from me, Moyann the Prince?"

The Master of Pharès took a breath. The air flowed down his windpipe, inflated his lungs, and minuscule things struggled and yelled to keep it from purifying his blood. But it succeeded all the same, once more, before it withdrew. Then the minuscule things subsided. In the time of a breath.

"I'm going to give you back your freedom, Emidhin."

It's strange, thought the Prince suddenly, how that spider spins its web. He gazed at the dark little creature on the wall near him. He couldn't see the spider very well, but its movements seemed unnatural. It climbed the wall slowly, no more now than a moving spot on the green background, and presently the sick eyes of the Prince lost it. Perhaps it was only an illusion, he thought. But suddenly the creature reappeared before him, motionless a few centimeters from his face, hanging from the ceiling by a slender thread that glimmered blue. Is it you, Sickness? thought the Prince. Is it you, come to announce your victory? Or to watch me while I enter the edge of darkness? Or are you the image of Death that watches me sinking slowly into the marshes from which no one can escape? The mud is up to my neck already and it's harder and harder to breathe. The gray sky above me. And all this silence. I'm sinking into the mud and into silence. I don't cry out and I don't struggle to escape from the darkness crouching below me. Why break this silence which gives me its last salute? For many years the Princes of Pharès have committed an offense which nature does not pardon. The mud pulls me slowly, sucks me down, swallows me. What is there left for me to do? What should the last Prince of Pharès do, before disappearing once for all into the marsh of oblivion? I have no pardon to beg. I've restored to Emidhin all that I can restore and the Sickness has punished me for the crime we committed. I've paid. There's nothing left for me but to let myself be swallowed up in that darkness, looking at the landscape while I still can. The landscape of Shangui-H'e, which gives this silent salute to the last Master of the Western Provinces, the vanquished. The gray sky. There's no wind today, and the leaves of the tomb-trees are motionless and silent. The blue-gray marsh has almost no ripples in it, only those caused by my slight movements. All this is beautiful, for it's the very image of my planet, calm, harsh and marvelous. And there's that little black spider sitting on a reed and watching the bluish mud rise to my mouth.

"But not my body of light?"

The spider is gone. This room is very cold, thought Moyann. The light? That minuscule glimmer lost somewhere in the depths of space?

"No. I don't know how to send you back."

I don't know how and none of the others knew either. The only one who might have known was Tahn, the little man, the one who sold you to us. No, the one we *forced* to lure you here. But who knows his secret? What evil we have done!

"In fact, I've suspected that for a long time. What do you intend to do?"

He is calm like our planet. He is of the race of stars.

"I'm going to set your Enashins free. Perhaps with their help you will find a way to regain your body. I hope so."

"Thank you."

"No, don't thank me. I wish I could have helped you more."

Outside, the morning breeze from the sea rises over Pharès. It helps the ruins crumble a bit more.

"You have already done much for me."

So little. I'm dying and you are being reborn.

"Do you think your planets are still alive?"

"I think so. They are good planets."

Moyann painfully got up out of the chair and moved slowly toward the metal wall. The little camera turned in silence. The Prince pushed the wooden button and with a faint click a punched metal card thrust itself half out of a console. The Prince took it. Now, he thought, nothing ties you to me henceforward. You are still a prisoner, but I am not your jailer. The oppression of the Princes of Pharès is done with forever. He would drop this plaque into acid and no one would ever be able again to enslave a sun, at least with the little man's machine.

"Now I'm going to leave you."

He turned and went out, dragging his dead leg.

"Farewell, Moyann the Prince."

The last Master of Pharès stopped and glanced at the metal wall. Cold prison.

"Good luck, Emidhin the Sun," he said, then left without closing the sanctuary door.

Look, child, look, the dune!
I see.
Well, come on, child, come on. We're here!

The spine of the universe curved a little more.

Wide-eyed, turning for centuries around the exploded carcass of an old Haggirian ship. His guts like a cortège.

Or else:

Swollen cadaver coming apart in tatters, a choice meal. At the bottom of a blue lake on Samoth.

Or else:

Eyes hollowed by age, white hair like a waterfall. Motionless. Leaning against the trunk of a lyre-tree, under the clear sky of the planet Douce. Insects in his mouth.

Dead.

Most of the Enashins.

Come, child, I beg you, come!
Cold.
We're almost there! The dune is there! Come on, child, try to get up. I can't carry you. I beg you, child!
Cold . . .

The metal creature advanced down the main street of Pharès and the sand crunched underfoot. The sea wind blew softly and murmured the song of time among the ruins. The metal creature came to the deserted great square and stopped to examine the palace of the Princes of Pharès, its green façade almost intact, windows useless.

The sun, still high over Pharès, gave the building a little of its old splendor. That splendor of the great ones, built on the oppression of peoples.

The metal creature turned its head when it heard the crunching sound.

Out of the shadow of a collapsed building a man was coming toward him. Wearing a long blue coat. Sandals. And on his right cheek the mark of the Diatshins. His eyes put out. To sing better. As the barbarians did long ago to birds, to make them warble.

The man went toward the metal creature with slow and tired steps. Then he stopped in front of it and put out his hand to touch the metal breast.

"You are Emidhin the Robot," he said. "You have journeyed very far and very long. You have traveled in other universes and you were once a sun."

"Can you tell me how you know that?"

"If you like, I can. I haven't much longer to live, but you will lend me your eyes and I will teach you marvelous songs."

The metal creature entered the palace and followed the long corridors. The ancient seat of the Princes of Pharès. Cracks along the walls. Rotted tapestries. Decayed paneling. Then a bare corridor. A half-open door. A little room. Walls that had once been painted green. On the floor, tiles that had once been white. At the back, metal. A spiderweb in a corner of the ceiling. A little camera. A tired voice that came from the little loud speaker.

"Here you are at last."

(Face to face with myself.)

"Here I am."

(You are me and you are different. I could not follow you out of this universe and I gave you your freedom. And since then you are no longer entirely myself.)

"You have found it."

(I had no one but this spider for company after all the others died. Then it died too. Then there was no one left.)

"I found it."

(I'm going back to my planets. There will be much heat to give.)

(Much love.)

(Yes. Much love.)

The robot went up to the metal wall and pressed down a steel lever. Then another. Then a third.

"There. I'm setting you free."

(I press this now and you'll go back to your body of light.)

(Wait.)

"Are you coming back with me?"

(You will not come back.)

"No. Farewell, sun." The Enashin pressed down the fourth metal lever.

On a frozen planet. Two corpses at the foot of a dune. Dead without having seen the ocean.

Emidhin the Robot left the palace and rejoined the blind man who was waiting in the square.

The man stood up and the two of them went together under the summer sun, making their way through the ruins of Pharès, the blind man's hand on the shoulder of the android.

And at the back of the sanctuary, on the metal wall, was graven the inscription the robot had put there before it left the palace:

I was a sun, and they made me their slave.

GOLEM

And time, and the wind, and the rain were very long in wearing it away.

—Translated from the French by Damon Knight

HEARTLAND

There are few things in marriage that mutual
toleration and good humor will not cure. One of
them, however, is being a horse.

Gustav Hasford

Wherever man has left his footprint in the long ascent from barbarism
to civilization, we will find the footprint of the horse beside it.

—John Trotwood Moore, in
The Encyclopaedia Britannica

Marshall Frankfort comes home from work and does not notice
that for some unknown reason his wife has become a large grey
horse.

In the living room, Cecilia relaxes on a fat pink sofa with a *True
Confessions* magazine on her chest.

"Hello, dear." Her voice is dry. She eats candy orange slices.
Marshall bombardiers his black leatherette briefcase into the

formica German wasteland of his new dining table and opens his
fat white Frigidaire. "Hello, dear."

His wife asks: "Have a good day, dear?"

"And how was 'I Dream of Jeannie' today, dear?"

"That's awful, dear. You really should tell them at the office
that they're working you too hard."

Pouring Bavarian beer, Marshall pays scant attention to a thick
grey horsehair frozen to the lip of the ceramic stein he has ex-
tracted from the freezer compartment of his Frigidaire. Boldly,
his right forefinger flicks the ugly horsehair off the stein and it
falls forever out of his life.

The sports page. Too portly to participate in athletic contests
in person, Marshall secretly admires Joe Willie Namath and will
create a baby son of such sturdy timber when Cecilia grows weary
of the easy life and flushes her pills.

The late show.

And Christmas.

"Marshall? *Mar*shall! Do I look tired? Run down? Does my skin
look crooked?"

Marshall (talking to Johnny Carson, exploring for Christmas
presents in *TV Guide*): "You look real good, dear." An aside:
"Would I pull your leg?"

She touches her face. "Still . . ."

"So for sure I couldn't fix it myself, so . . ."

"—that damn Andrews kid, the little bum. Pirates my new
accounts with my ink wet on the contracts. Why, I'll bet—"

"—plumber took off that shiny thingy and promised it won't
cost more than—"

"—and the boss walks in, right? Just as I'm trying to—"

"—but sometimes I don't feel well, Marshall. I get these
pains . . ."

"—told him just what he could do with—"

"Marshall, I feel . . . heavy . . . I . . ."
"—but no—no way. Said there was just no way I was—"
"Marshall!"
"What? What did you say?"
"Marshall . . ."
"What? What's *wrong* with you?"
"I'm scared."
Marshall walks into the living room, locks the door.

Cecilia flumps around on all fours in ways much flumpier than
the casual lifestyle cultivated by her past.

Marshall notices subtle signals—sobs, complaints about sore
legs, snorts, whinnies. Irrefutable evidence manifests itself: wet
hoofprints all over the bathroom floor, breakfasts of dry oats and
grass in a bowl with a heavy side order of horseradishes, and a
damp and gooey emptiness in the "Souvenir of Grand Canyon"
sugar bowl.

"We never fight," says Cecilia as though she were a key witness
at a trial.

Breaking coffee at the office water cooler, Marshall (the archa-
eologist) excavates a stack of little emotional newspaper clip-
pings about a Mexican standoff he had with Cecilia on their first
date way back when. She wanted to see *Don Rickles Bites a Cow* in
3–D Technicolor, but Marshall had tickets to see Pat Boone's
white shoes in *Bernadine.* Marshall devised a compromise: they
saw a double feature—*Self Abuse* and *Oral Communications.* Prehis-
toric dirty pictures were featured in a short cartoon, *The Paintings
of Reindeer and Bison on the Cave Walls in Southern France.* Marshall
was happy to sacrifice Pat Boone for the woman he loved. In
those shiny days he'd let her live it up all the time. Now, picking
the crunchy goodness of historical popcorn from his teeth,
Marshall decides to remind Cecilia of the old days to cheer
her up.

Home life gives birth to a silent event: Marshall finds Cecilia sitting alone in the kitchen in the dark. On a cracked saucer before her lies an incredibly old souvenir slice from their wedding cake—half eaten. In ten years of waiting, the cake—very much at home with the ice cubes in the freezer—has hardened into a yellowish sugar-coated fossil, as dead now as the curling full-color photographs of happy Cecilia and happy Marshall cutting the long-digested living pastry with a silver knife.

Marshall remains humble about his ability to tolerate Cecilia's crazy moods. The household disarmament treaty remains as solid as the Siegfried Line. No cruel tanks allowed in the living room, no hand grenades in the goldfish bowl, no Nambu machineguns or pastel-colored Fokker biplanes—and none of the thermonuclear devices which utilize the erotic potential of atomic fission.

Not even while Cecilia screams *"Look at me! Look at me!"* does Marshall break his cool. Rather, his response is calculated to suggest a more agreeable topic: "And so Jeannie turned Major Healy into a big chicken. What happened then, dear?"

Cecilia gallops into the living room, makes noise, mumbles clumsily, "I'm a horse, Marshall. I'm a horse. I'm a real horse. Really. I can see myself in the bathroom mirror."

"Oh, stop horsing around," says Marshall, chuckling behind his *Sports Illustrated*. "Use your horse sense, dear."

"I'm a horse, Marshall."

"Then you must eat a big bowl of fresh grass, dear. A person needs horse food to get enough horse vitamins, right? And frankly, dear, you haven't looked well lately."

"Marshall?"

"Yes?"

"I hurt. When I try to walk it feels like my guts are floating around inside my body. Sometimes I can't breathe."

"Horsefeathers. You'll be fine. Probably just a bug of some kind—the flu." He laughs. "Why, there's still a *lot* of horsepower left in you!"

In a drugstore, Marshall skims through a paperback copy of *Handy Horse Lore.* He learns that a horse will not step on a man. He reads that if a horse stays off its feet for a few hours, it dies. He finds these facts interesting. He decides to tell Cecilia that she'd better keep moving.

Roller Derby.

Cecilia does not produce TV dinners. Hours pass. Marshall waits patiently for the two small aluminum trays of cryogenically petrified food to be brought back to life with heat.

He makes a joke about putting Cecilia out to pasture for this, but he is alone and does not laugh.

The bedroom smells sick and hot with horsehairs and defecation, and Marshall's queen-size bed is sprinkled with decaying hay. A real elderly workhorse, sway-backed, shedding, bone-angled and dead, crumples in all kinds of directions, crushes fat pink pillows—half a ton of gristle and cold meat and big piano-key teeth and worn steel horseshoes staring out obsidian-hard over the hand-sewn watercolors of a butterfly quilt.

Calmly, Marshall calculates the extent of Cecilia's horseplay. This, he quips, is the last straw. It is bad enough that Cecilia refuses to talk to him. It's bad enough that she trots all over the house drowning in maudlin squalor, and won't cook. His heart is big for her. But this? This sloppy housekeeping?

"I can take a joke," Marshall announces in a loud voice, "but I'll be god*damned* if I'm going to sleep with a dead horse!"

Period.

Dirty sheets.

Marshall goes to see if maybe Cecilia is hiding somewhere in the living room.

On TV, Bob Hope and Bing Crosby sit in a big cooking pot and talk about love. They are surrounded by cannibals of the wildest design.

Marshall thinks: Have I seen this?

A Little Lexicon for Time-Travelers

afterhead	got	pfirstic	vanrangement
Ante Toasties	heanow	postposterous	venial sex
arewolf	Hucome Gernsforth	Pushman car	usouthodox
birth wish	isherwoman	rearquish	Wasaac Asimov
come-come girl	Katabaptist	retrophylactic	Waswas
earlyx	Math E'Nar	unisin	Zweifront

SANDIAL

Ach! Those German philosophers, how literally
they take everything.

Moshe Feder

Examine sand. It's not really white, but a halftone blend of many
shades. Some grains are white or beige, some clear quartz crystal,
and there are small black ones like the specks of bean in vanilla
ice cream. The sand at the beach is a loose conglomerate of
trillions of such particles. There they are piled in drifts and dunes
shaped by the imprint of seagull feet and other natural forces.

Sand is the primary ingredient of glass. In that capacity it has
some symbolic meaning, no doubt. Glass is a transparent non-
crystalline amorphous supercooled liquid. It's not a true solid at

all. Does that suggest anything? It was just such speculation that led Frierhoff to his theory of the universal metaphor. Ach! Those German philosophers, how literally they take everything.

Sand has other interesting properties. When mixed with a suitable amount of water it is the perfect medium for ephemeral sculpture. Sand castles are the most commonly seen examples. I wonder if Frierhoff ever built a sand castle? It might have done him good.

The day was ending with a warm red sunset. Henderson opened his eyes and saw that the beach was empty. Noting the imminence of evening, he rose from his place in the shadow of a dune. The fabric of his shirt and the shape of his back had left a concave imprint. He walked to just short of the line of tangled seaweed and shell fragments. Staring up the beach in each direction he saw that it was indeed empty. But there was a mound that stood out from the smoothness at the water's edge. He transferred the pair of shoes he was carrying from his right hand to his left and walked over to look at the mound. It was a sand castle.

The sand castle was guarded by a steep-sided moat that was a foot deep and was filled with water from a channel that ran to the tideline. Inside the moat there was a flat unblemished area three feet wide. The wall around the castle was as smooth and featureless as that surrounding plain; there was no gate, barbican, portcullis, or drawbridge. The wall was a foot high, square with rounded corners, had a flat top, sloped inward, and was about five inches thick at the bottom. The area enclosed by the wall was six feet long and five feet wide. This, the courtyard, was crosshatched with lines that simulated flagstone pavement. The keep with its attendant fortifications was square—four feet on each side. It was built in no easily identifiable style, but its massive solidity suggested Romanesque. The castle appeared to have three main stories and it was topped by a watchtower that reached a height of over four feet. The edges of the roof and the top of the watchtower were perfectly crenelated. The few windows were little more than narrow slits. On the ground level the outlines of doors were traced on the two sides that faced the larger sections of the courtyard. One was slightly ajar, and a hollowness could be seen inside it.

Stepping closer, Henderson put his naked foot in the area between the moat and the walls, violating its perfect smoothness. He carefully lifted his other foot and brought it down in the courtyard, erasing some of the delicate tracery on its floor. He bent down to examine the keep more closely, and grunted when he heard faint music within.

Henderson thrust his hand through the roof of the castle and rooted around for the radio he knew he would find inside. His fingers felt nothing but damp coolness. Curious and annoyed, he pounded the roof in, and in its collapse it took part of the supporting walls with it.

The sun was already behind the dunes, and the beach was grey, unlit by the yet unrisen moon. It was too dark to search any longer in the wet sand, and Henderson gave up. Stepping over the wall and the moat, he walked away. Discrete grains of sand detached themselves and fell away from the keep's perfect crenelations. The crumbling ruin dissolved in the moonlight.

Do you see what I mean about sand? This Henderson had obviously never read any metaphysics. Sand is certainly an interesting substance. Of course there are others: fire, air, water. But they are amorphous, they lack granularity. Not like sand. Only to Henderson are they the same.

Counting each step, Henderson proceeded along the beach. To his right, the barren ocean; to his left, just as barren desert. He walked rhythmically, deliberately.

He stayed on the beach as much as possible. The surf imparted a relative firmness to the sand that made walking easier. But periodically the splashing metronome would become too much to bear. His body's natural beat would lock into that of the sea.

His heart, his breath, his blinking, his steps, resonated with the waves. Then he would forsake the beach for the desert and walk among the dunes.

Only in the darkness could he travel any distance; in the searing daylight he slept. He was not yet weak and could still appreciate the chill night winds as refreshing. But he was fasting, and so he allowed himself regular rest stops. 9,994; 9,995; 9,996; 9,997; 9,998; 9,999; 10,000. Ten thousand steps since his start that evening from the sand castle. He stopped whenever he was precisely ten thousand steps away from his last stop. This way, at the rate of ninety thousand steps a night, he hoped to walk to civilization, whatever low form that might take on this thin margin between sea and desert.

He dropped his shoes and opened his volume of Frierhoff to page 335. *"Kapitel IX—Die Typen der Weltanschauung und ihre Ausbildung in den metaphysischen Systemen."* It was too bad his college German was so poor. Although he understood some chapter headings and many individual words, he was rarely able to make sense of a complete sentence. But reading did serve as a convenient timer. He would rest for as long as it took him to subvocalize his way through five pages, then he would get up and go on. So he opened his book and read by the lunar light. Fortunately the night skies were always clear, and the sandy white environment provided a uniform ambient illumination. His readings in *Die allumfassend Metapher* also served as a diary of his trek, an odometer that clicked over five pages for every ten thousand steps, before having to start again from page one.

On reaching page 340 Henderson snapped the book shut, got up, and started to walk. One, two, three, four, five, six, seven . . .

Sand. A geologist defines it as particles of rock between .05 and 2 millimeters in diameter. The shape of sand grains, transported by water and wind, is a clue to their history. When sand is used in an hourglass, to measure time, it sifts through cycles of move-

ment as top becomes bottom and bottom top. All the sand grains
in the universe go through great Hindu cycles, eons long, keeping always the karma of previous ages, holding it in their shape.
An angular grain of sand is young, the ancient ones are smooth
and polished. All are graded by the rivers and the breezes, separated into uniformity. If you could count all the grains you could
count the years of the cosmos, the days of creation.

Henderson thought of all his previous days of walking. He
would long ago have lost track of them if it had not been for his
book. But knowing that he walked ninety thousand steps each
night, he was always able to calculate how many days he had been
walking. He did not have to depend on his memory. Someday
Die allumfassend Metapher would sit in an honored place on the
walnut shelves of his library.

He jarred to a stop, realizing he'd lost track of his counting. His
thoughts had been wandering. He'd lost count. Grunting with
annoyance, he stood for a moment tapping his foot in a deliber-
ate rhythm. Then, sighing, he sat down and turned to page 340
of Friedriche Frierhoff's masterwork of philosophy.

When you walk barefoot in sand for even a short distance your
feet begin to ache. This is because the natural shape of the sand
fits into the curve of the arch so that the whole sole of your foot
is in contact with the ground. This is a condition your feet are
unused to. Also, notice how your toes throw out little roostertails
of sand that fall behind your heels. The motion imparted to those
grains is waste energy. Think of how many pounds of sand you
lift with your feet on even a ten-mile walk.

Walking again, hungry now, Henderson saw something scut-
tling along the top of the next sand ridge. A sand lizard! Maybe
he could catch it. He slid down the pile he stood on and with long
strides tried to climb the steep ridge. The sand underfoot cascaded away in sheets. He struggled to hurry more efficiently. He
reached the top of the ridge. There was nothing in sight.

Particles of quartz or feldspar that are larger than sand are called gravel. Particles smaller than sand are dust or the tinier constituents of clay. The parameters of sand differ from country to country.

Windblown sand is all-pervading. It acts as an abrasive and will erode rock somewhat faster than water could. If all the sand in the world were diamond dust, life on Earth would be impossible.

Henderson read the last lines of page 370, the last words of the night. His moonlight stroll had brought him ninety thousand steps closer to where he was going.

He looked for a well-situated dune, one that would provide shade and shelter from the flying dust that intermittently blew, as if, like rosin, to polish him.

He would sleep seven hours and then walk around the dune, or find another, or cool off as best he could in the simmering water. Then, awake, he would lie still and dream of philosophy and sand castles, until night came again.

Don't you wonder where Henderson is wandering? No doubt most of you do. But don't, it's not important. Sand is more important than Henderson. You don't think so? Well, it's very simple. Sand, after all, is real, and Henderson is nothing more than a figment of his own imagination.

Friedriche Frierhoff opened his eyes and saw that the beach was empty. He realized that he had succumbed to sleep, though he had tried so hard to stay awake. His readings in the book of the American master, Henderson, had convinced him that he would never truly comprehend his situation until he saw the desert beach in the daytime. Only with the aid of the sun's direct rays could he hope to jar his world view back into focus. But today's attempt, his second, had failed like the first. He simply found it impossible to keep from sleeping after a whole night of walking. Perhaps he should stay where he was, attempt to sleep in the cold, without a blanket. No, that probably wouldn't help, and it wouldn't bring him any closer to where he was going. He would get up and continue on his way. Perhaps further reading in Henderson's *Sandial* would suggest some alternate method of analyzing and resolving his dilemma.

That Henderson! What a frivolous title he had chosen for his masterwork of ontology. Perhaps the man fancied himself a poet as well as a philosopher. We all have our idiosyncrasies. The gemlike perfection of his thought was undeniable.

Friedriche got up and began his nightly wandering. It was too bad his memories of his *Gymnasium* course in astronomy were so faint. He vaguely feared that the star he chose as the polestar was different each night.

Friedriche walks. He has no illusions about his abilities or his lack of plans. He can only hope that someone will find him. He walks because he finds his predicament boring. He is used to pacing as he thinks, and anyway it keeps him warm. Over the course of a few hours he digests what he has read. Then he sits down to rest and he reads a few more lines of Henderson's book. Sitting with the book in his lap, he realizes that he has no idea how long he's been lost. Then he remembers that it doesn't matter. He reads on slowly, pondering each word.

A concern for time is a characteristic most typical of human-ness. Perhaps that is how we shall judge the alien species we will someday meet. Do they have clocks? If they do, if they are as obsessed with time as we are, we shall nobly grant them the patent of humanity.

The exiles and refugees of our civilization must often surprise themselves with their adherence to the patterns that are almost a part of their genetic legacy. Even when they no longer wait, they wait. They note the time, feel the need of a clock. It is hard to escape one's own madness.

A man lost where he knows not the local rites of Cronos has a special dilemma. He can estimate the advent of noon and mark the limits of night and day as they are passed. But at any single moment he is at a loss. His lame guesses are only less futile than the knowledge that his wristwatch, if it has stopped, is right twice a day. In desperation he may seek to resort to the venerable expedient of the sundial, only to realize that he is not sure how to read one, and to remember their inaccuracy. If he is floating on the sea he lacks a screen for a shadow's projection. If he is in the desert, he lacks even the stick to cast it. When he realizes this he will grumble and rack his brains, until finally he drops his head in defeat, and looks, vanquished, at the ground, only to see his own shadow.

Exhausted, Friedriche shivers. The fat tome under his arm has begun to be a fatiguing burden. He holds it in his left hand for a while, and then in his right. He holds it with his short fingers, spine up, then down. He holds it with his elbow against his ribs. He holds it in his armpit, and against his chest. He shuttles it from place to place on his anatomy. He tries balancing it on his head; he laughs. The transfers come more and more rapidly; each resting place is used up after a few steps.

The book falls from his limp hand, he drops after it, and lies, legs out, a T square. He leans back and his scalp feels the grating of the sand. He aches with concentration after trying to unravel the convolutions of Henderson's thought in a long, long sentence. It refuses to fall into place with satisfying clinks like a chain when it is laid down link by link on a hard surface. He decides to read the passage in question over again. Doing so, he finds the problem, a key preposition he had missed. He smiles.

Language is not a natural element. But like sand it has granularity. It is not amorphous, but composed of discrete particles. Units of energy modulated by meaning, sometimes encoded in print. As with sand, the contemplation of the particle does not lead to comprehension of the whole. The contemplation of the whole may leave, still, the particle in doubt. The one can be many, and the many composed of indistinguishable ones. This is the paradox that Henderson treats of in his writings.

Friedriche lacks for nothing. He shapes himself to the circumstance. He sleeps in the oven and lets the sun fire him with a glaze. His surroundings lack identity and substance. Homeostasis is maintained within him; locked in his mind are its reference standards, templates for the truth.

The ancient Egyptians discovered glass in a primitive process that gave a shiny glaze to their pottery. It sometimes left a noticeable layer of glass on the surface of the utensil. They soon realized that if they made the glass thick enough it could stand alone, without the pottery.

Sand alone is very hard to melt; very high temperatures are necessary. Adding potash facilitates the process; lime is added as well. The lime, for the glass as for us, gives sturdiness. Without it glass would crumble, as without our bones we would collapse inward upon ourselves like the morbid white stars, to a cold, compact existence and a colder end. Many times have men likened themselves to pottery. What then is the glaze—the veneer of civilization, or an externalization of the spirit?

Friedriche retires, to anneal and fix in the cool gray heat of a sand dune's shadow. Henderson has molded him, shaped the contours; the desert and the beach, the silent walk, run over and away from him like water, and leave no sign. Gradually he relaxes and slumbers.

Frierhoff is a master of metaphor. He rarely reads a page number, but gauges the progress of his studies by the thickness of the remaining pages between thumb and forefinger. So should lives be measured.

Awake and walking again, Henderson began to have hallucinations. The sand turned to ashes. Obviously, he had been dwelling too long on the symbolism to be divined in his situation, too long on universal metaphors and world views. Strange that he should have hallucinations now; the juice and flesh of raw lizard fill his belly, and his morale is high. There are irritating grains of sand caught in his mouth, and between his teeth. They grate there. He spits some out, but there are always a few left. He enumerates them with his tongue. His morale is high. Civilization is surely just over the next ridge.

Breaking his rule, Henderson counts aloud, calling out the numbers to the cupped ears of the sand. Not even an echo answers. Finally he hears his own voice, and telling himself that he has a sore throat, he counts softly, and then silently, but he grins. What matter if silica chooses to become a crumbly combustion product? All that can be counted is identical. Distinctions cancel out. Henderson traverses the lunar plain.

We mistakenly isolate Earth from the milieu of the galaxy because of the trivial fact of our existence on it. Some writers dream wild dreams of exotic worlds circling alien stars and perfunctorily dismiss the wonders of their home world. Familiarity has bred ennui. Perhaps we should leave the old place and hit the high spots in the next star cluster. Give the Magna Mater a chance to rest from the hectic task of raising her mad children. Let all the old echoes die, the associations fade away, until the silence of a world refreshed is untainted by a human noise.

The ash has turned to sand again. Henderson wryly considers the transmutation. It isn't hard to believe himself an alchemist. Certainly the subtle book he carries is appropriately obscure and profound. His readings continued and he made regular progress. One night, after he'd caught a sand lizard, he added five pages to his regular program. He walked one hundred thousand steps. He was tempted to make the effort every night. He hurried to reach the end of Frierhoff's book. The words slip by like the sand underfoot.

Earth and sky are one. There are rains that provide a tenuous communication. They drop stones and fish, frogs, angel hair, ice, and blood, signaling the dirt in some mystic code. In a wide swath from China to Australia there are one hundred million tons of tektites: aerodynamically shaped pieces of moon glass, the chips chiseled from the crater Tycho. And every day ten tons of meteorites and one thousand tons of stellar dust add their mass to the Earth.

In darkness relieved only by starlight, it seems to Henderson that he stands at the edge of the world. Behind him there is nothing, and before him, far at the opposite horizon, the sky closes around the sea. *Die allumfassend Metapher* is tied in his belt and hangs over his left shoulder. He stands slackly, in the manner of a schoolboy, and fingers a seashell. He throws it in the water. He knows it will come back again. In his mind he counts the waves that will pile themselves on the beach before it returns. Henderson puts his right hand in his pocket and walks on.

For men, time is rhythm. We divide time into discrete units, then count them as they pass. The ticks of moving gears and balance wheel, with the hands of a clock. The vibration of a quartz crystal or the resonance of an atom, with an array of alphanumeric tubes. Or the grains of sand that are the hallowed model for it all. We count them, not one by one, but as a whole. Thus is half a paradox resolved. Though the contemplation of the particle reveals nothing of the whole, the contemplation of the whole hints something of the indistinguishable ones.

Friedriche is sitting in the sand. He has finished *Sandial* and it has left a warm glow behind it. Barely breathing, he is afraid to hasten the inevitable end of the spell. He looks at the book fondly, and considers rereading it. Looking up from page one, he sees a figure on the horizon.

Henderson sits; page 605 is the top of the highest ridge for a mile in any direction. The ocean can be faintly heard. He wonders that the sound fades at all in the silence. The sun sets at his back. He closes the book on his index finger and scans for sand lizards. Looking behind him, he notes his own footprints, undisturbed since the previous night. Squinting, he sees a dark figure on the dunes yet ahead of him.

An hourglass has the seductive shape of a houri; the great erotic hips, the parabolic breasts, the slim waist. Sand and its transparent son join in the hollow algebraic shape. The discontinuous crystalline grains and the smooth, unit, amorph. They join, and together take the measure of infinity.

They get up.

The Memory Machine

Termites will destroy the foundation of the Taj
Mahal and it was the rats that killed off the
dinosaurs by eating their feet.

—W. C. Fields

Our Own Correspondence Corner

After looking at the cover on the March issue, I am weak and
wobbly. It is the best that Wesso has painted by far.

I only read "Poisoned Air" because it was in A.S. "The Affair
of the Brains" was good. "Vampires of Space"—what else could
you expect?—swell, of course. "The Hammer of Thor" was just
another doom-of-the-world bunk-bunk.

Yours till space ships drink milk.

> James Blish
> 4250 Kenwood Ave.
> Chicago, Ill.

—*Astounding Stories,* September 1932

Here is an announcement of great value: For a long time our
fair magazines have been defiled, and now the SPWSSTFM has been
organized to combat the evil.

Our society needs your help. If you are in sympathy with our
great cause, drop me a post card, giving your full name and
address.

The society (Society for the Prevention of Wire Staples in STF
Magazines) is bound to wield power among publishers and edi-

tors with your help. Every one—readers, authors and printers—is invited to join this campaign. Our motto is: PULL THE WIRE STAPLES OUT OF STF MAGAZINES!

Drop us a card now!

> Bob Tucker
> P.O. Box 260
> Bloomington, Illinois
>
> —*Astounding Stories,* November 1934

According to Einstein, the mass of a body increases with its speed until at the speed of light that mass, no matter how small originally, is infinite. Now it seems to me that this rule should apply to light itself which HAS mass (as is evidenced by the fact that a ray of light will bend in obedience to a strong gravitational field such as that of the sun). This mass should, at light's speed, be infinite. Consequently, the inertia of a beam of light should be infinite.

Now an object with an inertia amounting to infinity could not be affected by any conceivable force. If at rest, it could never be moved. And if already moving—as is the beam of light under question—it could neither be stopped nor turned from its path. Yet light can be stopped by a piece of tissue paper. How can you explain this paradox?

> Isaac Asimov
> 174 Windsor Place
> Brooklyn, New York
>
> —*Astounding Stories,* December 1937

And her left ear was a plumber's friend: gurgle, slurp, tiddly-um-tum, blork!

She might have been just twenty years old, with the look of womanhood just settling into her features. Her hair was light

188

brown, streaming rebelliously down her back. Her eyes were siphons, greedily sucking in all around her. Her nose and mouth were music in counterpoint . . .

> —"Of Love, Free Will and Grey
> Squirrels on a Summer Evening,"
> by Stephen Goldin, *Vertex*,
> August 1974

Whom, Heem?

She lifted away some of her shining hair and revealed an ear which had obviously been designed by whomever it is that holds the patent on the chambered nautilus.

> —"Agnes, Accent and Access,"
> by Theodore Sturgeon, *Galaxy*,
> October 1973

He put out feelers to some leading socialists whom, he thought, might be induced to join the Fabians . . .

> —*H. G. Wells,* by Norman and
> Jean MacKenzie (Simon and Schuster,
> 1973)

Academic Humor Department (Division of Near Things)

Just as genetic differences at particular loci are not sufficient to indicate racial differences, similarities for particular gene frequencies between two populations does not necessarily indicate racial identity. An apt illustration of this is found in the tests performed by Fisher, Ford and Huxley to detect PTC tasting among the chimpanzees of the London zoo. As with humans, this ability in chimpanzees is a genetically determined characteristic, and can be measured by observing their reaction to a PTC solution; the nontasters swallow the solution and the tasters spit it out. Remarkably, the frequencies of nontasters among the chimpanzees were found to be similar to the frequencies of nontasters among Englishmen. Of course, Englishmen and chimpanzees differ in other respects!

—*Genetics*, by Monroe W. Strickberger

Crazy Like a Foux, etc.

"If you're thinking what I think you're thinking, I think you're *foux*—crazy," the mathematician interrupted in a voice that was only half jesting.

—*Sledgehammer*, by Walter Wager

On another level, it is fantasy with the inherent appeal of all fantasy, with drugs forming the *deux ex machina.*

—"Science Fiction: Above the
Human Landscape," by Willis E.
McNelly, *Edge*, Autumn–Winter 1973

No, But Our Mother Was a Mez-cohen

Abruptly they started as a great section in the wall swung outward. Five strange things came out, warily, watchfully. They were tall, taller than Jan, nearly seven feet tall, and their bodies were small in the abdomen, and large in the chest. Their limbs were long and straight, and seemed more jointed than human limbs, but they were covered with cloths, as the Gaht-men covered themselves in the ceremonies, only these were finer cloths. . . .

"Who are you?" asked Meg, her voice soft and silvery in Jan's ears. The five made no direct answer. Only the leader said something in a strange way, like the Mez-kahns—the brown men from

the south—something Jan could not understand.
  "You aren't Mez-kahns?" asked Meg doubtfully.

> —"The Invaders," by Don A. Stuart
> (John W. Campbell, Jr.), *Astounding
> Stories,* June 1935

Or If Not Quite, Almost

Like an evanescent mote in a beam of sunshine, they vanished into the illimitable inane.

> —"Lost in the Dimensions," by
> Nat Schachner, *Astounding Stories,*
> November 1937

IN DONOVAN'S TIME

What we need is a goal, a purpose—something to
lift up our heads and our hearts and make us
realize that it's truly good to be alive. . . . Right?
Right?

C. L. Grant

Once in a very great while, and getting greater all the time,
Donovan tried to remember what it had been, could have been
like before he started walking; but the effort, a weak one at best,
was momentary and rewardless, and now that he was so close to
the end, quite without purpose. Whatever it had all been like, he
decided, it really wasn't worth knowing. Today was the time, and
tomorrow the time to be. So he waited.

While, round his neck, prominent in a soiled pouch suspended
from a tarnished gold chain, his coin: a wafer silver and worn that
he would use only once, half of a dollar for a lifetime view. He
twisted his neck to rub against the chain and anticipation forced
a grin, a small one, a sly one, but still it was a grin, and he was
heartened by it. Whatever had been was no longer, and perhaps
had never been, a concern: the coin demanded his waiting. So he
waited.

The people were quiet, and the crowd they formed all along the Avenue was not moving. It was a period of relief, too infrequent not to be savored. Those braver and stronger were able to relax and take their minds off their footing. Now there was no worry about stumbling, being pushed, being downed, being caught in a deadly intersection flux where they could easily be turned around so they would be moving dangerously, fatally backward. They were quiet; they were resting. Some looked up while stretching their necks to renew their acquaintance with the haze of might-have-been blue sky. Others twisted shoulders and hips gingerly, then vigorously to ease and bury the cramps and stiffness. Almost all of them dropped their hands from the shoulders of the person in front, first to pockets and pouches and secret places to touch their coins and offer brief thanks, then to flex their fingers and arms before swiftly repositioning them to prevent themselves from being pressed forward.

A May wind that hinted of winter and summer in alternate gusts cascaded down the Avenue. A noon sun glinted blindly off glass, aluminum and polished blue steel.

The crowd waited to move again.

Then, apparently without reason, someone laughed, loudly, with such natural gusto and infectious good humor that a silent dam was flattened, and it was at last the time to talk.

Donovan, a full head and more taller than most around him, looked anxiously to the woman at his side. She was pale, and even without the pressure of advance, he could see that her arms were already beginning to tremble.

"You okay, Alice?"

Her answering grin was hard and quick, her mind obviously concentrating on feeding her muscles strength she did not have. Her post, a squat, dark-skinned man in front of her, had straps on his overcoat, and Donovan wondered how long it would be before she clutched at them for support and was angrily, fiercely shaken off. He tried to judge whether or not it would be worth the trouble to figure a way she might be saved. And he knew he was dreaming. It had been at least two days since she last even made an attempt to answer his questions or laugh at his jokes. She was losing, and they both knew it. And she was beginning to hate him for his strength, and they knew that too.

I wonder, he thought, if all great leaders had troubles like mine.

I wonder, he thought, if she'd give me her coin.

"Hey, Donovan," someone behind him shouted impatiently (it sounded like the man who claimed to have been a plastics president; not that anyone cared). "How are we doing?"

Donovan, slightly shaken by his last, almost ghoulish thought, stretched up off his heels, squinting past the glare of the windows at the nearest signpost half a block away. "It looks like Fiftieth coming right up."

"Are you sure? I thought we were there last night."

"Positive, pal," he said, showing his displeasure and disdain by not looking around.

"Okay, Donovan, if you say so. Thanks anyway."

"Don't mention it. Again."

Then he ducked his head to rub his neck in an effort to hide the fact that he was smiling. It felt good, putting down a man with a voice like that. But Donovan did understand how much easier it was now to lose your place when you were so close to the Building. Tensions were higher and anxiety easier to succumb to, and more often now than before, there were some who tried desperately to bull ahead through the crowd. They seldom lasted long; their screams were short. Donovan looked again and nodded to himself. They were nearing the surge from the West Side out of the Lincoln Tunnel. The going was slower, the casualties more frequent. He considered himself more than a little lucky that he was in the center of the street, away from the grinding pressures at the crowd's edge, where those who normally fought to stay away from shop and door windows were those immediately faced with the crossbuck of every intersection flow. My God, he thought, it must be hell in Times Square.

There was a sharp, splintering crack. Despite the danger of losing his balance, Donovan turned quickly toward the sound, searching until he spotted a whirlpool movement. Someone, or two or three, had been tripped, pushed or just squeezed out, and through plate glass. If they were still alive, they would probably starve to death. Once out, there was no getting back in. The helicopters that came twice a day and dropped tiny packets of food paid no attention to the pieces of clothing that sometimes waved weakly from upper-story windows. Some, in a grand gesture, would throw their coins into the crowd, but it was only a gesture, because few dared to bend down to retrieve them.

"How many, Donovan?" a woman called.

"How the hell should I know, Sal?"

"Well, dammit, boy, go on over there and look!"

And the crowd laughed.

"Donovan?"

"Yes, Annie."

"Will my coin fit?"

"They all do, dear."

"Thank you, Donovan. I just wanted to know."

"That's all right, dear."

And the crowd, well trained, did not laugh.

Somewhere, back when there was time, they began to call themselves Donovan's Doers, refusing him a title but remembering his name. They depended on him to be wary of the traps, the sudden forward lurch that resulted when a group ahead of them fell. They assigned him the task of keeping track of their progress, telling them jokes, making them laugh, forcing them to move when they could move no longer. Whenever the time for talk ended, there was always his voice; and it seemed to them, and to Donovan, that he had always been there. He was the only constant. The Doers were always changing.

"Hey, Donovan, tell us a story."

It wasn't a child.

"I don't know if I have enough time. Seems to be a movement up there, a block or two, give or take."

A woman called out something in Italian and several people laughed. Donovan frowned, not wanting to be the butt of a joke he couldn't understand. In his position it wouldn't be right.

"Hey, Donovan, you know what she said?"

He shook his head as if he really didn't care, and the crowd laughed.

"She said maybe you're too busy cuddling up to your post."

There was more laughter, echoing now, and Donovan looked down at Alice, hoping for a smile. But she was staring dead ahead, her fingers twisted weakly in her post's shoulder straps, her arms so bent that her elbows nearly touched the squat man's coat. He started to say something, but a man, a new one by the voice, interrupted him with the beginnings of "Row, Row, Row Your Boat," and those who still had the energy joined him. They were mostly off-key, but uncaringly so, and the words eventually swung to a ribald burlesque of the original. A fat man began to jounce in time to the music until he was kicked into stopping. The pitch rose slightly, the tempo picked up; an old woman suddenly screamed hysterically and fell. There was a moment's hesitation before ranks formed and she was helped to her feet. She sobbed, put out her hands, and was silent. Damn, Donovan thought, and marked the place where she stood. He decided he didn't want to look that way when they started again. There were times, he admitted sourly to himself, when he hated being a leader. Sometimes it just wasn't any fun.

And thinking of the old woman reminded him of the girl beside him.

"Hey, Alice," he said softly to the sweep of her dark hair and the slope of her breast. "Keep your eye on the Building. Believe me, it's the best way, girl. Just watch it, don't let it go. See how it grows, the closer we get? Just think of it, Alice, the whole world, the whole damn world at your feet. At last. No more dark streets, no more buildings to blot out the sun; nothing but sky and sky and a hell of a lot of more sky. Free, Alice, and we're getting there. Damn, but we're getting there."

She nodded once, but did not look up.

"Hey, Donovan, tell us a story!"

And what did she see? he thought with questioning bitterness. Was she trying to remember the black street long since colored in red and pink and papered with layers of cloth? Was she trying to bring back that first-day stench of excrement and sweat that too soon faded into the equally meaningless pulp beneath their feet? Or was it the Building that bowed her head?

"Donovan!"

An elderly man had been his post once, too short to see anything, so he had spoken to himself of the street beneath his shuffling, filthy shoes, constantly reconstructing the lives of the people he trod upon. Then he died, was carried along until Donovan saw him slip and heard the man ahead cursing. "Ease," Donovan had ordered then, and the woman behind him shortened her steps, Donovan slowed and the old man fell. "Done," Donovan said, and stepped over him.

"For Christ's sake, Donovan!"

Damn their souls, he thought, why the hell don't they leave me alone!

And they were moving again, with millions of shuffling feet numbing him into automatic response, with pressure just great enough to keep his arms bent. His eyes stared until they watered (once he thought he was going blind), searching for the traps (he would have been cast aside), the sudden speedups (to die by the road without seeing), the tides of the streets emptying into the Avenue, upsetting the delicate balance between pushing and falling. He saw hair and hats, and one or two faces that whitened before they sank. He called out, demanding, screaming until he was hoarse and lesser men spelled him, though it wasn't the same. There was an hour and a half and he heard and considered the rumor that the George Washington Bridge had finally collapsed; and it took him only a moment to believe it. There was a panic second when he tripped and refused to look down, only grateful that his post had stiffened in time to save him. Two more hours and he was into the Fiftieth Street flux.

Squeezed. Pressed. Shouting above the din. Raising perilously an arm to mark the way. Kicked. Elbowed. Squeezed. Pressed.

And the passage was done.

For the first time in weeks, he wanted to sit down and rest. But they were cheering him, and it was a rare thing and he wondered, as they eased to let his arms spring up in a V, what the rest of the world made of it.

They moved on; there was a lurch on his right and a vacuum quickly filled but he ignored it, willed himself to forget it until he was able to spare himself a look, and saw a tweedy, sniffling man where Alice had been. God, she must have been tired, he thought.

Then they stopped. There was silence. Heavy breathing. The May wind of summer and winter.

Donovan, shaking off Alice's defeat (who was she? he wondered), judged this to be the time, lifted his head and intoned, "In the beginning—"

"All right, Donovan!"

"Tell it, Donovan, tell it!"

"A bit louder, Donovan, we got some new people back here can't hear you!"

"In the beginning, I said, there was a man, a most ordinary man who said: It's such a beautiful day, I think I'll take me a walk along the Avenue. And this man he said as much to his friends and neighbors and boss and doorman. Walk with me, he said, aren't you weary of looking up at lights and buildings and people and just plain things that sneer and leer and laugh at your living? Well, they nodded and looked and puzzled and wondered. I have an inspiration, the man said. For one thin, very ordinary fifty-cent half-a-dollar coin, we can look down on this goddamned world and tell it what we think; a lifetime view to put us in our place."

A lurch. A scream. Hush. Amen!

"Don't ask me any more, he said, but by God I'm going to walk, and I'm going to climb. And by God he did."

A window cracked but the commotion was muffled by the cadence clapping that picked up his words.

"And believe it or not, he was joined by every one of those

friends and neighbors and his boss and the doorman. And where
do you think he went to get that fifty-cent lifetime view of the
whole goddamned world?"

"To the john, you stupid idiot!"

A chorus of laughter one beat later.

"To the movies!"

Jeers now.

"No no no, you benighted heathen, to the Building!"

Cheers now, and applause.

"To that beautiful Building, my Doers. And when they saw
what he was doing, they went with him, and before him, and after
him. They emptied those air-conditioned buildings, they fled
those creepy darkened movie theaters, they streamed from every
borough, every town, every state. And by God, as I stand here
now, every last one of them was going to the Building!"

There was shouting, incoherent and tumultuous. Donovan
grinned and perspired and nodded, and took time out to flex his
fingers, touch the pouch.

"Now you won't believe this, friends, but they came from
Frisco and Detroit and L.A. and Dallas. From Mobile and Bis-
marck and Prescott and Nome. To the Building! NOT some fat-
assed mountain; NOT some swollen-bellied plane; but, goddam-
mit, to the biggest, bestest, most King Kong famous Building in
the whole goddamned world! That's what they did, my Doers. By
God, that's what they did."

"Why?"

There was silence after confusion, stunned and shocked, and
the wind turned winter. Donovan glared and did an unexpected
thing: he dropped his hands and turned around, showing his face
and the eyes that hated. It was his first challenge, and he was too
angry to be afraid, and those around him too amazed to close in
and crush him. A woman gasped and not a few began to cry.
Donovan was furious and it hurt them where they lived.

"Who . . ." He stammered, stuttered, blinked rapidly in anger.
"Who's the son of a bitch who said that?"

"I did, you scrawny misbegotten slob."

Donovan, slipping in mire, whirled around beneath hysterical arms. "Well, where the hell are you, you coward?"

The crowd, reacting now, called for the man and Donovan turned, facing straight ahead, waiting. When the shouting abated, the voice sneered again and this time Donovan looked up two stories, into the face of a shirtsleeved man, dried blood on his face, his skull more visible than his skin. He leaned forward out of the window and pointed a crooked finger down the Avenue. "Tell me, you addleheaded sap, do you have any idea what they are doing down there at your precious Building? Do you know what you're heading for?"

Donovan quickly, not thinking, twisted the tarnished gold chain over his head and whirled the pouch into a halo above him. "The View, old man, the View!"

"Why?"

A woman screamed in rage; claws raised; spit to froth.

Donovan replaced the pouch carefully, closed his eyes, trembling with inarticulate rage. Finally he looked up again and shouted, "Why is the sky blue, you coward?"

"What the hell kind of an answer is that?"

"All you deserve, you bum!"

And the crowd cheered. Donovan was heartened.

"What are you trying to do, take a shortcut across the rooftops? What's the matter, old man, you too damn lazy to do it the right way, the man's way, the goddamned human way? What the hell are you, old man, a freak?"

The crowd roared.

"I know where I'm going," Donovan screamed, "do you?"

There was nothing in the history of the Avenue to match it. More noise, more screaming than all the world's winds. Suddenly a boot flew out of the crowd and struck the man in the face. He staggered, disappeared. They waited. He returned. He wiped blood across his forehead, blinked it from his eyes. Another boot struck the sill and he winced, but didn't back away.

He addressed the crowd. "The View?"

They answered.

He pointed above their heads. "And what the goddamned hell are you going to see with all that smog?"

"I have my coin," a woman shouted back.

"And I," the perhaps plastics president yelled. And they all yelled, and Donovan knew they were his.

"Well, tell me this," the old man said, the contempt running thick as his blood, "how the hell are you going to get back down?"

A shower this time: glass, twisted metal, shoes, boots, unnameable debris scooped from the street. The man screamed and was gone again. Donovan waited, panting. The crowd waited.

Not breathing.

There was nothing, and they started moving again, forward, wearily.

"In the beginning—" Donovan shouted.

The crowd stiffened.

"In the beginning—" Donovan shouted.

The crowd screamed wildly.

Damn, Donovan thought, but it's great to be alive.

AMBIENCE

Death, the great obscenity—how odd that we spell
it with five letters!

Dave Skal

The anti-technologists are taken far too lightly. They want only to
clean up the smog, the sewage, you say? Think again. These politicians,
"intellectuals," all the sundry voices, who, like asthma, choke the lines
of discourse, reason, and progress—these are our real enemies! *A return
to natural beauty,* they cry, a return to wildness, irrationality, savagery!
The basic inhumanity of their goals is so obscene that any doubt about
their moral character is in itself an obscenity.

> —Ona Ransome, *The Doctrine
> of Dionysus,* a polemic

She had turned her apartment into a greenhouse, just as the
world itself was turning into a greenhouse, lush and tropical,
environmental affectation justified by ecological necessity. Afri-
can violets, miniature cacti, Aloe Vera and hindu ropes. Rugged

201

plants. Delicate plants. The withered dendriform phantoms of bonsai. You breathed out, and they breathed back. At least that's what she read often enough—usually twice, first in the morning faxsheet, and later at dinner, when the sans-serif pronouncements were shredded into elaborate salads. Unlike many of her contemporaries, who shredded the equally edible but noncommittal advertisements, *she* believed in Involvement. Nutrition of the mind as well as the body.

So. The icecaps were going. Santa Claus would have to learn to swim, and her cacti and rubbery fronds would give way to seaweed. One couldn't stop progress.

Cynic, she chided herself. She would make up for it that night, with a more relevant salad than usual. CANCER CURE HOPEFUL, with Roquefort dressing.

Her name was Gudrun Maxa. Maxa: the name suggested an abundance, the upper limits of a scale, the tops. She had a wide, inviting mouth, brown liquid eyes. The large frame that had embarrassed her as a child had melted into a woman's generous sensuality. Gudrun Maxa.

As usual, it was raining; black sooty water streaked her apartment windows. She paid attention to the elements, as a rule; this was only natural, since she worked as a weathermaid on a local television station. The job had built up a certain resiliency in her character, a toughness if you will, but a toughness tempered by a pervading optimism. Her twice-daily spot, "Weather Break" (the subtle psychological suggestion!), was a testament to these qualities; no matter how caustic or deadly the atmosphere might become, no matter how many fatalities there might be (which weren't broadcast anyway, but Gudrun got the figures), Gudrun Maxa had a sunny smile for everybody. And if after watching her program, people came away feeling, why, yes, the weather *has* lifted a bit, then wasn't it all worthwhile?

"The persistence and ubiquity of denial! Its survival value has been long overlooked . . . consider yourself an angel of mercy in a world starved for miracles."

That was the way Andrew had explained it to her—Andrew, the program director, when she had been picked for the job. Hand-picked, as it turned out—although now she and Andrew hadn't slept together in months.

She wasn't quite sure what had happened. There were no hos-tilities, just no sex. They still had lunch together, smiles, studio gossip . . . but something else had fizzled out. Andrew didn't talk about it, and Gudrun didn't think about it. It was easier that way.

She wasn't thinking about it that day as she stood before the bright-blue matte screen, modeling a photosynthetic shift for the cameras. Her natural complexion was pale, but not so pale as the white-white makeup she wore, enabling the technicians to tan her an unhealthy but attractive Scandinavian bronze (her contract, like most nowadays, had a cancer clause).

She often wondered what backdrop was being electronically keyed in, what canned three-dimensional footage of open, wind-swept fields. A spring thaw, perhaps . . . clumps of straw-colored grass like the bowed heads of flaxen-haired women . . . virginal . . . fresh . . .

Without warning, someone started coughing—violently. Gu-drun felt herself blush. The cameramen cursed.

"Get her the hell out of here!" It was Andrew, but Gudrun couldn't discern who had caused the disturbance. The techni-cians muttered angrily to themselves, they had already run over-time. Gudrun stepped out from under the hot holographic illumi-nation, which had already begun turning her costume to hot spinach, and saw Andrew collaring one of the office girls.

"Who do you think you are, bringing your filth in here, costing us time and money? Answer me, you bitch!"

The girl trembled in his grasp. She had high, sallow cheek-bones, and the little makeup she wore was inexpertly applied. "I'm sorry, sir—they asked me to deliver these papers—they said it was important—" Although she could have been no more than twenty, from a distance she appeared much older; she had the crabbed aspect of one of Gudrun's bonsai trees, an unhealthy, foreign complexion. She skittered around the floor like a crustacean in her worker's smock, picking up lost scraps of paper, handing them up to Andrew, an offering.

Andrew looked at the papers, then burst into laughter. "Do you know what these are?" He addressed the room. "Plumbers' invoices! For fixing the toilets! Crap!" He shoved the papers under the girl's nose. "Somebody in *my* department gave you these? Yes? And can you think of any earthly reason why a man in my position would want or need the deeds to a shitcan?"

Tears welled up in the girl's red eyes. She started to answer, but was suddenly seized by a coughing fit, worse than the last— obscene ripping sounds, a cord being pulled through a bellows. Was she spitting up blood? Gudrun couldn't tell.

The men gathered around her, taking up a low chant, almost inaudible: *Scum, scum, filthy scum . . .* Gudrun had a mental image of a ritual exorcism. The girl's mouth was pressed against the floor, her eyes glued shut with pain. *Scum! Scum!*

"Andrew—"

"Don't look!"

"Oh, for heaven's sake, Andrew, I'm not a child." But she was blushing all the same. Did it show, even through her thick layer of paint?

Andrew ignored her. The girl was being hauled out. "I just don't get it," he muttered. "You see stuff like that all the time now."

Gudrun tried to be helpful. "But don't they have . . . places?" *Tubercular, cancerous ghettos.*

" 'Equal opportunity employment,' they call it . . . Christ, they're nothing but animals."

Gudrun couldn't help feeling some measure of pity for the girl; she had obviously been set up by those goons in Andrew's department. The malicious pigs had been on the girl's back from the moment she started on the job. Gudrun had seen it all. But still—

"Get cleaned up and we'll go eat," said Andrew. He pressed

her hand and went into his office. Gudrun started for the dressing room, then remembered a script she had left with Andrew. She went back and knocked on the door. Inside, there was loud music.

"Andrew—?"

She pushed the door open silently. And froze.

Andrew was bent over his desk, coughing explosively into a tissue. The sound was masked by the music. He did not see her at the door, his eyes were tightly closed. The desk blotter was spattered with blood and sputum.

Gudrun saw nothing.

She quickly shut the door and went to remove her makeup. The face in the mirror was puffy and worn. She felt oddly dissociated, vaguely sick. She waited for Andrew. He came.

"All ready?" he asked, patting his stomach. The events of the morning had apparently been an appetizer.

They talk of natural beauty. They talk of a world uglified, desecrated by technology. They see one side only, discarding the whole of man's *rational* achievement like the very garbage they rail against. Who among us has not witnessed the unearthly beauty of a latter-day sunset, the roiling clouds of orange, magenta, puce—nature itself acknowledging submission, testament to man's triumph? No preindustrial civilization could witness such a spectacle.

—Ona Ransome,
The Doctrine of Dionysus

They lunched alfresco at the art museum, on a garden patio with a view of Rodin's vandalized "Thinker"; dynamited years before, the sculpture had been reinstated as a symbol of Sickness in Our Society. The anti-intellectual element. The Dionysians. Most of the sculpture's base had been shredded away, and now its hollow remains rested in a wooden cradle, reminding Gudrun of Quasimodo riding a huge bronze bell.

Hidden oxyjets moaned softly.

"I know we don't usually talk about . . . serious things," Andrew began, folding his napkin. He had a lopsided but expressive face, lacking the regular good looks required of an on-camera performer. He laughed nervously, as if to weaken his delivery. "I'm sorry. Let's drop the whole thing, okay?"

"No," said Gudrun quickly, leaning toward him. But her gaze drifted to a nearby table where an airbrain sat with a watery-eyed little man.

Airbrains . . . They grew them that way, on special aerobic farms. Big, boyish, musclebound . . . superoxygenated specimens of health and vitality. Trained to deal with any crisis of identity or faith, they were sought out particularly by the infirm or chronically doubtful. The voice was soothing and unctuous: ". . . nothing really ends . . . only rebirth . . . a continuous cycle . . ." The little man doubled up, wheezing, and the airbrain took him gently in his arms. Gudrun looked away.

"No, Andrew . . . I mean, if there's something you really want to talk about—"

"I wanted you to know that I didn't like what happened this morning any more than you did. The girl, I mean. Yeah, I know, I'm one to talk. But I had my orders, and—well, to be brutally frank about it, I'm in no position to argue." He paused, pressing his lips tightly together. "Ever since that girl—Carla, her name was—came in three weeks ago, things just haven't been the same. Like a morgue." Gudrun blushed. "You know how the tech crew has been. The secretaries have been the same way—cranky, irritable—just having *her* around is what did it. And today, that . . . coughing. It's depressing."

Gudrun shifted her weight uncomfortably.

"I've been doing a lot of thinking lately," he continued. The usual things—money, status. Sex." The nervous laugh. "It's funny, the way things are. The way the world just kind of belches us all up out of nowhere, lets us run around on a leash for a while, then sucks us all back. Sophomoric, I know. Existentialism 101, right? Not worth talking about. I flunked philosophy in college, you know. Had to take it three times . . . there was this damn

genius chink for a prof—I *swear* that man believed with his entire
soul that the 'relativism/absolutism controversy' was the single
driving force in the universe. Sometimes I feel so stupid—it's
silly, I know—for having never taken an interest in the big questions. What it all means. Christ, I must sound like an ass, a kid.
Deep down, I know it's all a lot of semantic drivel, philosophy and
the rest . . . but sometimes I wonder, especially lately, whether
or not it would make things any . . . easier." He stared at the ice
at the bottom of his glass. "Am I making any sense? Any at all?"

Gudrun didn't listen to his words as much as the tone of his
voice, the controlled rigidity broken by bursts of nervous, self-
depreciating laughter. She looked at him, sitting there in that
ridiculous coat with the padded chest and shoulders that she
really didn't want to think about. It embarrassed her. She felt a
need to escape before he revealed too much, before they were
bound together, inextricably, by some secret and terrible knowledge.

"I'm dying, Gudrun." He looked her straight in the eye. "Don't
tell me you haven't noticed."

His tone was becoming belligerent. Gudrun felt anger rising,
defensively. *I'm not one of your office girls! Leave me alone!*

"Look at me!" he snapped. "That's the very least you can do.
I'm dying, for godsake. They don't know what it is, exactly, but
they do know it's fatal."

She tried not to hear him.

". . . the body stops using oxygen efficiently, for one thing—
there's a theory that it's all part of a new evolutionary step, the
organism trying to adjust to a poisonous biosphere. In the meantime, we're nature's bloody guinea pigs."

"Andrew," she blurted, "I've been meaning to say this for a
long time and I don't care what it sounds like but I don't think
we should see one anoth—"

He was incredulous. "You haven't heard a word I've said, have
you? I'm dying, Gudrun, the way this planet is dying, and you
can't seem to appreciate either of those two facts."

"Andrew, please—"

"Are you blind? Can't you see that I've lost thirty-five pounds
in the last six months, that I wear prosthetic clothing to hide the
fact, and that I'm probably going to lose my job because I stink
of death, Gudrun, death and graveworms and a hundred other
terribly realistic things our society doesn't even pay lip service to
anymore!" He slammed his fist on the table. Heads were turned.
Gudrun shut her eyes.

*You are twelve years old and your father is a man named Gerhard Maxa
who gets up every morning and coughs out his guts into a toilet bowl. The
sound wakes you daily, raking, horrible, and you lie in bed and want to
scream, it's dirty, it's filthy, these perverts your family—but who is there to
tell? And you carry your shame to school with you, while your father goes
off to work in factories decent people don't even think about.*

"We have to survive, Andrew!" It was out in the open. "You
people make it so difficult—"

"I know." Andrew was no longer looking at her. "The persistence and ubiquity of denial," he said, clucking his tongue. "That
used to be my line, didn't it?" His voice was cool and ironic.
"You've learned your lessons well, Gudrun."

She spoke clumsily. "I . . . I won't forget you, Andrew. Really,
I won't . . ."

"No hard feelings. We live in an age of transience, right?"

She bit her lip. "Thank you, Andrew. Thank you."

After they parted, Gudrun's head began to throb. Something
in the air. A tension at the base of her skull. She didn't have her
mask with her, and her eyes began to water. She tried vainly to
remember the pollution-level figures she had recited that morning. Above her, blue-grey clouds of vapor writhed like ectoplasm.

Vision blurred and eyes burning, she got in line at an oxygen
booth. Nearby, a Ransomite rally was underway. Ona Ransome
herself was speaking, a tough, intransigent knot of a woman,
locked behind a gold-plated gas mask engraved with the sign of
the dollar. She harangued the crowd in husky, accented tones:

the threat of the neomystics . . . the threat of an unconquered nature . . . the threat, always the threat. Gudrun's head pounded agonizedly. She felt as if someone were driving an icepick into her brain.

"They do not stop at cleaning up the air and water, they demand a stop to shopping centers, expressways, transportation! In short, these Dionysian brutes are screaming for an end to America, a stop to civilization!"

Her audience was an undulating mass, responsive to her every cue. And why not? Wasn't she right, after all? Why carry an onerous burden of guilt when Ona Ransome clearly placed the blame?

A commotion was starting at the oxygen booth; a man refused to relinquish his place after the allotted thirty seconds. Gudrun took a handkerchief from her purse and covered her face.

Who are these people? she asked herself. Gaunt faces; brown-yellow skin stretched hot and tight across the bone. Hollow-chested women with cracked lips, the skin showing through their hair in leprous patches, their flesh seared and burnished by the air itself! Bandanas and scraps of cloth pulled across their mouths like gags. A few Ransomites shouted insults; the man in the oxygen booth stubbornly held his ground.

"The Dionysian motivation is clear—a return to nature in all its ugliness, a mode of life best described by three adjectives: harsh, brutal, and short!"

Men from the oxygen line itself—businessmen, public servants —joined the Ransomites in removing the protester; he twitched and shuddered like a weasel being extruded from the womb. He was stomped to the ground. There was blood. His attackers were met by a dozen ascetic-looking men and women brandishing signs and placards as well as their bony fists: AIR NOW! POLLUTION IS GENOCIDE!

Ona Ransome could not be heard. The sirens of riot police sounded monotonously in the distance. Gudrun felt herself crowded in from all sides, so tightly she could barely move, could only sag and sway with the movement of the mob. Screams. Rushes. Beggarly men falling of their own exertion, trampled.

All at once the crowd parted and Gudrun stared directly into the ratlike face of the man in the air chamber. His face was torn, his eyes maddened with blood and pain. Gudrun's head spun. She was about to faint. She extended one hand toward him in a meaningless gesture.

The man took something from a package at his side and hurled it with all his strength. Like a tough pink fish encrusted with tar, stinking of some foul preservative, it fell at Gudrun's feet.

A human lung.

She entered the bar quickly amid sounds of natural ambience; fluttering birds, tumbling water. She saw him almost immediately —the barrel chest heaving beneath a mesh shirt of photosynthetic weave. The state emblem on the sleeve.

She took a place at a corner table and cleared her throat once, self-consciously. The airbrain yawned.

Her pulse quickened. Again the signal, as delicate and tempting as the crumpling of sheets . . .

He set his milk down on the bar and rose to face her, deltoids flexing, his chest a muscle playground. "You have doubts?" he asked. A standard question, to which she nodded sheepishly. The airbrain had no doubts.

"It is important to have faith. . . ."

The oxygen made her dizzy. She inhaled deeply, relaxed. In and out. The world melted away. The airbrain smiled.

She did not breathe as he laid his hands upon her in a lingering benediction.

BINARY JUSTICE

To paraphrase Thoreau: Beware of any enterprise
that requires you to buy new skirts.

Richard Bireley

The water on the freeway canal didn't show a ripple. I eased my
skimmer down the ramp and watched the flashes from the fish
darting for the bottom. The new skirts of the aircar made it ride
a good twelve centimeters higher, and it was smooth, really
smooth. I sort of had to grin when I shoved the vanes to full
forward and cut in the afterfan. When I hit the speed channel, I
was already up to an even hundred kilos. Those fish were in for
a bad time later—on a day like this, everybody with a cool skimmer that could lift off the water would be pulling revs. But right
then it was quiet. I had to laugh when an old clunker with leaky
skirts lost power and plunked down right in front of me. I gave
him a blast with the afterfan, just to watch him bob, then scurried
in to work. I breezed into the parking marina with plenty of time
to spare and strolled into the shop. By the time I got to my bench,
I didn't feel so good.

Somehow a transfer day always does that to me. I don't owe too much. The usual. Rent to the city for my pad at the collective. A meal tab for two intervals. Payments on the skimmer. Except that I had gotten a bit carried away with those new skirts. My credit was down to the edge of my C5 credit limit. It really wasn't fair. The more you made, the more you could owe. I had heard the C12 limit was a thousand credits. And here I was stuck at a miserable hundred and fifty. So I shot my balance, and then some. And today Trim Skimmers, Inc., was due for another transfer. I hoped Karl would bail me out. It wouldn't be the first time.

I dropped into my seat at the bench and picked up the first visiphone. The tag read "Broken View Switch." Well, that computed. No one would believe how many came in like that. The view switch "somehow" jams on. Then when the user answers the call straight from the shower, they are terribly surprised and flustered when somebody *sees* them. I remember one time . . . Well, anyway, I was fixing the switch when Karl arrived. He worked at the bench next to me.

"Unity, Len."

"Unity, Karl. Hey, Karl, how about transferring a hundred credits until tomorrow?"

"Sorry, Len. I'm into my limit now. What's the trouble this time?"

Then I really didn't feel so good. I gave him the whole story, complete with dulcimers and moogs. He nodded.

"Bad break."

That didn't help much. I had a date tonight, too. Free-fall games. Then he got my attention.

"Look, you can take care of the credit problem real easy."

"Sure," I said. "I'll break into the Center with a magnet and wipe them out."

"Naw. That doesn't work, anyway. But I can show you how to get a start on the next interval."

"Watch your program, fella. You know that new credits are entered for everybody at the start of an interval. No sooner."

Karl laughed and sat down on my bench. "Yeah, I know. What time is your payment due?"

"No later than nineteen hundred hours."

"And what time does the credit center shut down for the day?"

"At seventeen hundred."

"Correct. Are you getting the program?"

"No." I could see that Karl had something interesting going, so I shoved back my chair.

"Retrieve, man. Retrieve," he said. "What says you got no credits? A little strip of plastic on your ID card. Just a few little magnetic spots. Now! What is that interesting piece of machinery next to us? A coder for the key strips in the phones. A coder for little magnetic spots."

I put the visiphone down with a thump.

"Run complete, Karl. Just add enough to keep the smiling dealer smiling. By the time my transfers hit Central tomorrow, my credits for the next interval are already in. That's the first run of the day. Then I go to an update booth, get my new balance recorded, and everything is square. Could work."

"Does work. Do it myself sometimes. Here, I'll show you."

Well, it probably would have worked, too, except that I went out at noon for a quick hairstyling. I wanted something short for free-fall. I was cruising into town when this water beetle pulled me over. They hate that name, but what else can you call those little pill-shaped black-and-whites with side jets that look like legs? So the monitor herded me into a control slip and looked me up and down.

"Unity, citizen. Ridin' kind of high, aren't you, son?"

I sort of thought I knew what he was getting at.

"Uh, what do you mean, Monitor?"

"Looks to me like you're a bit over the legal maximum on skirt length," he said.

"I don't think so. I always heard if you didn't go any higher than the long side of a credit report form, you were okay."

"Sorry, son. Eight centimeters. No more. Anything over that

and things begin to get unstable. I'm going to have to punch this up." He pulled the report box from his belt.

I knew what was coming, and thought of gunning out of there, but that's why they have control slips. His bug blocked the way.

"Citizen's ID," he said, holding out his hand.

There was no choice. I gave it to him.

He scanned my number and added it to his list. Then he checked his sheet of violation codes and entered a number on the keyboard. My card went into a slot at the end. A second later, his readout glowed. He scanned it briefly.

"No previous violations," he said. "They'll probably take it easy on you." As he spoke, he punched another button and checked again. "You got off easy. Only thirty credits." His voice became formal.

"The law states that you may post bail immediately, or you may appear in court at seventeen hundred hours on the day of the alleged violation. Objections may be registered at the time of transfer."

Oh, wow! Seventeen hundred hours on a date night? No way. Besides, that traffic computer probably didn't update more than once every twenty-four hours anyway.

The officer extended the box with my card still in the slot. I took a deep breath and thumbed the transfer button. The readout changed to an angry red.

"All rise."

I jumped to my feet nervously. The court calendar was crowded, so it was two very long hours before my case was called. My attorneys rose casually with me. One on each side. The older one winked at the prosecutor. Then a side door opened, and the judge in his symbolic white lab robes appeared. He stepped to the bench and sat down.

"Be seated." The clerk advanced, rustling a stack of papers. "Court is now in session, Judge Frederick Dove presiding."

The judge banged his gavel once, activating the large control panel mounted in the face of his bench. Some lights flashed, and the tape units started to twitch as the system was initialized.

The clerk faced the audience and intoned, "Now for computation, the People versus Leonard Verst."

More lights flashed, and across the top of the bench appeared pictures of the faces of the six jurors. A green light flashed on at the prosecutor's panel. The senior attorney, I think I heard someone call him Pike, began a series of pigtails in the corner of his printout.

"What happens now?" I whispered.

The number-two man flapped his hand in a hushing motion without looking at me. Nervously I ran my thumbnail along the lines in the molded-plastic tabletop. Deep grooves showed that a few other jokers hadn't felt too good about filling this chair either.

There seemed to be a pause while everybody took a last-minute look at their printouts. I didn't have a printout, so I leaned back and stared around. It was nice enough, for a courtlab, though the thick green carpet didn't seem to go too well with the white tile walls. Each wall had a large mural set into the tile.

On the right side they had a statue of Justice, extending from floor to ceiling. That was fine with me, but she was wearing a blindfold. And her right hand was holding a sword. Not so good. The left hand was a little better. In it was a punched computer card. I could understand that part. A scroll across the top had a motto printed on it in Old English letters: "Equal Justice Under Electronic Law." I got to thinking, when you're really guilty, equal justice doesn't seem all that good.

On the other wall there was a picture of a big building, shaped like a computer, with citizens going in the front door. They left on opposite sides, smiling on one side, heads bowed on the other. I scratched at the tabletop again, and wondered if a computer had ever missed a date because it was low on credits.

The prosecutor pushed back his chair and stood up, clearing his throat. Consulting a sheaf of printouts, he moved to the terminal in front of his table.

"Your Honor, members of the jury," he began. "I intend to

show that the defendant, Leonard Verst, is guilty of the crime of Alteration, as defined in Program Fifty-three, Subroutine Alter, of the State Master Penal File." As he spoke, his fingers moved over the keyboard. The recorders began to whisper, and lights started a march across the big panel. The prosecutor continued in a matter-of-fact tone.

"I shall prove beyond reasonable doubt that the defendant did willfully, and with intent to defraud, alter the record on his Citizen's Credit Card to indicate credits that did not exist."

I started to jump up. "Wait a minute. That's not right. I just . . ." A hand on my shoulder forced me down, hard. No one seemed to notice. More squiggles appeared on the sheet next to me. The prosecutor turned and smiled toward our table. I didn't feel included.

"The attorney for the defense will present the position of his client." He stabbed a button with his thumb, and the green light shifted to our terminal. The attorney for the defense doodled a last pigtail and eyed the results. Then he nodded and got to his feet. As he approached the panel, I glanced at the pictures of the jurors across the top of the judge's bench. The one on the left seemed to be smiling, but that didn't help much either. I wondered what he was thinking about when they made that picture.

I tried again. "Where are the jurors?" I whispered to the assistant. He gave me an irritated look and pawed through a stack of papers. Finding a small pamphlet, he checked a page and pushed it toward me. My lawyer was making his opening remarks, but it didn't make much sense to me, so I glanced at the book. It was titled "Facts for the Defendant—A Citizen's Guide." The figure of Justice with her punched card appeared just below.

Most of the stuff I already knew. Like how all the laws and decisions are stored on computer tapes, and each court computer is updated daily. The jurors report each day and are put in little rooms, where they are wired into the computer. A plastic band goes around your head that holds the pickups for your brainwaves. Then they fasten a bunch of little sensors all over you that beam data to the master receiver. You lie on a couch like a big damp sponge and watch the proceedings on a full-sized visiwall. As the trial progresses, the computer monitors the jurors' emotional responses and stores them. When the presentations are complete, the computer evaluates all the responses and weighs them, along with the points of law programmed by the attorneys, to arrive at an absolutely unbiased verdict.

My attorney cleared his throat and raised his voice. "It is clear that one essential element of this crime is not present. That element is intent. My client had credits legally due him which he expected would more than cover the amount drawn."

Now that sounded better. More lights flashed, and the tapes turned jerkily. One clicked and began to race ahead. The judge's eyes were closed.

The defense moved on. "I would like to introduce a statement from my client's employer attesting to his reliability and work habits." The green light went out, and a big red flashing job appeared on the main panel.

"What's that? What happened?" I said.

"It's an objection," muttered the assistant.

The prosecutor stood up. "Objection, File OBJ327, your Honor."

My side was not to be outdone. "File DEM828," replied the defense.

There were lights all over the panel, and the tapes got busy for sure. A printer clattered briefly on the judge's bench. He reached out and tore off a strip.

"Sustained," he announced. Then he checked the timer on the far wall. "This hearing has now reached the twenty-minute first-period maximum. Court will recess for ten minutes."

We all rose, and I went along with my defenders to a room next-door. They told me to sit while they analyzed the first session. I couldn't follow much of it. There was nothing about me, or what I did. Just subroutines, jumps, and things like that. Now and then one of them would go to a small keyboard and punch up something. Then they would both mutter over the resulting printout. Finally one of them kicked back his chair and began to pace the room.

"I see how we might be able to pull this off."

"How's that?" I should have kept my mouth shut. They both glared at me, then bent back over the table.

"There used to be an operation in early FORTRAN called a DO loop. The idea was that a subroutine could be set up to repeat until some limit or result was reached. Like testing an equation by substituting all the numbers between one and one hundred for constants. You didn't have to write one hundred instructions. Just use a DO loop with one hundred as the upper limit. The equation would be solved and one hundred solutions printed out. Nobody uses that anymore, but if we could slip one in after the instruction regarding intent, maybe we could give the idea many times the weight it would normally have. That might be enough to swing it."

The other nodded. "Why not? There's nothing else going for us."

Back in the courtlab, we all rose, and we all sat; then the prosecutor got up for his summary. Most of it was about programs, routines, and weighted averages. He did a good job. Minus the buzz words though, one thing came through very clear: I was guilty as hell. Then my team got the green light, and it was more of the same. I think I saw him enter the DO loop. There was one time when his hands were awfully busy, while he wasn't saying much. The prosecutor was frowning about something.

Finally it was all over. The last entry was in. The green lights were gone, and a big yellow one on the main panel came on. The tapes were all going at once, and the indicators were a blur. After about a minute, a printer clattered briefly and was silent. The tape decks all switched to fast rewind. Everyone sat quiet for a moment, then the clerk stood up and headed for the printer, where he tore off a strip of paper. He handed it to the judge without even a peek. I held my breath. My attorney drew more doodles. The judge took the slip, then, with his eyes fixed firmly on the statue of Justice, he announced the verdict.

"The computed verdict finds the defendant innocent of all charges. The electron knows no favorites."

I let out my breath in a rush and jumped to my feet. The prosecutor was up too, shouting.

"Your Honor, I appeal this verdict as provided for in the master file of court procedures."

The heavy hand was on my shoulder again, and a voice told me to sit down.

The judge nodded. "Granted," he said, and bang went the gavel. The clerk did something to his panel, and we had a yellow light again.

"Now what?" I wanted to know.

My attorney looked around. "There has been an appeal. The appellate court will review your case." I felt honored. He had actually spoken to me. Might as well keep him talking.

"Where are they? Are they here too?"

"No. They're probably playing golf right about now."

"But . . ." I nodded toward the yellow light.

"Oh, that. Their Honors have all been on record since they were appointed to the bench. They just stop by in the morning for an emotional index reading, and the appellate computer takes it from there. We're linking up with it right now."

As he spoke, one tape spun briskly, then stopped. Another wait. I munched a mangled thumbnail and watched the flashing lights. They stopped, and the printer clattered again. Once more the clerk tore off the paper and handed it to the bench. The judge looked, then nodded. This time, he looked straight at me.

"Decision reversed, by a vote of six to one. Counsel for the defense is commended for a job well done." My team nodded and smiled. "The prisoner will rise." This time I was hauled to my feet.

The judge began to punch some buttons on his own private

console. Twice he shook his head and made some more entries. Finally he nodded.

"Leonard Verst, in accordance with the laws, programs, and procedures of this state, you have been found guilty of the crime of alteration. You are accordingly sentenced to a term of thirty days, these days to be served consecutively as a member of the jury of this court."

As the gavel banged for the last time, a flicker of motion at the bench caught my eye. I glanced up at the jury. The left-hand face had been changed. I was staring into my own eyes, and I was not smiling.

THE HOUSE BY THE SEA

She only wanted to be alone with her melancholy
there in the windswept house beside the sea with
her troglodytes and her holovision, but alas, her
sensitive nature could not ignore the burning need
of Craig—and Ricardo, and Ming, and Harry: until,
one storm-swept night . . .

Eleanor Arnason

I was happy enough in the old house by the sea before Craig
returned. Many people would have minded the almost continual
mists and the sound of the sea below the house, the grating roar
of pebbles which the waves sucked back and flung, at their return,
up the high strand. Not to speak of the noises the troglodytes
made at night in the basement. But I had lived in the house my
whole life, as had my ancestors for half a millennium. I felt comfortable walking on the great stone terrace, wrapped in a warm
cloak of grumbler fur, hearing the sea's slow, tremulous cadence
far below.

Of course my heart had been broken that night, two years
before, when Craig had stepped into the transmitter and disappeared, forever I had thought. There'd been a thunderstorm, and
my troglodytes had been nervous, padding restlessly around the
house, their silver-grey fur standing on end. I'd begged Craig not

to go. The new settlers and the city dwellers don't believe the troglodytes are psychic, but we who belong to the old families know they are.

Craig had shaken his head, his dark face set and stern. He had decided to go to Newport that day, and go he would. He believed that a person should give in to circumstances as little as possible. Into the glassite box he stepped, and activated the machine. At that moment, lightning struck the house. The lights went out. I heard a great crack of thunder directly overhead. Then the auxiliary generator came on. The lights glowed, dimmed, brightened, and I saw that Craig was gone. Worried, I called the main transmission station in Newport. Craig had not arrived there.

"Oh, no!" I cried, and fell to the floor in a faint.

When I awoke, a man was bending over me: tall and slender and silver-haired, though his face was unlined. His eyes were an extraordinary bright blue.

"Are you all right?" he asked me.

"Yes," I said, and he helped me to my feet.

In that manner I met Ricardo. Ah, that summer! He was a troubleshooter for the transit service, and he kept coming back to check my transmitter. First he took it apart, hoping to find Craig in the storage matrix. Then he checked the transmitting mast from top to bottom. Then he checked the house's electrical system. Everything was in order, he said. Craig had apparently transmitted just as the lightning struck and the power went off. Either the lightning had garbled the transmitter signal, or there hadn't been enough power to transmit the signal to its destination. Craig was gone forever.

By midsummer Ricardo and I were in love. *Poor Craig,* I thought, wandering hand in hand with Ricardo along the stony shore. But least said, soonest mended. Ricardo and I embraced in the mist at the sea's edge, our ears full of the waves' melancholy, long, withdrawing roar.

Early in the fall Ricardo was transferred to another district on the other side of the planet, and I met Ming at a party in Newport.

Half Chinese, he was stocky and broad-shouldered, brown-eyed and brown-haired. He was a collateral descendant of Mao Tse-tung and the present head of the family, paid by the state to return to Earth every several years and perform certain necessary rites of ancestor worship. He and I stayed together all winter, spending our days on one or another of the Pearl Islands, which were halfway around the planet from my house. We swam in the warm water and basked in the sun on shimmering, pearl-grey beaches. In the jungle behind us, birds darted from branch to branch of the flowering bloodroot trees. Out in the lagoon, broad-backed grumblers sometimes surfaced and made loud grunting and mumbling noises. Our nights were spent at my house, while the wind moaned around the old stone walls and snow whirled down onto the terrace. My faithful troglodytes brought us baked apples and hot wine. A fire burned in the fireplace. Warmed by it, we embraced, and my troglodyte musicians played water drums and chimes.

After Ming came Harry, a red-headed oceanologist. With him I spent the spring and summer, commuting daily between my house and his submersible laboratory. What nights we spent in the ocean's depths! Beyond the laboratory's portholes, deep-sea fishes glowed. I brought him brightly colored mosses and lichens from my rock garden and shells from the shore below my house. He gave me hard, delicate pieces of sea lace which his nets had dragged off the ocean floor.

We kissed and parted in the fall, and I was alone for a while, except for my faithful troglodytes. I stayed home a lot that winter, troubled by melancholy and the sense that life was passing me by. Those were dark months. Even the merry antics of my troglodyte tumblers couldn't cheer me. The house seemed cold and drafty, though it had excellent central heating. I took up embroidery to help pass the time, took holovision courses in Amerindian cooking and flower arranging, and tried to get the family library in order. Nothing helped. I remained as melancholy as ever.

With spring came hope, however. My spirits lifted, and I set to work in my rock garden. One by one, my plants revived. The scarlet parasols opened their round red leaves and tilted them toward the sun, and the silverspears thrust their white, slender stalks up through the sandy soil. My troglodytes cavorted on the terrace on nights when the mist cleared and the moons were visible: three tiny yellow disks lighting the dark sea.

Early in the summer Craig returned, my stern, bold, starfaring lover, back from the dead.

The night before he came back, my troglodytes were nervous and wandered through the house, mewing. They clutched at my hands with their small, soft, furry hands and stared up at me with huge dark eyes. What could it mean? I wondered. Restless myself, I walked on the terrace. The sea was calm that night. The tide was full, and the three moons shone. North and south of me, I saw the cliffs that stood, glimmering and vast, out in the tranquil bay.

I went to bed finally, but couldn't sleep, got up and walked again on the terrace. At dawn I went to sleep.

I woke late in the morning, when someone shook my shoulder. Opening my eyes, I saw Craig. I gasped and passed out. I woke again when he slapped my face. I said something silly, such as "You're dead."

He grinned and shook his head. "No, no, my love."

I sat up and looked at him. His face was unchanged, but his body was entirely different. Or had I forgotten him so completely? It wasn't possible. The Craig I remembered was tall and thin and muscular, a keen-looking sword blade of a man. This fellow was squatty and apelike, with too-long arms and too-short legs. He grinned again. "It took two years of surgery to get this result, my love. You should've seen me before."

"What happened?"

He shrugged. "All I know is I came out in Landingtown instead of Newport. Half crazy, with half my memory gone, and my body looking like—" He shrugged again. "Something went wrong with the transmission, obviously. Well, that's done and I'm back." He bent and kissed me lightly on the lips. I drew back.

"Oh, no," he said, and grasped my shoulders. I saw his hands as they came toward me. They had no little fingers. Craig pulled me toward him and kissed me again, this time ruthlessly.

"Why didn't anyone tell me you were still alive?" I asked after he let me go.

"I asked them not to. I didn't want to see you. I remembered enough to know I hadn't looked that way before."

I realized with sudden outrage that Ricardo must have known what had happened to Craig. He had told me he was looking for Craig in my transmitter's storage matrix, when he had known perfectly well that Craig was in the hospital in Landingtown. *What perfidy!* I thought.

I got up and we had breakfast in the sunroom, my troglodytes serving us, their grey fur all abristle. There was no sunlight that morning. A grey mist swirled outside the glassite windows, and the clear panes were beaded with water. The sea was quiet. I could hear the fountain at the other end of the room gurgling softly, surrounded by pots of azalias. When we were done eating, Craig leaned back in his chair and sipped at a final cup of coffee. "I got invalided out of the space service. After they finished putting my mind back together, I couldn't pass the psych tests. So here I am."

"Why?" I asked, sipping at my own café au lait.

He grinned. He hadn't smiled that way before, I thought. This smile was twisted and wry. There were lines around his eyes now, and his face was a little thinner, so there were hollows below his high cheekbones. "What else do I have?"

I set down my cup. "I don't want you to stay, Craig."

"I have to. The transmitter's no longer working."

"What! Why?"

"When I arrived, you were asleep and your troglodytes were all in the basement. I shorted the transmitter refrigeration unit. By this time, the transmitter brain ought to be too hot to function."

"I'd better call a repairperson," I said, and stood up. "The radiophone isn't working either."

I looked across the table at Craig, who was still sipping at his coffee, and I thought about asking my troglodytes to take care of him. But troglodytes are a peaceful folk, which is why they have disappeared from most parts of the planet. They survive only where there are old houses, and members of the old families able to protect them.

What could I do? I sat down and asked my troglodytes to bring me more café au lait. Craig grinned. "One of the things I've always liked about you, Lucia, is your calmness."

After breakfast Craig said he wanted to walk on the beach. I got my grumbler-fur cloak and a brooch an ancestor of mine had found three hundred years before, lying on a beach on a distant planet. There had been no other signs of intelligent life anywhere on the planet. The brooch was a gold disk, engraved with strange characters. I used it to fasten the cloak and we went outside. The mist had lifted a little, and I could see smooth, dark-grey billows coming slowly in to break against the grey gravel beach. I was, of course, afraid. What was this strange, new Craig planning? Was he dangerous?

"What are you planning?" I asked.

Craig stopped, turned and stared at me. I was sure that his eyes had been dark brown before. Now they were light brown, almost yellow. "I don't know," he said after a moment. He put his hands on my shoulders and pulled me toward him, murmuring, "Ah, love, let us be true to one another." He kissed me. For a moment I remembered I had loved him once and returned the kiss. When he let me go, he laughed. "That's better."

We walked farther down the beach. Craig kept hold of my hand. At last we turned back. What I needed, I thought, was a weapon. There was my grandfather's collection of death rays and shock whips, which covered the wall above the big fireplace, but it had been a century since they had been recharged. Why hadn't I taken karate or kung fu? Then I remembered that Craig was a black belt in everything. I sighed.

We went back into the house, and I fixed an Aztec luncheon while Craig wandered around. My troglodytes were still upset and pattered around the kitchen, mewing sadly while they helped me. Was there worse to come?

"The flower arrangements are new," he said when he came back. "And all that sea lace. Are you starting a collection?"

"No," I said, and set food on the table.

After lunch we made love, if love is the right word, in the red bedroom. It had always been Craig's favorite room. When we were done, he went to sleep. I got up and took a shower. I considered getting a knife out of the kitchen and stabbing him while he slept. But I've always been squeamish. I put on a houserobe with a band of embroidery around the bottom that I'd done myself and went back to look at Craig. He was still asleep. One arm was outside the covers. I looked at the abnormally long forearm and the four-fingered hand. I sighed and went down to the kitchen. There were several troglodytes there, cleaning up. They came over and touched my hands gently and looked up at me. "It's all right," I said, though it wasn't, and the troglodytes, being psychic, knew it. I got myself a snifter of brandy and took it to the sunroom. How long would it be before someone tried to reach me and couldn't? How long before a repair crew was sent out? What would Craig do then? The sunroom ceiling glowed, giving the plants the sunlight they needed. I sat down in the shade of a potted palm.

He would have to go back to the hospital, of course. The doctors had done a terrible job of putting him back together. Could he sue them? I wondered. I was certain that I could sue them, and I intended to. He should not have been let out in his condition. That was negligence, if I ever saw it. My troglodytes brought me more brandy and made soft growling sounds which were intended to reassure and comfort me. I smiled at them, patted them and said it was all right. After they left, I looked out the windows. It was raining. Drops of water ran down the panes. The mist was so thick that I couldn't see the parapet on the other side of the terrace. Craig ought to be able to sue the transit service, I thought. Or was the lightning an act of God? In any case, that wasn't my problem. I drank the brandy.

Shortly thereafter, Craig came looking for me. He stopped when he saw me and grinned. "I thought you might've run away."

Now why hadn't I thought of that? It would not be easy, of course. There were barren mountains on three sides of the house, and no other habitations for a hundred kilometers. On the fourth side was the unplumbed, salt, estranging sea. Would it be possible to escape Craig in the mountains and stay alive there till help came? I wasn't sure.

Craig went and got some brandy, coming back to sit beside me. "How long are you planning to stay?" I asked.

He shrugged and cupped his hands around the snifter, warming the brandy. "Are you so eager to get rid of me, Lucia?"

I looked at his worn, weary-looking face. *Poor fellow,* I thought.

There's no more dangerous emotion than pity, except guilt, of course. Both make you put up with intolerable situations. "No. I'm not," I said softly and took hold of his hand. He smiled and set down the brandy snifter. We kissed.

That afternoon we walked on the beach again. At night, we slept in the crystal bedroom, which was my favorite room. The ceiling shone and shifted like a kaleidoscope. Multicolored gleams of light slid over the glassite furniture. The floor was silver. My troglodytes, calm at last, brought us glasses of cold wine and clusters of crystallized grapes. When I woke in the morning I heard Craig singing in the shower. That at least was unchanged. He couldn't carry a tune any more now than he could before.

I spent the morning working in my rock garden and the afternoon making an Aztec dinner. In the evening my troglodytes entertained us with music and tumbling. When they were done, Craig put a music cube into the player. I turned off the ceiling. We danced in the firelight, one of the old, slow dances that were coming back again, after I forget how many centuries. When we started to get tired, we went up to the red bedroom.

Early the next morning the repair crew came in a fanwing that landed on the beach below the house. Neither of us woke till they rang my doorbell. That woke me. I rose and put my robe on. Craig groaned, rolled over and sat up. I kissed him good morning, then went down to let the repair crew in. They asked me what had happened to my transmitter. I told them, and they called the law service. A few minutes later the cops arrived. They found Craig in the silver bathroom, shaving in front of the mirror wall, and they arrested him and took him away.

EUCLID ALONE

Which is more important: the truth, or an error
that holds the whole world together?

William F. Orr

1

The elevator was passing the tenth floor when Dr. Donald Lucus
started from his reverie into the panic of embarrassment he always felt when he had passed his floor unknowingly. His mind
shifted with reluctance from one program to another as it was
drawn to the demand for a decision by the illusion of a sudden
decrease in gravity that indicated the elevator would stop on the
eleventh floor. He would have approximately ten seconds to
decide. He could stay on this elevator, possibly all the way to the
twenty-fifth floor, and get off at six on the way down, wasting a
large but certain amount of his time, resulting in only a brief
moment of embarrassment before unknown engineers on the top
floor, who would realize his foolish mistake when he remained in
the elevator, who would smile and wonder why this absent-

230

minded old fellow hadn't been retired by the Institute yet. Or he
could get off now, at eleven, and wait for the next down elevator
to take him to his own floor. Again, it would be apparent to the
secretary at Genetics that he had gone by his floor, and he would
be aware of her, sitting behind him at her desk, thinking he had
been a section head much too long and ought to be replaced. As
an alternative, he could resort to subterfuge and walk down the
hall to knock on the door of an empty office, pretending that he
had legitimate business there.

But he had neither the will nor the energy to act out such a
pantomime, when his mind needed urgently to be occupied with
another problem, which it had been drawn away from by this
trivial face-saving decisionmaking. In the end, he decided that
getting off at eleven would waste less time than any other course
of action, and that was, after all, the most important consideration.

As it was, he made this decision too late to avoid another
embarrassment, that of being hammered on both sides by the
elevator doors as he stepped out, while the secretary of Genetics
looked up and smiled. An automatic mumbled "Pardon me"
crossed his lips as he pulled free of the gentle vise-grip and
turned self-consciously to push the down button.

Only then could he relax and let his mind sink back to
the complex but ordered patterns of proof which were its
true medium. And that order had form quite as real as the
world of elevator buttons and social ineptitude, of old men
and young men and publishing deadlines and hiring policies.
There was an intricate structure made entirely of straight lines
in a plane that intersected in named points and formed identifiable triangles, all related to one another by a carefully chosen
pattern of congruences, similarities, and equal sides and
angles.

This structure had been built very carefully to its present state
by a process of repetitive partial construction. All the way along
the freeway he had occupied himself with the task of mentally

rebuilding the structure which he had spent almost the whole night examining. He would begin each time at the same starting point, building one line at a time, noting each label, each equality and similarity, until the structure reached a degree of complexity, as it did each time, that exceeded his ability to assimilate new information and which became manifest in the sudden complete loss of.a necessary fact. At this point the only possibility was to begin again at the foundation. Each time, he got a little farther in the proof, and while it might seem at first a most inefficient method of construction, it would eventually result, not only in a completed proof, but also, and more importantly, in a complete intuitive familiarity with that proof, both in its overall conception and in all its particulars.

It was a learning method that Dr. Lucus could remember having employed successfully for over forty years, and even his loss of mental agility resulted only in a longer amount of time spent with any one proof and not in any loss of total comprehension once the process was completed.

He had taken temporary comfortable refuge in the beauty and symmetry of this proof, which he could do now, shutting out all thought of the threat, the horror of its ultimate implications. The four cups of coffee kept him awake and uncomfortably numb to the eventual attack on his one sure foothold on reality. He stepped into the elevator and forcibly turned his thoughts from what he must do in the next few hours. For he was not certain what he must, could, or wanted to do. Too many roads were open to him, and they all seemed to lead to eventual dead ends. But that was only, as Hans used to tell him, his own lack of imagination, his lack of initiative to build his own road. So be it. As he began once more to piece together his elusive triangles, he was aware more than anything of the face of the secretary of Genetics, frozen in the last narrow inch between the closing elevator doors, smiling at an old, absentminded man who held in his mind the cursèd flame of destruction of this whole temple of reason.

If Ruth was aware of the worn, drugged look of his eyes and face when he entered the Math office, she did not betray this. She turned from her typing, pulled her glasses down on her nose, and regarded him with what she supposed was a friendly smile, as she always did. After the obligatory good-mornings, he paused, trying to force efficiency into his reflexes, confused over what were to be his instructions to her.

"Uh, Ruth," he began at length, "Ruth, would you get the Director on the line for me?"

"The Director, sir?"

She was not, in fact, asking for confirmation, only registering surprise. Dr. Lucus seldom had any contact with the Director, except at executive board meetings. When he did contact the Director, it was always through interoffice memo, and Ruth had shown her surprise at this breach of tradition before she had a chance to check herself. One telephoned subordinates and colleagues. One wrote to superiors.

"Uh, yes, Ruth, it's rather important."

Was there something else to say to Ruth? He had to call Publications, but that could wait until after he got the go-ahead from the Director.

"Oh, uh, Ruth, is the mail in yet?"

"No, sir, but there was a telegram. It's on your desk." She was impatient to get back to her typing, impatient with his slow talk and his hesitation. But she would not return to work until he left the room. Office etiquette was her one comfort in this job.

"Oh, uh, thank you, Ruth." He turned to his office. At the door he paused a moment, as she said, in accordance with custom, "Would you like me to bring you a cup of coffee?"

He had anticipated the question, so his answer was immediate —in fact, clumsily abrupt. "No, thank you, Ruth."

As the door swung shut, the steady patter of her machine resumed. She would type one page to allow him time to take off his coat and get settled. She would sip her own lukewarm cup of coffee, which she nursed for three hours every morning, and then turn to the telephone. Her wrinkled face would show no sign of the joy she felt at hearing her own crisp, stiff voice conducting business efficiently and properly.

His hand was strangely empty as he took off his coat. He had left his briefcase in the car.

"Damn," he muttered. That meant he would have to go back for it during his lunch hour. He would definitely need to have the papers in it before he saw the Director. In fact, he had wanted to review Professor David's paper this morning and to check the mental construction he had prepared in the car. In any case, he would need the paper itself before he could run a computer check on the validity of the proof.

All these trivial irritations made it even more difficult to see through the haze of a sleepless night that he was caught up in something historic, in something frightening. He was not made for scrapping a lifetime of firmly held beliefs in a day, as Hans was. He was not made to be forced suddenly and rudely into a crucial position of responsibility. Hans could handle that sort of thing; he could not. Hans could submerge himself in madness and come up smiling, happy and sane. But for Donald Lucus madness, if it came, would be the end. He rested a hand on Hans's sculpture as he sat at the desk. In the outer office, the sound of typing stopped.

There was a thin wire human figure suspended inside a cage, which was formed by the edges of an irregular icosahedron, slightly skewed on its axis. Two edges of the polyhedron were broken, and the figure was falling, one hand stretched out vainly toward an edge, a bar of the cage. Its mouth was open.

"This," the artist had said to him years before over a game of Go, "this is you, Don. Not now. This is you at sixty-five. This is you and your twenty-faced monster and your quintic equation. I want you to save it for your old age and then tell me if I'm right."

He had clicked the cigarette holder between his teeth and grinned that diabolical smile that always dared you to guess whether he was joking or serious.

"Look at it, Don. And when you finally recognize yourself,
write and let me know."

The telegram was brief and clear.

DON.

HANS DIED OF A STROKE FRIDAY. BETH ASKED ME TO LET YOU KNOW. FUNERAL
WEDNESDAY AT ONE ST. PAULS, CINCINNATI. WILL NOT BE THERE AS THINK
THAT WOULD BE BETTER FOR BETH. HOPE YOU CAN THOUGH. MUCH LOVE.
                                                                  MARY

"Dr. Lucus, I have the Director's secretary on the line. The
Director will not be in until ten this morning. His schedule is full
today, but I can make an appointment for you Tuesday afternoon."

Tuesday afternoon. He set the telegram down and covered his
eyes to think. Tuesday afternoon. He could make an appointment
for Tuesday afternoon, and that would give him another day to
relax, another day before he really had to do anything about the
situation. But no, that was impossible. He couldn't put it off, and
he couldn't *be* put off. Of course, he must see the Director immediately.

"Dr. Lucus?"

"Uh, yes, yes, Ruth. Uh, thank you, but I really must talk to the
Director as soon as he comes in. It's . . . it's quite important.
Would you leave a message for him to call me? It's very high
priority, Ruth." He thought high priority sounded better than
urgent, more professional. It was a term the Director would probably use.

"Yes, sir. Will that be all?" There was only a faint sign of
reproach in her voice for this break with tradition.

"No, that's all, Ruth. Thank you."

But there was more. There was much more he had to do before
lunch.

"Wait! Ruth? Ruth, would you get Publications on the phone?
I want to speak to Jack Hudson. That's right. Thank you, Ruth."

He sat frozen behind his desk. He had to talk to Hudson and
stop today's mailing, to recall any copies that had already been

sent out, to hold them until someone could make a final decision.
Someone. He should run a check on the computer, and a projection too. Ordering these things in his mind was a difficult task.
There were too many factors to tell what to do first. The whole
pattern of his schedule was torn, and he had left his damn briefcase with that damn paper in the car. Construct angle $F'G'H =$
angle $GG'B$. Then, if AJ is dropped perpendicular to BG from
A, $BJ = AJ$ and $BG = F'H$. Thus triangle ABG is congruent to
. . . is congruent to . . . He rose, rushed to the blackboard, and
began drawing furiously, attacking that hideous proof directly,
headlong. He *must* find a fallacy. It *must* be false. He drew in three
colors of chalk, erasing and redrawing segments in new propor-
tions, stepping back across the room to view his diagram from a
distance, making quick notations on the back of the piece of
yellow paper on his desk, pacing the room jerkily and returning
to the board to scowl, erase, and redraw. He hardly noticed it
when Ruth buzzed to tell him Hudson was on the line. He strode
to the desk, one eye on the board, and surprised himself by his
handling of the situation.

Was the autumn number of the *Quarterly Mathematics Publications
of the Federal Basic Research Institute* ready for mailing? Good, hold
it until further notice. No, no serious problem. A rather important error that would have to be corrected. A paper might have
to be removed. Had any copies been sent out? Five review copies
had gone out earlier. Please have them recalled. As soon as
possible, yes. Lucus himself would write to the *American Mathematical Monthly*. No, it wasn't a serious problem. It would be
rather difficult to explain to a nonmathematician. Thank you very
much for your cooperation, Mr. Hudson. Terribly sorry to cause
your department all this bother. Yes, thank you. Good-bye, Mr.
Hudson.

It took only a moment at the blackboard to regain his balance,
to recover his position. His construction started at the bottom,
spread out on both sides, and then began climbing upward, just
as it had in David's paper. Like some sort of tower. That's what

Hans would call it, if he were here. A tower of matchsticks, something like that. Then he would insist that he was going to do a painting of it. And he might, in fact. It was rather attractive, quite nicely symmetric. The whole picture had a neat look of innocence about it, as if it were nothing more than a new proof of the Pythagorean Theorem, for example. Hans would call it "The Tower That Demolished the Tower" or something like that and find the irony of it hilariously funny. The destruction of centuries of mathematical thought would mean nothing to him. It was a joke. A joke on Lucus, a confirmation of everything Hans had said over those interminable Tuesday-night games of Go.

As the tower neared its peak, it became increasingly obvious to Dr. Lucus that the proof was correct, that there was no fallacy. After six times through it, he could no longer tell himself he was not following it well enough, that he would see the obvious hole in the logic the next time through. David had been meticulous, he had left out no steps. His paper was densely written and quite thorough. Euclidean geometry was not Donald Lucus' field. He was not used to its methods of proof. But by now he could feel each lemma and corollary of David's Theorem in his guts. He knew it was true. Only a computer confirmation remained.

He called the computer office and arranged for some time that evening, asked for three tapes to be sent to his office: first, CØN-PRØØF 2: Confirmation of the consistency of a proof in a mathematical axiom system given as a subroutine; second, EUBERT: Hilbert's axioms for Euclidean geometry, subroutine for CØN-PRØØF 2; and finally, LØBACHEVMANN: Lobachevskian and Riemannian geometries, subroutine for use with CØNPRØØF 2.

Then he called the head of the computer division and explained that he wanted to run a social projection later in the week. The man was incredulous—and amused.

"In Math?" he asked.

"Yes," replied Lucus. "And I want the problem and the output to be considered Limited Interest."

The man paused only a second at the other end of the line, his mouth hanging open an inch from the receiver.

"I . . . I'll have to have an okay from the Director on that first, but all right, I'll see what I can keep open for you Friday night."

Lucus thanked him and hung up. His palms were covered with sweat. The use of the term "Limited Interest" had frightened him and impressed on him the seriousness of the thing he was doing. There was no classified research at the FBRI; its fundamental philosophy was one of "basic research in a free and open environment." All the work done in the building or under FBRI grants was published and widely disseminated. However, it occasionally became clear to the Institute officials that certain results could prove dangerous in one way or another if prematurely released to the public or to the scientific community at large. Therefore the code "Limited Interest" had been developed to refer to such work: unclassified, but kept strictly under wraps.

It was nine thirty, and he had done all he could until he talked to the Director. The tower stood flat against the blackboard, a dead, crystalline, cutting blade of red and blue and orange. Outside the window, a squirrel darted along a branch and vanished down one of its countless customary routes in the maze of almost leafless branches. The Institute was built into the side of a hill, so that Dr. Lucus' office, which was on the sixth floor if seen from the front, actually appeared to be no higher than the third floor. He had a peaceful view of grass and sky, held fast by the swift, layered lattice of branches. Often he felt that he did his best thinking while he was standing here, running his eyes peacefully along the branching lines, like one of Kaufmann's illustrations in *Graphs, Dynamic Programming, and Finite Games.* But today he could not think in leisure. The soap-white walls that rose to enfold his world were too close now, and he was trapped, trapped and falling.

He did have one thing left to do, although he did not feel like seeing Ruth. It must be done, and it would give his mind something to grasp until he could talk to the Director. He had her come in, and he dictated a polite letter, a bit too long, to the editor of the AMM, explaining that an embarrassing error had crept into the fall *Quarterly* and asking that it be returned, so that it could be replaced by a corrected copy.

As Ruth got up to go, her steno pad pushed the yellow paper off his desk to the floor. He bent to pick it up and smoothed it on his desk, staring blankly at the calculations on the back. His watch said 10:05.

At ten fifteen he still sat, frozen, his eyes open and filled with the erected sword shape plastered flat against the blackboard. It was cutting deep into his retinas, but his mind was suspended in dreamless waking sleep that numbed the wound and held him in inanimate rigid repose. Solidity of metal and wood near him and touching him melted, and only the neat impersonal sword hung above, simple, clear, no longer threatening, neutral now as all things were within the asbestos web which held him.

He had to force his head down, to force his eyes to see the desk, the wrinkled yellow on white metal. To force his arm up, pull back the sleeve, and decide to act. Only then did his focus return, caught by the jittering watch, and then the office took clear familiar shape again around him. And fear returned.

"Ruth? Would you call the Director's office again and see if he's in yet?"

When the Director finally came on the line, he was curt and impatient. He didn't like to be bothered by petty problems; Lucus knew that.

"It's really quite urgent. I don't like to upset your schedule, but I'm afraid it can't wait until tomorrow, sir."

"Well, what is it in Math that you can't handle yourself, Lucus?" His voice was overamplified by the receiver, and there was no comfortable position for it. "If there are problems with funds or payroll, that shouldn't be handled through my office. I should think you would be able to take care of your own distribution of grants."

"Well, no, sir, it's a more important problem than that. It's research that I feel needs . . . uh . . . special attention. I mean there seem to be possible . . . possible dangers in publication of certain discoveries."

"In math, Lucus? You're exaggerating. What sort of research in math could produce . . . uh, dangers? I mean, you're surely getting carried away with your formulas, aren't you?"

"I'd rather not discuss it over the phone, sir. It is of rather . . . of rather Limited Interest."

"Oh?" Lucus could feel the younger man's eyebrows rising. "What sort of 'Limited Interest,' Dr. Lucus?"

"If I could make an appointment, sir . . ."

"My schedule is terribly busy, Dr. Lucus, and I don't see how I can fit in another appointment—unless you will tell me the nature of the problem."

Lucus was not ready for this, not ready to reveal to anyone else the secret that, as far as he knew, he alone shared with Professor Paul David. He had not thought this far. He would have to tell another man the horrible thing that had been discovered, the horrible thing that had lain in wait for discovery all these centuries. His face covered with sweat, his hand sticky against the plastic receiver, he controlled his voice as much as he could and said, "A disproof of Euclid, sir. One of our fundees has produced a proof of the inconsistency of Euclid . . . that Euclid is not true, *cannot* be true . . ."

There was no reply, no sound. He didn't know if the Director was as shocked as he, or if he was incredulous, unable to believe such a thing. Did he perhaps share Hans's sense of the cosmic joke of the whole thing? Was he smiling with the chemist's triumphant smile at the defeat of the abstract theoretician? How would any man react to such knowledge? Lucus decided that the Director did not believe him, that no man could accept such a horrifying conclusion without rigid proof. Surely he himself had spent two days and sleepless nights in the attempt to shake the unshakable conclusion. Finally the voice answered. It was a short answer and made its point perfectly clear.

"Is that all? I think you should be able to clear that up by yourself, Lucus. After all, I don't know much about math, and I don't see why you have to bring it to my attention."

And that was it. He was unimpressed. It meant nothing to him.

"I think, sir, that it is very important that I explain the problem to you in more detail."

"All right, Lucus, all right. Come by at three, will you? I have an important call on the other line. Sorry, I have to hang up. At three."

The sigh of resignation in his voice had been almost theatrical. He hated to be bothered with petty departmental problems.

Dr. Lucus cradled his head in his arms on the desk, shaking uncontrollably with the release of tension, still alone in his fear and in his knowledge.

2

"Don, you're using strategy again. It's the same strategy; it's a textbook play." Hans Kaefig blew a thick puff of smoke at the stilled Go board. "Blurd your vision a little, Donnie. Come on, find a play that doesn't have a proverb to go with it."

Hans leaned back in his chair, hands behind his head, cigarette holder rising out of his bushy grey beard like a radius vector tracing minute burning circles in the air. He closed his eyes tight in a pantomime of cogitation. "What you need to do, Donnie, what you need to do is . . ."

Don smiled and fumbled with his pipe. He knew Hans could go on like this all night, fighting his own eternal battle with rational thought out loud, using Don's career as his battlefield, giving him advice, often self-contradictory, on how to break from the confines of Aristotelean logic and soar like a bird on the soul of his intellect. Or the intellect of his soul. The words varied proportionally to the amount of brandy consumed every Tuesday.

". . . what you need, Donnie, is to state a theorem without a proof—with no hope of a proof. Write a paper, Don, with ten or twenty wild, impossible theorems and lemmas and corollaries—no proofs . . . absurd theorems. I'll help you. I'll give you some ideas, you can rewrite them to sound mathematical. We'll publish them—inside a year someone will have proved half of them, done all the work, but they'll all be called Lucus' Theorem or Kaefig's Conjecture—and we'll have it made."

"Wouldn't work, Hans. No one would publish them without proof."

"Well, then—we'll publish it as a novel. That's it, a novel. You write the theorems, I'll write the sex. We'll call it *Propositional Calculus,* and start a rumor that it was written under drugs. We can cut the verbs out of all the sentences and make it look all Burroughs-y. That's the way to do mathematics, Don. Get out of the mainstream . . . underground math . . . subversive topology, that should be your field, luv."

"Hans, I appreciate your help with my career—"

"It's only that I pity you—I'm determined to make an artist of you, if you don't make me into a scientist first."

"Now have I tried to do that?"

"Oh, you're subtle, Donnie. You're subtle. And that's what I'm not. You can see my plan of action right away. But you—well, you just leave those books lying around open so I'll sneak a peek. You try to draw me to those dirty pictures: a truncated cube, a stellated dodecawhatsit, two pyramids stuck through each other . . . it's warping my brain. I go to my studio and find my mind all hung up in your simply connected sets and those tragic asymptotic curves—Tantalus damned to approach without reaching forever. What can I do? You have told me a doughnut is a coffee cup, and I have believed you. I used to paint the city and garbage and reality. Now all I know are points in space. I dream each night of being trapped in Königsberg, forever recrossing those bridges, while Euler stands by the river and laughs. Oh, don't deny it, Don. You are slowly turning me into what you are, enveloping me in symbolic logic and set theory. And I keep coming back and asking for more."

"And why do you come back?" asked Don, finishing off his brandy.

"Ah, you force me to say it! You are my muse, Professor Lucus. Without you my art would die. Without you, my dear friend, I would paint only the city and garbage and reality."

"Oh . . . I thought Mary was your muse."

"Mary? Of course not. A muse must be unobtainable, mysterious, the artist's opposite, the soul of what he can never be. You might as well say I am Mary's muse. After all, she did dedicate a quartet to me. Am I flattered? No. We're getting divorced this year, or next year—whenever there's time."

"You're not serious, Hans!" Don hated the terrible uncertainty. In fact, he never did know when Hans was serious about *any* subject.

"Of course I am. It was her idea. Or maybe it was mine. Anyway, we talked it over and thought it would be fun. But now you've sidetracked me. I was explaining your role in my art. Ever since I started playing Go over here, look how I've improved. Look at that sketch I did of your continuous function theorem. The critics love it. They think I'm a genius."

"It's ugly, you know. It's really ugly." As much as he liked Hans, Don had never been able really to appreciate any of his work. He found it childish, simple, and sometimes repulsive. Since Hans had begun basing his things on diagrams in Don's math books, he liked them even less. They seemed to make art lifeless and mathematics unprincipled.

"Yes, it is," agreed Hans. "Very ugly. And you see, before you inspired me I'd never been able to paint anything quite that ugly. I'd tried . . . Lord, I have as good a sense of what is offensive to the eye as any other artist, but I'd never been able to put it down on canvas. I would walk around in the slums and look at the *dreck* in the alleys and think it was ugly. I would eat starch sandwiches at the Automat and wipe my beard with a used napkin and think that was ugly. But then when I looked into your Hocking and Young and saw that wild sphere—I knew I had found it! I knew other men had seen the true vision, and I could learn from them."

"You're crazy, Kaefig," Don intoned, shaking his head.

Hans clicked his teeth against his empty cigarette holder and drew a pack of Camels from the pocket of his Levi jacket. "You've said that ever since college, my dear Professor, and it hasn't made it any less true, you smug sane bastard. Let's put away the game and get drunk. I think I've done quite enough to try to save your soul for one night."

And so it went for over seven years, from Don's thirty-eighth birthday deep into his forties, until Hans and Mary finally split up and he moved to the Midwest.

And Don never tired of his friend's harangues, because he knew there was something important there, something he should hear. And so he listened to all the nonsense and rambling, trying to sift out the bit of informational content, the little he could really learn from Hans.

Mary had been hired as conductor of the Denver Symphony, and Don had heard little from either of them since, except for sporadic Christmas cards. He had left teaching to come to the Institute at fifty-five, and there he had remained, sitting—how had Hans put it?—sitting on top of that pile of elephant tusks, lord of what little he surveyed.

A few years ago, a journalist had interviewed Dr. Lucus, because Hans had said he was the only man who could explain his sculpture *Ragtime Band,* that sprawling monstrosity that was the culmination of his fascination with the wild sphere in Hocking and Young and, according to many critics, the culmination of his career.

And now all that remained of those endless games of Go were a couple of Hans's paintings in Donald Lucus' house, the wire sculpture on his desk, and a telegram with few hasty calculations on the back.

He worked on the program until past his usual lunchtime, carefully cross-referencing the manuals spread out on his desk.

The first step had been to write out the entire proof, as well as he could remember it, but with the diagram on the blackboard to help him. This was written in his own private notation, a hybrid of FØRTRAN, mathematical symbology, and abbreviated English. The next step was to translate this into symbolic logic, using the special terms and syntax laid out by CØNPRØØF 2 and EUBERT. Not only was it necessary to translate from one code to another; in order to avoid an impossible mass of detail, Lucus also had to augment the Hilbert axioms for Euclidean geometry with statements of all the Euclidean propositions called upon in David's proof. There was a list of these in the supplementary notes on EUBERT, and so he didn't have to worry about coding them, only that he had inserted all the necessary ones and correctly labeled them.

This was only the Euclidean part. For a while, he was afraid it would be necessary to duplicate all this work to program his Lobachevskian and Riemannian checks. But then he discovered a special tie-in in LØBACHEVMANN which would allow him to use the exact same input as was used for EUBERT and have validity checked in both non-Euclidean geometries at the same time. He was familiar enough with the use of the old CØNPRØØF 1, but only in conjunction with such systems as TØPØSPACE and ENSN, which he used constantly in verifying topological proofs. The axiom systems for synthetic geometries had been a complete mystery to him for over thirty years, and what he had relearned in the last three days was hasty and incomplete.

So his office, normally neat to the point of sterility, took on the aspect which it had only a few days a month, those few days of feverish inspiration when he had all the business details of his position out of the way and could allow himself the luxury of creation. Directly in front of him were a programming pad, on which he was writing his final version, and a pile of scratch work. Across the upper part of the desk the three program manuals lay open; to his left was his recent reproduction of David's proof, continuous on the back of last month's budgetary output, and a stack of used scratch paper which contained calculations important enough to be saved; on his right, a well-worn FØRTRAN manual on top of the three books which were almost the only customary adornment of the desk: *Webster's New Collegiate Dictionary*, Whittier's *Trilingual Mathematical Encyclopedia*, and a book of Go proverbs. The wire sculpture and desk calendar had been moved to the file cabinet to make room for all the necessary reference material.

By twelve thirty Ruth had gone to lunch, but the programming was not nearly completed. He had to pull himself away from the pad and pencil almost violently. His hand, his whole body, and a portion of his mind were unwilling or unable to stop writing. Once the trance was broken and he was putting on his coat, it began to frighten him. Surely he worked efficiently in such a hyperactive state, but it was dangerous. He could easily push himself too far, almost unknowingly, uncaringly, if he were allowed to give himself up to the immersing impulse too often. Even as he walked through the outer office, he noticed a stiffness in his legs and neck, an ache in his back and hand, that he had been oblivious to minutes before. Returning to awareness of his body's torture, he found the temporary divorce from objectivity even more frightening, as though it had been imposed not by himself but from the outside, as though he had been driven too hard by some other being, with little or no concern for his complaints or his safety. He had been abused. And he was tired, very, very tired.

His stomach was feeling upset—from the two cups of coffee he had had with lunch, he supposed—when he returned with his briefcase and David's paper at one fifteen. He found that once he lowered himself into the swivel chair it was necessary to sit still for several minutes to catch his breath. He knew he needed rest, but there was much more to do before he saw the Director. He tried to weigh the priorities in his mind, to reach a reasonable plan of action, but it was difficult to pin down ideas, and his thoughts were constantly intruded upon by images of congruent triangles and hyperbolic planes. Each attempt to list the tasks of the afternoon and assign time estimates to them was met with frustration, and his ears rang with the faint sound of laughing voices chattering in FØRTRAN.

Finally he decided that the only really necessary task was to finish the programming for CØNPRØØF 2 and have it sent to the computer division.

This took about half an hour. The work went much slower than it had in the morning. He constantly found himself looking blankly at his own notes, confusing output statements with axioms, losing his tenuous grasp on the details of David's proof.

When the whole thing was finally sent out to be punched up and compiler-checked on the A50 unit, it was ten minutes to two. He told Ruth to call him at five to three and gratefully laid his head on his folded arms on the desk, not even bothering to darken the room.

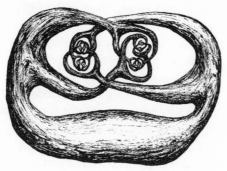

At first sleep would not come, only sharp-edged pictures, alternately threatening and soothing: his small house, his books, Mary as she was thirty years ago, when he had thought he might marry. Unrelated images swam about in his mind: a snatch of old rock music, a lemma from the Side Approximation Theorem, the smell of lilacs, and slowly one figure emerged from the mass and began to grow and dominate it all. At first it appeared to be only a smooth, featureless, somewhat metallic topological sphere. But this was only the bottom portion. Above, the figure split into two parts, not so much like a branching tree as like a squid with two plump arms, spread in a gentle flattened circle and coming together again—but not quite. Before the arms met, each of them split into two parts again, a thumb and an index finger, which linked together like a chain—but not quite. Before each finger reached its thumb, it was bifurcated, as was the thumb, and again the two arcs linked to form a chain—but not quite. This process continued infinitely, each step increasing the number of parts geometrically. The result was a figure simple in its construction, frighteningly complex in its final appearance.

"My God in heaven!" exclaimed Hans. "What in merciful hell is that? I never expected to find a book on demonology in your home, Donald."

Don had been at the bar pouring brandy and didn't know what Hans was referring to. By the time he got back to the table, Hans was standing silently, biting the side of his thumb and staring fixedly at the open copy of Hocking and Young's *Topology*.

"That's Alexander's horned sphere," explained Don evenly. For a moment he too felt an uncanny horror at the picture. But it passed, and what was to Hans the image of Satan became only a wild embedding of the two-sphere in Euclidean three-space.

"You see," he went on, setting down the drinks, "it's topologically a sphere, but its complement is not the same as the complement of an ordinary sphere. For instance, you could link a circle around it, just like you would around a torus, and it won't come off. In fact, there are an infinite number of ways you can do it."

Hans seemed not to be listening. He did not respond when Don sat down, but continued to bite his thumb rhythmically.

"The one thing that amazes me," he said at length, "is that I have seen it—" He paused, running his fingers through his beard. "—that I have seen it . . . and I still live. What is it, Donald, and how has it found its way into your neat religious parlor?"

"I told you: it's a wild sphere. It's called Alexander's horned sphere. It's really not so extraordinary, Hans. There's a wild arc

on the next page. Here's your brandy; now let's get started with
the game." Don was impatient to forget the thing, for Hans to
close the book and change the subject. He didn't like this reaction
to a simple mathematical object, as though it were something
more than it actually was.

"One could imagine Dali painting it," Hans continued, still
fixing his gaze on the picture, "all ugly, bleeding lumps of flesh.
That would be the obvious way. But I think I see it as a sculpture.
It would have to be tremendous—say, thirty feet high—so that
the branches start out fat as sequoias and end up—and end up
microscopic—and never end. They should go on to the atomic
level and beyond. Alexander's horned sphere. Can you see it
squatting in the sun in the middle of Chicago, like some horrid,
slimy crab? Yeah! Come on along, come on along. A sculpture,
yes, a sculpture, that's the way I'd do it."

He slammed the book abruptly and laid it on the floor.

"Donald," he said, more in his natural voice. "Donald, if you
have looked at that picture before and not felt the fear of the
darkness in your veins, then all I can say is—you are hopelessly
lost in your salvation. Have a Camel?"

Don shook his head, smiling, and Hans fitted a cigarette into
his holder, continuing to talk between his teeth as he puffed life
into it.

"Donald, the only man who is on such good terms with the
devil that he can look him in the eye so casually is the satisfied
theologian. You are a priest, not a prophet, and you must learn
that even the bestest church what am will not protect you, your
doctrinal orthodoxy will not save you, when the prophets begin
to quake and wail outside the temple."

"And you are the prophet?" asked Don, egging him on.

"Hah! No, not *your* prophet. No, honey lamb, you've missed
my point. Or else my analogy doesn't work out right. The prophets. Donald, I'm talking about mathematics, not art."

"Well, then I wish you wouldn't use a religious analogy. There
is a fundamental difference in approach between religion and

mathematics, and— No, let me finish. I know what you're going to say: that mathematics is predicated on the worship of reason. Well, that's wrong. Reason is only a tool to certain ends."

"Well, I agree, of course, Don. Reason is a tool to certain ends, and in your case those ends are basically theological. It's clear, you know, in this baroque fascination you have with the intricacies of your own proofs. You're only interested in plastering over the cracks in the temple. You've grown too dependent on it; you're afraid to worship in sunlight. Don't hide behind reason, Don. Your enemy will use the same tool. It's not reason that's against you, sweetheart; it's history."

"Anyway," Don interjected, annoyed at this turn in the conversation, "let's start playing or we'll never be done by ten."

"All right. But, Donald, I am going to do that sculpture, that Alexander's whatsit, someday. If ever I get a big commission. And you will be the only man who will understand all of its . . . all of its deeper meanings, my friend."

It was to be another fifteen years before he would get that commission and carry out his threat. It would be only twenty feet tall, not thirty, and in Cleveland, not Chicago. But it would shock, amaze, and frighten thousands of art lovers/haters, just as the original conception had shocked, amazed, and frightened Hans Kaefig.

Hans Kaefig, whose thoughts enveloped, surrounded, like rows of black disks, moving, shifting, unpredictably, while Donald Lucus' white disks coiled and struck, each move a step in a plan, each play a proverb. The patterns of black and white tessellations became too intricate to follow, and then there was no pattern at all, only the flashing black and white and a buzzing behind them, an insistent buzzing; as seconds stretched and expanded, he groped for his thoughts, sorting out the buzzing, reached for his glasses and the button on the intercom.

"Yes, Ruth?"

"It's two fifty-five, sir."

"Thank you, Ruth. Thank you."

He sat another minute, not really awake. Then, both hands on the chair, he lifted himself to his feet and did his best to tidy his suit. The Director was twenty years his junior, and yet he felt like a truant student being sent to the principal's office to explain himself, and knowing that the principal is never disposed to hear explanations.

3

He hadn't prepared a lecture in years. He had spoken of math only with other mathematicians. He had lost the knack of translation. There were English words, phrases, similes, that could say the same thing as a few swift logical statements, but he had forgotten them. And so he did not prepare a lecture. He had no idea what he was going to say to the Director, whether to present him with a neat, clear proof or simply to shout *"Gott ist tot,"* and make his point loudly and emotionally. He knew the Director was not a believer in any of the fundamental truths that were at stake. He would view a breakdown in the fabric of logic the same as a breakdown of the subway system. It was a nuisance to him, but it was certainly not his job to address himself to the problem; that was what metro engineers were paid for. That was what mathematicians were paid for. Lucus could not approach him on that level. What level he should direct his strategy toward he was not certain. He had, however, foreseen his opponent's moves well enough to expect the reception he received from the Director's private secretary.

"I'm sorry, Professor Lucus," the young man clipped, his glasses sliding down his nose in what seemed a studied parody of Ruth. "I'm sorry, but the Director is extremely busy this afternoon. I can make an appointment for Wednesday, I think . . . Of course, the Executive Board meeting is coming up next week . . ."

"That's all right, young man, I arranged to see him for a few minutes at three. I'll just slip in, and you can go back to your datebook." He would not be stalled any longer by the technical shunting about of the organization.

The Director looked blankly up from his desk as Lucus shut the door. He mumbled something feeble about thinking it was to-morrow that they were to meet, hoping to be rid of Lucus. As it became apparent that the math head had no intention of being put off further, he graciously conceded the skirmish and turned in an overly friendly manner to the problem itself.

As they talked, he leaned back in his chair, making full use of the physical advantage of his position. He sat comfortably in his shirtsleeves, collar open, bulky arms raised with his hands behind his head. Lucus alternately stood and sat—neither position was comfortable—in coat and tie, sweating through his shirt in the overheated office.

The Director was in his early forties, had held his position for three years. He divided his time unequally between his office, wife and children, and a girlfriend in San Jose. He drank more than Lucus had at his age, but seldom drank brandy. He was a mediocre chemist and an excellent administrator. He played golf one weekend out of two and worried that he was growing too fat. Lucus knew all this and very little else about the man. It was probable that he had studied calculus in college and forgotten a good deal of it by now, that he would be surprised to learn that an excellent mathematician might be very bad at arithmetic.

"Wait a minute," he protested before Lucus was very deep into his subject. "I thought Lobachevsky did that. I don't know much about math, but isn't that what non-Euclidean geometry is? Didn't they prove that Euclid was wrong? If it wasn't a big catastrophe then, why should it be now?"

And so he had to backtrack and try to give a ten-minute summary of the history of axiomatics. That Euclid's main contribution was not in his specific theorems, but in his method of assuming a very small number of "self-evident truths" and deriving all his results from them alone. That the question in the nineteenth century had only been over the notion of "self-evident," and then only over the fifth postulate, the so-called parallel postulate, and the exterior angle theorem. That non-Euclidean geometries had never denied the *consistency* of Euclid, but had only proposed alternative, equally consistent systems.

The Director balked at the word "consistency."

"But what's the difference between consistent and true?" he asked innocently.

"Truth has no meaning in mathematics," Lucus began. At the Director's scowl he corrected himself, for he was no logician, and these distinctions did not come quite naturally to him. "Or rather, truth is defined only relative to a given system of assumptions, you see. A statement is true in this system if it can be proved . . . I'm not sure if that's quite right . . . Well, anyway, if it necessarily follows from the assumptions. But a system of assumptions is consistent if you can't prove a contradiction from them, you see? If they could be a description of something that really exists."

"Okay, let me get this straight," said the Director, fishing a pack of Marlboros out of his pocket. "Something is *in*consistent if you can prove a contradiction from it, right? And what your Professor David seems to have done is prove that Euclid's postulates—is that the right word?—that his axioms or postulates or whatever are inconsistent. Am I right? So that means the whole notion of Euclidean geometry is nonsense. Well, I'm no mathematician, but I don't see the problem. Luckily this Russian has given you an alternative. So if, as you say, Euclid is scrapped, you still have this hyperbolic geometry and this other one, the one like the sphere, to choose from. It's very interesting, but hardly the kind of thing that requires any sort of executive decision."

Lucus bit his lip in frustration. He had always been a bad teacher, and Hans had said that . . .

"The non-Euclidean geometries were proven consistent by Riemann and Lobachevsky—" he began.

"Yes, well, that takes care of it, doesn't it?" the younger man interrupted.

"No, it doesn't!" said Lucus, too loudly. He sat down and tried to control his voice. "Non-Euclidean geometries were proven consistent by constructing models of them *within* Euclidean space. They are *conditionally* consistent. They are consistent only if Euclid is consistent. And, in the same way, Euclid depends on them. David's proof is valid for all three."

"You mean to say that *every* system of geometry is . . . is inconsistent . . . is meaningless?"

"Yes, sir. Not just geometry. Euclid can be derived from the real numbers. The real numbers can be derived from set theory. If Euclid is inconsistent, then the whole basis of mathematics is demolished. David's proof comprises the futility—" Donald Lucus' vision began to blur. His heart pumped blood deafeningly into his temples. There was a sharp pain in his chest. He spread his soaked and empty palms and spoke hoarsely. "—the futility of everything."

The Director was not unmoved by this display. He expected such an emotional plea on the part of a suppliant for a research grant on occasion. He was used to tearful outbursts from his girlfriend in San Jose, and he could react gently but unfeelingly in most emotional situations. But old men made him acutely uncomfortable. Emotional involvement in one's professional work puzzled and frightened him. He did not even yet understand the importance of the revelation which had been disclosed to him, but he did understand that it must be of some importance to bring this staid and dry old man to tears.

"You've checked it on the 666?" he asked.

Lucus looked away from him, embarrassed, fighting for breath, but trying not to breathe too deeply. "Not yet," he answered. "I have computer time tonight. I've made arrangements to have a social projection done this Friday, dependent on your approval."

"My approval?"

"For Limited Interest status."

"Oh." The Director rounded his lips meditatively and put his hands behind his head again. His cigarette lay in the ashtray, a long grey ash extending from the filter.

"Oh," he repeated. "Well, yes, of course. I suppose if it checks out, that you feel Something Must Be Done?"

"Yes, sir. I think there may be indications that Something Must Be Done about the problem."

And so Lucus knew that he had won the minimal confidence that he needed from the Director. The matter was to be given priority at the Executive Board meeting next week. He would have to go through the whole explanation again, many times. But it would be easier, the responsibility would no longer be entirely his. His white pieces coiled and struck across the board like a snake, squeezing the black ones out of strategic positions, reducing Hans's forces to a few holdouts near the edge. The brandy was sharp and exhilarating this evening.

4

With that trying interview over, Lucus felt a change in his mind and body. The oppressive burden was gone, and he could look forward to a great deal of time- and energy-consuming work. Responsibility was his, but it was the sort that he could be comfortable with, responsibility to get things done, to keep things moving. He spent the rest of Monday afternoon debugging the CØNPRØØF 2 input, which had arrived from the A50 during his absence. The work was routine, undemanding, and gently satisfying. By five thirty it was in shape to run, and Lucus went home to dinner and eleven hours of cool and dreamless sleep.

Tuesday he worked continuously, stopping only for half an hour for lunch, fortified during the day by three cups of Ruth's dark but tasteless coffee. He had called Bibliography as soon as he got in and had his checklist headings augmented greatly. Every month articles containing certain key words or phrases in their titles or abstracts were sent to all the department heads. The controlling program was sophisticated enough to produce some very worthwhile information and very little that did not hold at least some interest for him. Now, in addition to his standard topology codes, he added a few checks in various kinds of geometry—it was, after all, likely to be his field of specialization into the foreseeable future.

David's proof had checked out perfectly in all situations, which did not surprise him at all. The program—which turned out to supply much more detailed output than he remembered from cØNPRØØF 1—even made some suggestions on simplification of certain steps in the proof. It was indeed valid. There could be no doubt of that. He began writing up a short report on the program, which he would eventually include in his report to the Executive Board.

All day Wednesday was spent in conference with the head of the computer division, explaining in detail the results of David's proof and its connection with the rest of mathematics. They finally decided that the social projection could be done fairly easily with existing programs and data tapes, and it wouldn't be necessary to confer with Sociology—at least not until after the initial run. Lucus found himself working especially well with the man, developing an instant rapport and communicating the details of the problem much better than he had with the Director. In fact, the entire day he felt especially energetic and happy, almost euphoric, and he finally went home after seven with a genuine sense of accomplishment, disturbed only by the itching occasional thought that there was something he had meant to do but forgotten—nothing very important, but some detail that was left out, that destroyed the symmetry of the day. But this thought was eventually buried by the mass of other details, important details, enjoyable details, that competed for his time until late Wednesday evening.

Thursday and Friday were spent shuffling between two projects: the social projection and his report to the Executive Board. The Executive Board meeting, which had been scheduled to begin at two o'clock on Tuesday, was rescheduled to the morning, and all section heads were advised that some very important business might well cause it to run into most of the afternoon. The mere fact that the nature of this business was not mentioned, of course, tipped them off that it was "Limited Interest" and probably involved the sort of executive action that the Institute was theoretically not empowered to take. Actually, the Institute did stick literally to the guidelines in the Congressional bill which had authorized its founding. It served in an advisory capacity to the agencies which carried out the occasional difficult decisions which the board was sometimes forced to reach despite the seeming incompatibility of these decisions with the supposed concerns of the Institute. And if employees of the Institute were called upon to aid these other government agencies in the regrettable but necessary enforcement of decisions made in the interest of the general good, they clearly cooperated with their government as private individuals, usually in "special consultant" positions, and not as employees of the FBRI itself.

And so by adhering to the letter of its charter, the Institute managed to stretch the spirit of the charter when that spirit became a threat to more important considerations. No one on the Executive Board took this responsibility lightly. Indeed, it was the gravity, the solemnity with which they were bound to weigh questions of ethics and then exercise their own benign power in the interests of the whole of society—it was this gravity, the awesome weight of obligation and the crucial necessity of judicious application of their superior skills which secretly thrilled many of the board members and added an unequaled zest to these meetings. There had been one department head who opposed all such actions, but he had left the Institute to return to teaching some years back. Now there was usually a broad and healthy range of opinion and discussion on questions of "interference," as it was called, Genetics holding out against exercise of such power except in the most extreme cases, Biophysics being perhaps a bit overzealous in his enthusiasm for the Institute's potential control of future events, and the rest of the departments arranging themselves variously between these two poles as befitted their individual politics, esthetics, professional ethics, temperaments, and digestive difficulties.

Mathematics, that is to say, Dr. Donald Lucus, was never entirely sure where he belonged in the spectrum, being, he knew, too easily swayed by each side of the debate in its turn, and most often casting his ballot with the majority. The issues were always too vague, uncontrollable, and, as he put it, "political," and they seemed very far from his real concerns in his work. This time, however, he had no doubt which side of the issue he would take. He would have to hold the floor himself, and he knew for certain that the Institute must take appropriate measures to head off the catastrophic events that could be instigated by David's proof.

The initial surprise of the board when they realized it was he who was going to read the report was the customary reaction he got from everybody whenever they learned that Mathematics might be involved in something important. He was the out man in the building, and he now felt a bit of pride in presenting his case, in being allowed to overshadow their scientific concerns with the problems of *his* field for an entire morning, perhaps for a whole workday.

He began by giving a precise and ordered account of David's proof, its connection with the previous history of mathematics, and the interrelation of geometry with the foundations of all modern mathematical theory.

After this, and before the presentation by Computers and Sociology of the social projection, there was a period of questions directed to Lucus, as was customary, to ensure that everyone had a clear understanding of the issue. As it was, a number of them did, but the others were often reluctant to question a speaker in another field, less for fear of exposing their own ignorance than out of professional courtesy and a desire to avoid any question which might appear as a challenge to the speaker's competence. It was usually understood that each head considered his colleagues as the final experts in their own fields, and their private terrain must be respected, as they respected his. An attempt to gain too complete an understanding of his territory was dangerously close to a takeover of his sovereign province. So the questions were only halfhearted requests for clarification about Hilbert's axioms and the independence of the parallel postulate. Until Genetics raised a fluttering hand and asked with a Socratic smirk, "You say that the principles of Euclidean geometry can be derived from set theory, and, of course, this can be verified on the 666?"

"That's right."

"And so it all falls back on the principles of symbolic logic, and theoretically you could put the whole thing in terms of a proof in logic?"

"Yes, in fact, there is a program which can do just that with most mathematical proofs, and once I get around to it I intend—"

"Yes, yes. Well, very good. But isn't it true that your whole method of proof is based on symbolic logic?"

"Yes."

"And since you use this same method of proof in David's Theorem—"

Lucus smiled. He knew what was being suggested.

"Since you use this same method of proof in David's Theorem, and since you have *shown* that this method of proof is not valid —I mean, that's what you've shown by proving the inconsistency of symbolic logic itself—then you really haven't proved David's Theorem at all, have you? I mean, have you?"

Naturally, most of the board members were made acutely uncomfortable by this want of tact, and especially by Genetics' toothy grin as she spread her hands and waited for an answer. She was most unpopular, and it was rumored that she was not likely to remain much longer at the Institute. These rumors, however, had been circulated for a number of years with no noticeable effect on her position or her unwillingness to initiate a change of career herself. She was fifty-five now, and if she remained at the Institute many more years she was quite likely to become the Grand Old Lady, in which case her position and power would be unchallengeable until her own gracious retirement.

But now she was a minority of one, smiling at Lucus that same

wide friendly smile that her secretary had conscientiously striven
to imitate, smiling and waiting. He was not prepared for this
particular question, but he had taught basic math courses long
enough to be familiar with its general tactics. It was, put on the
grossest level, to dismiss mathematical jargon as a lot of nonsense. But, applied more subtly, it consisted of pointing out
illogicality in the nature of the mathematical approach, in the
detection of ubiquitous paradoxes, all of which eventually boiled
down to some variation on the Russell paradox: the serpent of
mathematics was forever swallowing its own tail. But Russell had
long ago found a solution in the simple expedient of multiplying
the number of serpents and lining them up to swallow each
other's tails, a much more plausible situation, and happily one
which introduced no further problems until the level of transfi-
nite numbers was reached, and here the mathematician was again
swimming in his own medium.

"But your argument can only serve to confirm David's proof.
You are arguing from a paradox, from the absurd." Lucus returned her smile, feeling around his shoulders the temporary,
illusory mantle of the Grand Old Man.

"How so?" she asked.

"Well," he continued, "simply because the method of proof of
David's Theorem is invalid, that does not insubstantiate its result
—no, wait, let me finish—at best you would have to conclude that
it is proven neither true nor false. Now suppose you assume that
the basis of logic is in fact *valid.* Then you are forced to accept
David's Theorem and the proof of the *in*validity of your logic;
you are led to a contradiction. Therefore the assumption of the
validity of logic is untenable."

"But, on the other hand," she objected, "if you assume that
logic is invalid, then David's proof is invalid."

"Precisely. And that is a perfectly consistent position. David's
Theorem does *not* say 'This sentence is false.' It says 'This sentence is unprovable,' and therefore it must be true."

"I think you're talking in circles," said Genetics.

"It's all very well for you to think that, but the fact remains that this position is sound—it can easily be verified on the 666."

The remaining questions were dutiful inquiries into the nature of the Russell paradox, and each answer was followed by a polite "Oh, yes, I see." Lucus was calm and confident by the time Computers and Sociology began their description of the social projection.

The problem had been of quite a different nature from that of most of the projections that had been introduced to the board. Usually, a discontinuity was introduced into a percentage prediction pattern and the other initial conditions were varied within certain ranges, so that the effects of the invention of some new device or some new discovery in physical law could be ascertained, both short- and long-range effects. The discontinuity had some direct and immediate effect on material or political conditions, on arms capabilities or projected population figures or the economy. A good deal of such research had been done, it was true, with discontinuities of a religious or philosophical nature, and the sort of results obtained was quite well understood by those in the field. The Institute as a whole was seldom concerned with such results. It was the responsibility of other branches of the government to deal with the possible detrimental long-range effects of new religious or philosophical movements.

The projection for David's Theorem showed remarkably unperturbed figures for a long period. Even in the mathematical world, it was predicted, little notice would be taken of it for fifteen to twenty years, notwithstanding its immediate effect on Dr. Lucus. It would be dismissed and ignored—at first. But within thirty years the disruption of the mathematical world would become violent and begin spreading into other fields. Still it would remain an academic debate. There would be much name-calling and side-taking, the introduction of heated emotions into decisions of hiring, tenure, structuring of mathematics and science departments. But still the public at large would remain entirely unaware of the issue. New schools of philosophy would arise to address themselves to the problem. Within forty years the issue would be taken up in the public press, the result being an increase in the polarization of scientists in all fields, and within fifty years, sixty at the outside, a violent antiscience reaction at all levels of government, huge cutbacks in funding, reduction of departments in universities all over the country, massive shutdowns of laboratories, and even elimination of many industrial research programs. The original issue would be mostly forgotten by this time; it would be the widespread fear of being dominated by scientists, scientists pictured as caricatures from Vincent Price movies, that would be the main concern of the public. But the effects would be disastrous for the scientific community.

There was heated discussion on this projection until one o'clock, when the board took an hour break, and then reconvened for the afternoon session. There was particular objection to the long-range nature of the projection. Many members of the board felt it was not their duty to be concerned with developments half a century in the future, and some of them were highly skeptical of the accuracy of the 666's figures for such a period, although error estimates were given for all figures, and they usually didn't get beyond five or ten percent at the sixty-year level.

To many it still seemed incredible that a mathematical theorem could have such an effect, but the evidence of the 666 was hard to dispute. Only Genetics objected to the input and assumptions of the projection program itself.

"What you don't assume," she said to Lucus, again smiling with all her teeth, "is the ingenuity of the world's mathematicians. The program projects the proof of one theorem into the future, without considering what else will be proved in the future. If you scrap geometry, why shouldn't a new geometry arise? If you scrap Aristotelean logic, why shouldn't a new logic arise?"

"I assure you, madam," answered Lucus, "the proof is valid for *all* logics, for intuitionism as well as for the many-valued systems."

"And there are no other roads?" she asked cynically.

"And there are no other roads."

"Well, then, I would suppose your field is likely to come to a stagnant standstill in any case, with or without any help from Professor David."

There were shocked murmurs of censure up and down the table. Cryogenics, who had intended to question the methods of formulation of the theorem for the 666, thought better of it and folded his hands in silence.

The debate went on, but there was a marked increase of support for Lucus. By seven, when the final ballot was taken, he sat content, watching the other men and women folding their slips of paper. There was a sense of camaraderie, of common purpose, that he had never felt before with the Institute personnel. It was much like serving on the Honor Code Committee in college: the shared duty, the secret debates, and the final pride in the satisfying justice of the verdict, a day very well spent creeping, creeping to a close.

It was the consensus of the Executive Board that Something Must Be Done, and with that most of them could entirely forget the problem in good conscience. For Lucus, however, there were more meetings with the Director and Sociology, conferences in Washington, and an eventual temporary advisory post in an agency of the executive branch.

He returned to his work at the Institute, allotting a few hours a week to his new advisory position, the few hours he used to devote to research, research which seemed to lose some of its insistent appeal now that he had other important duties. The fall *Quarterly* came out only two weeks late, minus David's article, with a brief editorial apology for the delay. Letters had to be written, editors conferred with to assure the difficulty of David's publishing his article elsewhere in the near future. Meanwhile, the foundation was laid for the discrediting of any publication he eventually managed to achieve. The strategy was all laid out by experts in Washington who had handled similar cases, and Lucus had only to implement a few of the moves which required the prestige of his position in his field. Fortunately, David was up for tenure at his university that year. When it was not granted, he had immense difficulty obtaining a position elsewhere. He was quite a meek man, and certainly not paranoid enough to accuse anyone of being involved in a conspiracy against him. He ended up turning to high school teaching, which allowed him less and less time for any serious research.

The whole problem was neatly and efficiently disposed of, and Lucus could not help admiring the simplicity of the plan of action. He had carried out his own part of the program carefully and professionally. No one could reproach him. He had represented his profession admirably.

5

"You're a creep!" said Hans, coming up behind him on his way back to the dorm after class.

"What do you mean by that?" he asked without turning, gripping his books tighter, feeling the strength in his fingers against them.

"You're a creep, Lucus, that's what!" Hans held up the morning's edition of the school paper. "Look at this, you creepy bastard! That was really a rotten thing to do."

"Look, the whole committee voted on Jonathan!" Don left the brick walk and cut across the lawn, anxious to be rid of Kaefig.

"And I know how you voted too, you creep!" Hans insisted. "And now the poor kid'll be expelled, just because he got caught cribbing on one little exam . . . and you can be smug about it. Can't you find a better way to save the honor of your precious code?"

"It wasn't one little exam, Hans, and besides—let go of me!— and besides, it wasn't just Jonathan we had to think of; it was the integrity of the whole school and the Honor Code. How long do you—I said let go of me!—how long do you think the faculty would let us keep the Honor Code if we let everybody off who broke it? Hey, get away! I've got to go to lunch!"

He dropped all his books as Hans wrestled him to the ground. It wasn't much of a match; Don was a skinny kid, and he was more worried about keeping his glasses from slipping off than in putting up a fight. He was soon on his back with Hans on top. Hans swiftly pulled off his glasses and slapped him twice, hard. He lay still, his face stinging and wet, as Hans got up.

"I had to do that, Donnie, because of the rotten thing you did to Jonathan. You understand that, don't you? I mean, we don't have to talk about it anymore. That was all I wanted to say." He held up the palm of his right hand. "You okay now?"

Don nodded. His face was hot with fear, his eyes turned upward, away from Hans.

"See you tonight for a beer?"

Don nodded. He closed his eyes and dug the fingers of one hand into the cool soil. But Hans still waited, out of his field of vision, tired and afraid; unsure, Hans waited for an answer.

"Kaefig, you're crazy!" he whispered.

He lay there, not moving, long after Hans had gone. The tree above was blurred, but he could trace the pattern of its larger branches, and the smaller ones seemed to wink in and out of existence. If he concentrated and squinted, he could follow even those, tracing the patterns over and over with his eyes and his mind. He often looked at trees, never tired of looking at trees, sliding along the limbs with his eyes, absorbing the whole of the latticework.

Every year there were new branches on the tree outside his window. Even this year, strange as it might seem, new green branches on the tree outside the window of the elephants' graveyard. To lose himself on these branches. To reach up and out with his mind. To lie prone on earth and cease to ponder on himself, the while he stared at nothing, drawn nowhere. His breath came with more difficulty these days, his hands would not close with ease and pained him when they did. Walking was an effort and all chairs too hard and wrongly proportioned. He longed to—what was the verse?—to

seek release
From dusty bondage into luminous air.

But he was no hero. What lay on his desk was merely dry and inevitable. The morning's mail, a cup of coffee, the laughing icosahedron. He had thumbed through the journals marked for his attention by Bibliography late in the morning. And there it was, in a Polish journal of logic, to be sure. In German, yes, but there could be no mistake: *"Die Widerspruchlichkeit der Logikgrundsätze als Folge eines geometrischen Beweises,"* by Kálmán Kodály of the University of Budapest.

Of course, it had to happen; anyone should have known. He placed one hand on the icosahedron, no longer needing to look at it, and raised himself to his feet. He walked slowly to the window, knowing he would find something there, the vision of order and neutrality, of "light anatomized." It was waiting for him, soft and green and easy on his eyes. And for long minutes that morning, Donald Lucus stood at his window, tracing the lines, the beautiful lines of the tree, and wept for the death of his dear friend Hans.

Arcs & Secants

JOAN D. VINGE ("Mother and Child") wrote this story after dreaming that she was reading the second half of it in an anthology. ("Maybe I time-travel in my sleep!") She reports that she and her husband Vernor are a second-generation writing team—Vernor's parents were co-authors of two books on geography.

We wrote to a friend in February, "I think you can conveniently divide s.f. from straight fiction and fantasy by using the three bins you mention (actuality, possibility, impossibility), but if you try to be precise you find unfortunately that some stories don't fall into the right bin. What about stories taking place in the contemporary world in which the vice president has been assassinated or a new breakfast food called *Freebies* is on the market, etc.? Anybody would say these are straight stories, but you have to put them in the possibility bin because they deal with something that could happen but hasn't. If in trying to be precise you have to abandon the three bins and call some things s.f. that have not been called that before, I think that's okay if only because it dissolves an artificial barrier and calls attention to places we have not been going because the maps all say 'That's not s.f.' And I think this is happening or about to happen, and that's why all the ferment about defining science fiction."

A puzzled reader asked in March, "Do you actually want amateur writers to submit manuscripts to you?" We said yes. *Orbit* gets most of its material from previously unknown writers, and pays 3–5¢ a word, as an advance against a share of royalties.

R. A. LAFFERTY ("The Skinny People of Leptophlebo Street") wrote to his agent in April, "Hey, Mildred Virginia, about allegory, symbolism, metaphysical stuff, multiple depths, transcendental aspects, of course they are always present in everything. If we are the six or seven or eight dimensional persons that we are supposed to be, then everything we do is done in several worlds at the same time and has a complex of meanings. But I never liked to isolate minor aspects and pull them out by the bloody roots to analyze them. It's a little as though one should say of a picture 'Is the perspective right in that? Is it supposed to have depth? Let's see if it has,' and then drive a surveyor's stake through the middle of the picture to take bearings. Or say of a living arm 'Well, it's all right on the surface, but what is the hidden substance? What is the interior content of it?' and then a bodkin in to its hilt to start a little gusher. 'Oh, blood is the hidden substance, huh? But blood's old stuff. It's been done before.' Or to wander through a playing orchestra with a piano tuner's whistle to check on the pitch of everything, but maybe it will miss some of the harmonics anyhow. Integrated depth is what a thing is supposed to have (hey, that's a pretentious phrase, isn't it?) and if it's done right it won't let itself be pulled apart."

DORIS PISERCHIA ("A Brilliant Curiosity") is bemused by everything about the writing and publishing world, but is hooked and can't stop.

JESSE MILLER ("Phoenix House") drove a cab in New York after he got out of the air force, and loved it, but had to quit because of eye trouble. This story was written in a VA hospital; it is his first, although others were sold and published earlier. "I am black, I am twenty-nine, and I have a good sweet woman, whose name is Jean, and I am slowly going blind. That just about puts me where I am this morning."

JOE HALDEMAN ("Counterpoint," *Orbit 11*) sent us a picture postcard of a Spanish cathedral with the note, "This would really be a great hotel, but they keep ringing those damned bells."

ROBERT THURSTON ("Jack and Betty") is living with his wife and small son in the Washington Heights section of Manhattan ("quiet, with trees lining the streets"). In a way, this story is a companion piece to Thurston's "Stop Me Before I Tell More" (*Orbit 9*).

Technological regress dept.: On a recent visit to Louisville, Kentucky, we saw a supermarket advertisement for "Imitation Salad Dressing."

HENRY-LUC PLANCHAT ("Prison of Clay, Prison of Steel") is a young French writer and editor. This is the first story of his that has been translated into English.

LLOYD BIGGLE, JR., wrote in June: "Dean [McLaughlin] called me the other day. 'I've just invented a new antigravity device. It's called a ladder.' I said, 'Great idea—if you can keep the moving parts to a minimum.' "

GUSTAV HASFORD ("Heartland") is a young Southern writer who is working and starving on the West Coast. Pray for him.

Readers are invited to submit temporally scrambled words to be added to the "Little Lexicon for Time-Travelers" which appears on page 173. To be accepted, words must be ingenious, unexpected and *pronounceable*. The best entries will be published in *Orbit 18*, and the contributors of the five most outrageous words will receive copies of that volume in its hardcover edition. (To the writer of the most piteous letter expressing bewilderment about the whole thing we will send a copy of Lin Carter's *Black Legions of Callisto.*) Entries must be received not later than

August 15, 1975. They should be addressed to: Damon Knight, Editor, Box 8216, Madeira Beach, Florida 33738.

MOSHE FEDER ("Sandial") spent his childhood in a yeshiva and then went to Queens College of the City University of New York, from which he graduated, a year late, in 1974. Since 1972 he has been a part-time, unpaid assistant editor of *Amazing* and *Fantastic*. This is his first published story.

C. L. GRANT ("In Donovan's Time") is a former Army MP who was once assigned to write up the awards for bravery won by other MPS stationed in Quinhon, Vietnam. ("Most of them were a pack of purple-prose lies, the worst being an attempt by a career major to get himself a Purple Heart for catching his finger in the door of his trailer during an enemy rocket attack. *He* never got it, but the colonel who fell off an armored personnel carrier and skinned his elbow (he was drunk at the time) did. Thus did I practice science fiction while in the army.")

DAVE SKAL ("Ambience") reports that the Rocky Mountain Casket Company of Whitefish, Montana, markets a $180 coffin which converts into a wine closet.

RICHARD BIRELEY ("Binary Justice") is an electrical engineer, a former professional magician ("The Great Bikini") and disk jockey.

ELEANOR ARNASON ("The House by the Sea") makes great Christmas tree ornaments out of wrapping paper and egg-shells, and is the only person she knows who has written an epic poem.

WILLIAM F. ORR ("Euclid Alone") says he has been writing a lot, but not fiction: "Two mathematical articles, one NSF proposal, one popular science article in Esperanto for an amateur astronomy magazine published by an observatory in Yugoslavia, a short article for a Polish Esperanto magazine suggesting that Lem be translated into Esperanto . . . and some translations from Arnaut Daniel's Provençal poetry."